JUST PRETENDING

JUST PRETENDING

LISA BIRD-WILSON

COTEAU BOOKS

Edited by Warren Cariou
Cover designed by Tania Craan
Cover Photograph "Cyborg Hybrid Teressa (New York)", by KC Adams
Typeset by Susan Buck
Printed and bound in Canada by Imprimerie Gauvin

Library and Archives Canada Cataloguing in Publication

Bird-Wilson, Lisa
        Just pretending / Lisa Bird-Wilson.

Short stories.
Issued also in electronic formats.
ISBN 978-1-55050-546-7

        I. Title.

PS8603.I75J88 2013   C813'.6   C2012-908110-8

Issued also in electronic formats.

ISBN 978-1-55050-736-2 (EPUB).--ISBN 978-1-55050-737-9 (MOBI)

10 9 8 7 6 5 4 3 2 1

2517 Victoria Avenue
Regina, Saskatchewan
Canada   S4P 0T2
www.coteaubooks.com

Available in Canada from:
Publishers Group Canada
2440 Viking Way
Richmond, British Columbia
Canada   V6V 1N2

Coteau Books gratefully acknowledges the financial support of its publishing program by: The Saskatchewan Arts Board, including the Creative Industry Growth and Sustainability Program of the Government of Saskatchewan via the Ministry of Parks, Culture and Sport; the Canada Council for the Arts; the Government of Canada through the Canada Book Fund; and the City of Regina Arts Commission.

for my family

Table of Contents

astum

The full moon perches on the horizon, trying to look her in the eye. It floats on the water, kissing its own reflection, melding the two. She raises her arms to the spirit of grandmother moon, welcoming, submitting.

"It's time," the old woman whispers.

"At last," she breathes, her words carried away on the air, even though there is no breeze and she hasn't spoken.

She steps to the water, releasing her song. She sings in the language her own mother gave her as a gift. The language that couldn't be cut from her tongue with sharp words and boarding school straps. The language that survived smothering closets and retch-inducing brown soap.

Alerted, the grandmothers join their voices with hers, filling her with astonishing desire. She moves to the great moon, the spirit of the grandmothers, joins them there in the water. She spreads herself wide only to find she is no longer a single being but connected, within and of both the earliest women and those yet unborn. Teeming with ancient song and surrounded by the sacraments of the grandmothers, she cedes her earthly body, dissipating within the foam.

"Here she is," they murmur. "*Astum*, my girl."

From the shore, the old woman watches the tiny waves that ripple the surface. The heavy moon has begun to rise in the sky where she will take her place, watching, tranquil and unrepentant, over those she's left behind.

blood memory

Θvery pregnant woman dreams of what her baby will be like.
But babies shouldn't have to dream of their mothers. It's been
more than thirty years, and I still struggle to quell the haunting
voice at the back of my mind that urges *Find her find her.* Instead,
I invent her.

I want to start at the beginning, but beginnings are slippery
to pin down. What would hers look like? Was it the moment she
realized her period was late? I can imagine the instant of understanding that her actions, up to then carefree and light, came
with real consequences. Or maybe the beginning was the concep-
tion itself, when she and my father pushed the limits behind the
big barn that housed the cattle in winter, the small heated calf-
shack tucked into its shadow. What made her think she was
immune to it all, to the fecundity of the land and animals that
every day plugged her nose with pungent odours, filled her ears
with bawling bleating madness?

More likely, the beginning had something to do with the day
the gnarled, squashed fetus (she made herself call it a fetus to
avoid thinking of it as a b-a-b-y) squalled its way into her world
and she made her way out of its world – a double beginning.
Each a newly released hostage, not quite believing she had survived, fleetingly grateful before moving on as though nothing of
import had occurred. There's got to be a reason why babies and
mothers forget the pain of birth.

I picture it something like this. At the height of the ninth
month, swollen like an overstuffed olive, lungs and other internal
organs squeezed so tight she felt out of breath on the wide staircase of the antiseptic "home for unwed mothers" (read: "institu-
tion for misfits and fuck-ups"), she tried to understand, but she
could not find a reason for the mythical underwater creature
swirling beneath skin stretched so thin and taut that in her

3

dreams she popped herself with a shiny dinner fork. All the while, inside, the fetus (repeat: *fetus, fetus*) sank and swam in murky depths of blood memory, bonding secret-identity-mother to child. And a word bobbed about in the depths, tickling the tadpole, the word waiting to be picked up and held in the palms of two hands, examined then crushed to the chest rubbed into arms, over shoulders, across the belly, the word more than a word, to be inhaled then expelled bit by bit with every breath – the word *Métis*.

I don't know about the home and the wide staircase; she could have been kept like an animal in a barn for all I know. But going off to a home seems the kind of thing that would have happened, back in the day. I imagine them saying she'd been sent away to live with a sick aunt after her father made an angry visit to the neighbouring farm and scared the hell out of the farmhand, who was really just a boy, while her mother got on the phone with the priest. Sent away for five months before returning deflated, with large leaky breasts, eyes swollen from lying in the back of the family station wagon and bawling all the way home.

"Growing nicely," Dr. Dubious pronounces as he measures my belly from pubic bone to top of fundus – some of the new words I've been learning. What about the words she learned? Not the words of a fantastic and beautiful anatomy to be revealed during the rite of passage through pregnancy and birth toward mother-hood. Instead, the words she learned – truly learned in their deep and hurtful meaning, maybe for the first time – those words may have been *shame, wrong, bad, disgrace* – words that made her cover her head and stop her ears to deflect their blows.

I also learned, on my visit to Dr. Dubious, that it's awkward to have a baby when you don't know your medical history. *Any history of heart disease?*

No.

What about in your family?

Nana died when I was nineteen, and my mother struggled to

find the words to tell me her mother was dead. That's when I understood that my mother had been a daughter first. But Nana's stroke doesn't count for Dubious's question – he is looking for hereditary conditions. I have nothing to offer, only a great yawning blank. I give him the only thing hereditary I know: *Métis*.

Not a baby, not a baby. She must have willed herself to remain blank and distant from what was right below the sternum. No picturing startled fingers, tiny heels that would fit in her palm, a dark silken bloom of hair, down-covered shoulders. Instead, a fishy eyeless globe, a silent sea monster in the well of her incubator body, gnawing at the base of the cord that attached them, one to the other, trying desperately to escape as a muskrat will chew its own leg off to get out of a trap. She once saw her father open a ripe sturgeon, full of black eggs, and saw him lament the lost potential of those eggs, as though somehow he'd been a careless steward. But her insides harbour only a single shimmery orb shadowed by a thin stretch of tail. She imagines this thing contained; herself a container. She is filled with blue-green water, soft seaweed tendrils undulating in time with her movements, a secret underwater world like a dark aquarium. There must be a reason we're grown in the dark, submerged in water, hermetically sealed – what is it we're trying to keep out?

She dreams of gigantic garden shears sharpened to a razor's edge, oiled and free of catches, her hands holding the rubber-coated grips and cutting the briny cord, setting herself afloat as the fetus *fetus fetus* drifts lazily away like Huck on his raft, and she is laughing.

In one of her dreams, she finds a small blue jewellery box bobbing in the toilet. She scoops it out and holds it in her palm, wet and messy, leaking onto her bare toes. She's afraid to open it because she thinks it is ticking. She panics and tries to hide the thing before it explodes. She blurts out mock-magic words "*Ababa,*" grievous, faulty in a solemn voice, flicking her fingers over the box, a magician's black-magic flourish, *léger de main,* before flushing. A different type of disappearing act, she conjures me down.

I tell Dubious that I'll have my baby at home with midwives, that my baby must remain with me at all times, particularly during those few first lucid hours when the most intense bonding is said to occur. I mention my anxieties about "attachment capabilities" and "emotional glue." But I don't tell him that I'm teetering on the edge of an insurmountable regret, a loss so large it threatens to smother me – the loss of what was mine by birth, a deficit that I wear like a scar.

I know this because as a child I had two best friends – both adopted, both Native. This seemed incidental, but I now know it wasn't. It was an intuitive recognition of each other's wounds, as though we each saw, like an aura, the pieces that hadn't formed, the missing parts that would have made each of us whole. I only tell Dubious that I want the best for my baby.

"All expectant mothers say that," he laughs.

I don't tell him he's wrong.

During the last months of my pregnancy, my mind becomes watered down with the weight and change in my body. I sit for hours dreamily staring into space while the radio plays softly in another room. I relish the quiet, the peace, the opportunity to do nothing, which those with experience tell me will soon end. I imagine what these months were like for her, in that home, day after day, a prisoner serving a sentence, waiting to be set free.

At the home, there's a girl she has taken to calling Mary K. Mary K is lithe and sexy, even at nine months, while she herself is puffy, toxic with high blood pressure and nauseating headaches. She can envision Mary K sitting on an older man's lap and fiddling with his pants, toying with the idea of being taken advantage of, a spunky, sway-back, streetwise Lolita, her slippery seal's body a horny turn-on. If she'd had something other than sex to peddle, she'd be the queen of snake-oil sales. If life had dealt her a different hand, she'd be driving a big pink Cadillac with vanity plates that read *Mary K.*

As they smoke in the alley behind the home, one girl dares to confess she misses her boyfriend. The rest of them drag on their smokes and say nothing.

The days are long and bleed one into the next. The girls are not allowed out of the nuns' sight. Many resent not being free to walk and shop and pretend to live a different story than the one they do; many are from remote rural places, and being on the edge of the city only to be forbidden a trip downtown vexes them to the point of tears. Only Mary K, looking like a malnourished, pot-bellied orphan, manages to slither out under the cloak of night to secure cigarettes. She brings back small flat bottles of lemon gin, and the girls, with their skewed centres of gravity, tumble one atop the other with shrill delighted screams. The Mother Superior threatens to kick them out; to call their parents. She tells them how lucky they are to be there, how ungrateful.

One evening at the home, as she makes toast, she looks at her bloated reflection in the chrome and dreams of being thin again. The girls can talk of nothing else. As she reaches into the toaster with the point of a knife, she knows that it's a stupid thing to do. So when the shock throws her back onto her ass with a hard *hmph,* she's not surprised. Hours later, after the cold stethoscope with the doctor at the end of it is gone, and her hair still floats about her head with static, she thinks about the pond of dew she might have been standing in were it not enclosed inside her body, and how water and electricity make bad company. She wonders about the cloudy lagoon sloshing about in her distended belly, with its fragments and bits, if it had been electrified, touched the way she once saw a loose live wire send a blue-white spark to skip over puddles in the barn like stones over water.

I was one of those electrified bits, plotting my escape from inside the belly she was forced to wear like a blanket of shame. I know this happened because my own mother, the one who raised me, told me what the social worker had said. "There was an accident. You could have been lost." She told me this in order to impress upon me how much I was wanted even before they knew who I was, even before I was born. I want to be grateful, I *am* grateful. But still I know she wouldn't understand my feeling that I've always been lost.

As she completes her sentence at the home, waiting for me to be born, shameful words creep up on her. In Cree one word is spoken over and again in her head – *macitwawiskwesis,* a bad girl. Perhaps she had a note from her mother on her birthday, expressing hope for a better year, yet between the lines she reads her mother's desire for a good daughter, not such a bad *nitânis.* My heart twists, half with empathy and half with jealousy, for at least she got to know these words, difficult as they are. At least she was *nitânis,* no matter how *bad.* When my husband returns home from work, I chalk up my tears to hormones and he holds me until I sleep.

I imagine that all her dreams occur under water. The night she goes into labour, she floats peacefully, hair swaying about her face, hands gripping her garden shears, only to be tossed on shore by the insistent tides of her body. She gasps, lying in a puddle. Has she breached the thin membrane between dream and wakefulness, somehow exposing the netherworld to this one? She cries out with her first conscious contraction, and the girl in the next bed says, *Shuddup, fer fucksake.*

Hours into the labour and delirious with pain, does she finally hear me?

"FEE FI FO FUM," I bellow from below.

Her whimpering is lost on me.

"I'LL GRIND YOUR BONES," I holler as I grind my way through her childish pelvis.

A sentimental girl might name the baby. It never occurs to her, before, during or after the birth, that I am anything other than the black-penny-eyed tadpole of her imagination. She fills in the blanks as best she can – there are rules about these things – but no one can make her open her heart, and no one can force her to leave anything behind, not even a name.

I sit in my bathtub at home, riding waves of contractions, soothed by the warm water, two midwives amiably attending, prepared for the long haul typical of most first births. I can't shake the dream-world mother I've created. *Nitânis,* she whispers, as I let my head fall wearily between contractions; one midwife mops my brow with a cool cloth while the other perches on a chair and sips tea. Someone's put soft music on, my husband warms towels in the dryer, and I can hear the excited voices of our families downstairs in the living room.

My mother, real or dreamed, never had any of these things. No one whispered *nitânis* in her ear, mopped her brow, made the tea, warmed the towels, waited in the wings, treated my birth like a celebration. Instead, I imagine harsh words, harsh towels. Maybe a younger nun secretly attempted to soften the punishing experience of most births at the home. I'm confused and angry over the loss of what I needed: identity, blood inheritance, to be Métis, to know where I've come from, something to pass on to my own child, who will also be blind to what ought to be hers by birth.

Hours later, my child is born. "She's a *girl*," I say to my husband, surprised by the awe in my voice. I hold her warm, waxy body, a bent snail, next to my skin, and cover her with my hands. Curled like a comma, punctuation, an exclamation: the end of a sentence, making way for the beginning of something new. I palm her black-capped head, and she looks at me – looks and looks – her eyes wide and serious.

"Hello," I whisper. "Hello, *nitânis.*" My first blood relation.

the nirvana principle

f or the record, his real name's Dr. Semenchuk. At first I tried out *cement truck* and then expanded to *semen chunk*, but for some reason these never really resonated with me. Pink-o, Dr. McOink-Oink, and Shrinky Dink became my favourites to randomly rotate through. If you want to play shrink too, you might say that I use these names to dehumanize him, perhaps as a way to distance him from me, keep him from getting too close. I would say that if you ever saw Shrinky Dink, you'd try to keep your distance too. I only use *semen chunk* when my mother (a.k.a. grandmother) says his name to me.

"Did you go and see Dr. Semenchuk this afternoon?" or "How did it go with Dr. Semenchuk today?" she says.

"Dr. Semen Chunk was grand. He sends his love," I say. Or, "Dr. Semen Chunk says to tell you your money's going to a good cause – he had an *extra* patty of lard in his lunch today."

"Oh, Hanna," she says.

He knows it has something to do with the girl who died, but instead we talk about my mother. It's the obvious thing – abandonment issues and all that. I've been reading a lot of psychology books in my spare time lately, trying to guess what Shrinky Dink will come up with. Dry stuff, for the most part, until you get to some of the juicier bits of Freud. Most interesting is the patient named Anna O, who was the basis for Freud's theories. She didn't talk much, and then she would do this thing she called "chimney sweeping," where she would talk like mad to get it all out, as though she had been saving it up. Then she felt better. I believe

I'm on to Pink-o and his tricks now.

So he knows it's about the dead girl, and he knows I know he knows. I have the feeling he's just humouring me with all his unimaginative talk about my so-called real mother while he waits for me to get to the real point and tell him why I'm here (all this talk about "reality" makes my head spin. I'm in the process of converting from a blind faith in structuralism, that I didn't even realize I had, to a belief in post-structuralism. I'm finding that it really suits my cynical nature.)

I've been told that for fourteen, I'm a smart girl. I've also been told that I am deeply immature. "That's okay," I sometimes reply, "I like being complex."

"You're a smart girl, Hanna." How many times have I heard that? Or the somewhat sideways, "You're too smart for your own good" (Mrs. Connor, grade six). Or the much more interesting and straightforward, "You think you're pretty smart, don't you?" (Melody Perkins, member of so-called "peer group.")

"Hanna," Melody sing-songs in the lunch room, and giggles erupt from her table. "Hanna Banana." More giggles. "Hanna, want a banana?" Lewd gestures with the banana.

"Is that the best you can do?" I ask, picking up my untouched lunch tray to dump in the garbage by the door again.

Sing-song voice gives way to hard edge. Loudly: "But Hanna doesn't like bananas. I think Hanna would rather eat *flowers*." Louder still: "I heard Hanna's a lesbian who does it with Miss Flowers. She's the teacher's pet, or maybe she just pets the..." The cafeteria door swings shut behind me.

Of course I love Miss Flowers. Everyone loves Miss Flowers. But I have a deep and inevitable crush on her. Different, I'm sure, than everyone else who loves Miss Flowers. Maybe I've been underestimating Melody Perkins.

Dr. Shrinky Dink interrupts the sound of the ticking clock

steadily marking off our silent hour together (well, fifty minutes, or three thousand seconds, if you want to be technical) to suggest to me that I'm addicted to the "high" I get from the endorphins when I tell bold lies, or steal, or otherwise overtly oppose the so-called authority figures in my life. After he says that, he sits back with his pink face gleaming, trying to look benign, reassuring, and masterful all at once. The effect, more than anything, is to make him look pompous.

A little too convenient, I think as I stare at his round belly straining to escape his food-spotted shirt. Lunch, I wonder, or something (disgusting) much earlier, like last night's supper, perhaps? Or (more likely, I smirk inwardly in my special inward-smirking kind of way), a masturbatorial bit of goo that has something to do with the two thousand *Playboy* magazines that this creepy shrink keeps in his office as some quasi-political statement about the okay-ness of nudity that I am too young (thank god) to hear about but that all good post-war feminist hippies like my mother (a.k.a. grandmother) would likely agree with. I spend half my time here praying that this sicko isn't some kind of child molester.

His theory about the addiction to the endorphin high makes me say, "Isn't that a bit ironic?" right out loud, which I didn't really mean to do, and causes Dr. McOink-Oink to pause and cock his left eyebrow in such a way that I am left with the impression that this is a very practiced move. But he's keen now because he's gotten something out of me.

"Ironic? How so?" he queries, his fingers laced together over his tub-o'-guts.

I practice raising my left eyebrow at him as if to say, *Don't you know?* But both my eyebrows work in tandem, and I'm sure I only achieve the undesired effect of looking surprised. Damn. I am particularly annoyed with myself for having given this impression when I am most certainly NOT surprised.

Nothing this buffoon could do or say would surprise me. He could go into labour and have a baby right here on the mouldy green carpet and I would hardly be surprised. He could lunge from his chair and try to plant sloppy wet kisses on my neck (ugh) and I would not find myself surprised. He could slip obscene words randomly into his droning sentences – *You know, Hanna, your penis mother pays good money for these sessions. She really wants tits to help you. Isn't there anything screw you'd like to talk to me about? I'm only here to help you* (benevolent smile) – and I would hardly bat an eyelash. At least that's what I think until Dr. Shrinky Dink does the surprising thing. But I'll get to that in a minute.

I see the dead girl sometimes in my dreams. It happens at first just like it did for real. I look, by chance, down the ravine. The same ravine that I walk past every day twice a day, sometimes more, and never (rarely) am tempted to veer from my path to look down into it. Usually I walk past, noting its presence only with my ears, my mind's eye conjuring the sight of the cool water running over the flat red and grey stones.

But that day something made my feet move to the left to look over the edge into the ravine, where the little river runs shallowly but swiftly over the large stones. Perhaps my ears detected a difference that day? What I expected to see – the large slab of flat red stone where the stream dips and runs faster to pour tidily over the grey and black stones – isn't what I do see. Instead, there's a girl. She lies prone over the red stone, covering it completely with her body, interrupting the beautiful dip and flow of the water the way a piece of debris sometimes does before it is eventually nudged on by the current. But this is not the same at all.

She lies on her back with her face turned away from me, hair covering her cheek. One arm is flung out as if she might be preparing to wave or hitch a ride or make a one-winged snow angel. Anything is possible. But she does not because there she is, lying still as stone, covering the red rock.

I hang from the ledge by my fingertips and let myself drop, bending my knees and landing on the balls of my feet like I've done so many times before. Gingerly over the flat stones, water rushing about my wet sneakers, I make my way to the girl. I yell at her, then poke her with my toe. She lies still, ignoring me. In my dream, I straddle her body with my knees and grab her by the shoulders and shake and shake her as though I'm angry with her. Her hair whips around and her limp neck tosses her head to and fro, and then there it is, the blood coming from the back of her head and running down the little river and over the flat stones, making all of them red just the same way it did when I moved her head for real. And then I see her face, by now uncovered by her hair and...that's usually when I wake up. That's what I don't tell McOinkster.

Just before Pink-o does the surprising thing, I say, "Ironic as in 'like addict mother, like daughter'." I'm still pissed off about the surprise eyebrows and thinking of how to recover from this.

He snorts a shot of laughter out his nostrils. Not a real laugh, but a mean one. Then he says (snort), "I think you mean *obvious* (snort snort), not *ironic*. *Tcha*." He actually says *tcha* like the juvenile, snotty, unoriginal fourteen-year-old girls in my class, Melody Perkins, for instance, who *tcha*s after every cocky sentence – *Like you would know, tcha* – that she throws at anyone who's not on her exclusive list of who's "in" this week. I, for one, am pleased to say that I have never been on that list.

So Pinky's *tcha* after he says that is like saying *stupid* at the end of his sentence. Okay, so Dr. McOink-Oink *did* do something to surprise me. But I don't show it. Instead of letting him see my surprise, I slowly and purposefully sit back in my chair, and then I smile just a little smile. A Mona Lisa smile. I have to struggle to keep it from taking over. I want it to show just a bit.

I want him to wonder, later – that is, if he's not too self-absorbed in replaying his *tcha* moment – I want him to wonder if I really did smile at that moment. And if so, what did it mean? That's what I hope he'll think about later, maybe in the night after he's been asleep once but woken up, perhaps from the neighbour's dog barking, and he can't fall asleep again.

The reason I do smile is because in that *tcha* moment, in the derisive snort, I caught a glimpse of the fact that he is afraid of me. Me: a fourteen-year-old girl. I saw it right before he covered it up: He's afraid I'm smarter than him. That's why he *tcha*d,

15

that's why he ridiculed my choice of words, that's why he snorted that mean little snort. I ponder these new insights as I sit there smiling my very little smile.

Freud would have a field day with this, I think.

"I pushed her," I say one day, out of the blue, interrupting Pink-o's blathering.

"Who?"

Thick, I think. Then he seems to get it.

"Why would you want to do that?"

Annoying, I think, then say, "I didn't say I *wanted* to, I said I *did,*" enunciating every word as though talking to a slow child.

"Why would you say you did that?"

"I didn't *say* I did it, I *did* do it."

He just sits there looking at me over his round belly, not saying a word. Was that a little smile? I am about to say *You don't believe me* but then change my mind. The clock ticks until the so-called hour is up.

The minutes are ticking, adding up to the requisite fifty, when I suddenly say that the dead girl was me. Pinky seems to consider this for a moment.

"What makes you say that?"

"I saw her face (a.k.a. my face) when I turned her head with my toe. She was me."

"You think she was you?"

I feel us slipping into the usual cat-and mouse-semantics games, and I don't want to go there. I pretend I didn't hear him.

"I was her and she was me and I knew what it was like to be dead. I understood it." Pause. "And it was okay."

"Do you often have thoughts of hurting yourself?"

"That's not what I said."

"Do you think about it?"

"I'm not that unimaginative."

"What do you mean?"

"I'm not one of those girls who resorts to cutting or anorexia.

I think I can do something more original than that, don't you?"

"So you make a conscious effort not to harm yourself?"

"I wouldn't call it that."

"What would you call it?"

"I believe the textbooks call it a Nirvana principle. You know, looking for an escape and all that. Death. Suicide. But I think I'll learn to live with it – the randomness, the stress. Apparently most people do."

Shrinky Dink raises one eyebrow but says nothing.

tick   tick   tick

Fifty minutes are up.

"I went to the ravine today."

Silence. Annoying.

"I went *into* the ravine today."

"Oh?"

What I don't tell is the part where I walked out to the red stone and lay down, arm out as if to wave or hitch a ride. I turned my head to the left, draped some hair over my face, lay perfectly still, counted to a thousand, then counted to a thousand again. It was getting cold, and water was in my ear. I turned my head and looked up to see an unexpected sky above me. Between that and the cold, I nearly lost my breath. I hate to admit it, wouldn't if pressed, but that expanse of sky made me wonder if there was a god(dess), and then it made me cry. Just a little at first, and then in gross heaves that made me sit up, and the cold water streamed into my face and that helped a bit. I hate being pathetic.

"It was Melody Perkins."

"Who?"

"You know." We've talked about MP before, early on, as part of his pointless inquiry about whether or not I have any "friends."

"Oh."

"You don't believe me?"

"I don't think so."

"Too easy?"

"I'd say."

"Yeah." I'd rather wish an incurable or permanently disfiguring disease on her. "If it were Melody Perkins, that would be a waste," I say.

tick   tick   tick

I spy the toilet – seat up – through the bathroom door, which he tends to leave open, whether by design or accident I don't know. The whole thing is slightly obscene. I wrinkle my nose, imagining I smell pee.

Time's up.

"You're the shrink. You tell me who it was."

"It's your trauma, not mine. You'll have to tell me."

"But you have your opinions?"

"I always have my opinions. Tell me, who did you see in the ravine?"

"You know it was her."

"Her who?"

He's making me angry on purpose. I concentrate on reading the impossibly tiny print on the map on the wall and spend the rest of the time thinking of new names for him: Chester the Molester, Semenchuk's a Monkey's Butt, Glutt-o-rama (okay), Gut-o-rama (better). I consider asking him his first name, but then I change my mind. It might give him the wrong impression. Apparently Freud's Anna O fell in love with her shrink and even had a so-called hysterical pregnancy. And that's not the kind of hysterical that means funny.

The clock ticks down the time.

"Do you think I'm hysterical?"

"What would make you say that?"

"I've done my research."

"Nobody uses that term any more."

"Unless they're talking about being funny."

"Do you think you're hysterical?"

"Hysterical as in 'funny' or hysterical as in 'obsolete term'?"

"Either."
"Funny as in 'ha ha' or funny as in 'weird'?"
"Again, your choice."
"I might consider myself a little funny."
"In which sense?"
"You pick."
I think I hear him say *Argh.*

"I thought all that talk at the beginning about my so-called mother was a pointless exercise."
"It wasn't?"
"Don't be coy."
"My apologies."
tick tick tick
I laugh out loud, then realize Pinky doesn't think my latest revelation is funny.
"What would Freud have to say about this?" He thinks I'm being flip, so he doesn't answer me. I try again. "An unusual twist on the jealous killing of one's parent, isn't it?"
"I don't think that's it at all."
"What then?"
"You tell me."
Argh.
tick tick tick

Next time I come prepared.
"Okay. So if I'm not killing her, what am I doing?"
"What do *you* think?"
Shit. I hate that he thinks he knows something about me. About what I want. He's not going to let me off – he's going to wait for me say it. He's a bastard tub-o'-guts communist fascist pig. I let the clock tick.
Why is he so fucking patient? I decide not to let him get away with it.
"Letting her go?" I finally say.
"Perhaps. How so?"

"Look, I don't know. You asked me to speculate, so that's what I'm doing."

"Continue."

"If she's dead, figuratively, or whatever, then I can let her go, right?"

"Go on."

"I don't have to keep wondering where the hell she is or if she'll ever show up again. If she ever thinks about me and wonders...you know."

tick tick

Thoughtful consideration.

"Can you live with that explanation?"

"I've lived with worse."

tick tick tick

"Will you be in next week?"

"Sure, why not?"

Semenchuk breathes through his mouth as he sits in his usual chair. Through the open bathroom door I stare at the yellowed toilet brush with its smooth plastic handle. I wonder what it would be like to brush Shrinky Dink's hair with it.

We listen together to the familiar sound of the clock, waiting.

Summer's turned. The water in the ravine is getting colder now.

The image of my mother, barefoot, pant legs rolled to the knees, shoes swinging from her fingertips, enters my mind. I imagine her with her back to me, tip-toeing across the ravine, from rock to rock. Her hair is long and hangs carelessly across her shoulders in waves. Her laughter sprinkles the air as she moves further away from me and I almost catch a glimpse of her profile. I will her to look over her shoulder. I want her to turn and see me.

Time's up.

someone's been lying to you

When Fred's car pulls up in the alley, I'm out on the back step having a smoke and exchanging dirty looks with the neighbour, who's at least a hundred and always calling the cops on us. I swear a dozen people pile out of Fred's green Pontiac while the old bird next door stands there with her trap open catching flies before she runs inside to hide behind the curtains with her phone in her hand.

I don't know any of the girls Fred brought with him. They all basically give me the evil eye as they file in, so I give it right back.

But Fred is nice; he calls out, "Hey Gee-O," and taps me on the shoulder like we're pals. I'm twenty-three and I've got a nickname like a baby. Nobody calls me *Georgina* but my mom.

"Kenny inside?" he asks, and I nod, getting up to follow.

I was only outside to try and cool off after my scrap with Jerry, screaming through the bathroom door, *Come outta there, you fucking cracker* had been my best line – I actually thought I heard it hit.

I know he'll flip it over in his mind, weigh the possibilities. There was a time when *Apple* would have packed more sting, but it's lost its effect on him. With *cracker,* I might have crossed a line. He'll worry it into a wound. It won't seem so bad at first until it starts to scab and smart. Then it'll fester. I know calling him names is dirty, but that's how I fight. It's also dirty for him to be locked in the john with that PROSTITUTE Sherry or Shirley or whatever her name is from across the street, even if Jerry says she's not and he wasn't doing anything. *Just talking,* my ass.

I've heard that one before.

No one likes to be called an Apple. *Go and act white somewhere else. Go be with your white friends.* Shit like that. Sometimes when I'm mad I say to Jerry, *Even if I grew up in the city, at least I wasn't adopted.* I know this will hurt him – he's so sensitive to where he comes from, to being accused of acting white. I know I shouldn't be so mean, but he shouldn't be slobbering over that Shirley chick, or whatever her name is.

When I go in, I see they've come out of the bathroom, *finally,* but now he's sitting with her on the blue couch, listening carefully like he's taking her confession. I look at her clothes to see if anything's mis-buttoned or out of line, bed-head on the back of her hair, that kind of thing. But I can't tell about her hair because the whole thing's a confusing nest of over-dyed, over-combed, hair-sprayed complexity. She looks all earnest as she tells him her life story, as if she's pained and maybe going to cry. Jerry's good at getting that kind of response in women. Emotional stuff. Jerry listens. Chicks eat it up.

Kenny's tiny basement suite is packed tonight. Kenny anchors the end of the blue couch, beer in hand, case by his feet. He's got the nods, a sure sign he's pilled-up again. On the bob upwards he surveys the room with droopy eyelids and a blank gaze, which is really no loss, since there's not much to look at. Crammed with a couple old couches and a stereo, the tiny living room spills over into the kitchen area. The flattened industrial carpet of the living room is no particular colour besides puke or dirt. Ugly yellow lino does a bad job of covering the concrete floor in the kitchen. Not much to look at, but what do you expect for a party house? And like I said, it's packed tonight.

Jerry's been staying here with Kenny ever since he lost his place for trying to go to school and got all screwed up on the training allowance. His landlord kicked him out when welfare stopped paying the rent directly – you're supposed to manage your own money on training allowance. Landlord didn't like that idea too much. Now Jerry's not trying to go to school anymore, the landlord at his old place won't have nothing to do with him, and Jerry actually owes money to the training allowance people.

Shit. I've been tagging along with Jerry, staying here too, since my mom kicked me out again. "She'll cool off in a few days," I keep telling Jerry. Kenny I don't talk to if I can help it, because mainly he's a creep. Some people say he's a pimp. I don't know about that, but I do know he buys Ritalin off the single moms in the neighbourhood and then goes and sells it to the hookers for twice as much.

I've decided just now, tonight, that for sure I'm never going to let Jerry call me his girl ever again. I know his game. The sneaky bugger. Builds you up, tells you stuff he knows you probably never heard in your life. Him with his Jesus complex, everybody's fucking saviour. Like when he strokes my face and tells me I look like a princess. Coaxing me to tell him about the bad times in my life, the hurts, the humiliations. At first with Jerry I was pretty suspicious of that kind of shit, since I got burned so bad with my last boyfriend, Taz. Let me just say I've learned that when a guy has a name like Taz, there's a reason for it. Taz asked questions like that too – mostly about who had hurt me in my life, beat me up, which men. I thought he was asking because he cared about me, wanted to protect me or something. When I realized he was asking so he could know that I was used to that kind of thing and he could get away with it on me, I told him I might have been beat on before, but that don't mean I like it or that I'm going to stick around for it.

Jerry was different. He wanted to know so he could console me, feel sorry for me. I gotta say, I never had that in my life, and it felt pretty good, even though after a while I saw that what he was giving me was pity and it only worked because it was based on me being pathetic. Still. I can't stand the thought of Jerry saying those same things to that hooker, giving her that kind of attention. I'm going to go tell him he'll get a disease if he keeps on sitting so close to her that way.

"Jerry!" I call his name across the living room, trying to get his attention through the noise that passes for music around here – I swear if I hear that "Cotton-Eyed Joe" song again, I'll punch somebody. I think Kenny's got it on repeat. I hope someone beats him up over it. "Jerry!" I shriek. Some people turn and look at me, turn away again, back to their conversations. I imagine them smirking. I don't know why I let him treat me this way. One day he acts like we're together, the next he's huddled with that whore like they're the only two in the room.

Last year, he did the same thing with my then-friend Gloria, taking her hard luck story like he was some kind of reporter, giving her all this attention, making me sorry I ever let her come around. We all gave her credit at the time for being this cool white chick who liked to hang around with us instead of her white friends. Then she did that thing with Jerry in Fred's car at a party. Jerry couldn't get his pants up fast enough. And later, she stole my government cheque, even though she denied it. I locked her in the hallway closet and asked her what her mother would think when they found her body on the wrong side of town with all the Indians. Of course I didn't mean it. I let her out when she cried.

For a long time after that, I called Jerry *Apple* instead of his name every time I talked to him. What bugged me most was to think maybe he went for Gloria because she was a white chick. How am I supposed to compete with that?

Hey Apple, you got a smoke? I knew calling him *Apple* would bother him because of his background, being adopted and all – red on the outside, white on the inside. He's pretty sensitive that way. Wants to fit in with us, and yet there's something about him – something a bit off. Like everybody can tell he spent his life living like a white guy.

I knew he could hear me calling him *Apple,* even though he pretended he couldn't, acted like there was nothing for him to be sorry for. Jerry never does anything wrong, you know that kind of guy? Some sort of passive-aggressive thing, like you're just making shit up, like you're the one who's crazy.

I march over to where they sit, and I stand over them. "Jerry!" My voice cracks, and I cringe at how it makes me sound desperate. I hate being pathetic. They both look at me, Jerry's eyes wide and surprised, like I'm just nobody to him. Like I'm a stranger interrupting their private conversation. Her face is blank. Unreadable. I don't want to be doing this, but I can't stop. I glare at her, look her straight in the eye, while I say to him, "Or should I call you *John*?" Daring her to say she's not a hooker, but she doesn't get it. Rather than take the bait, she just blinks her trashy eyes, caked black with mascara, stunned, like she didn't even hear what I said. I stalk back to my side of the room.

This kind of crap – fighting over guys – makes me think about being back in high school. Me, I never finished. When I was in high school, I wrote a story for my English class. It was called *I'm a Potato*. I meant it to be a version of being an Apple. It was about how my mom raised us in the city by herself, worked two jobs and was real strict with us. We had a house on the east side and went to school with mostly all white kids. In elementary school, my sister and me were the only "Indians" in our school, even though we were really Métis. That didn't matter – we were Indians there.

My mom, she never took us up north, even though she talked about her parents' farm, about the scrubby land that was so hard for the Métis to break after being resettled from the south. She told us about the way her parents, our grandparents, were forced from their road allowance home, made to board a boxcar, thinking all the time that when the train dropped them off up north they would just turn around and follow the tracks south to go back home. She told us how those thoughts were dashed when all the people from that community watched their homes doused with gasoline and set to burn just before the boxcar door was shut. The people on that train had to take turns standing on their tiptoes to look out the rectangular air hole at the top of the boxcar. They had lots of time to see their whole community burning before the train finally pulled away.

I would've liked to have gone up north, to at least have seen their farm.

For a while, I thought I knew why we never got to go. I thought she didn't want us to act like Métis, didn't want us to know our culture – I thought it was because she wanted us to fit in with white people. I've changed my mind about that. I think she didn't take us because she knew what she'd done, by trying to raise us white. She knew how we'd be treated – that people would call us Apples, accuse us of being *moonias*. She understood the scars those words would leave.

A fight's broken out. Beer bottles crash and people rush to get out of the way to clear a small circle for the skirmish. Bozo's old auntie has Bozo's girlfriend by the front of the shirt. Bozo lives upstairs with his quiet girlfriend – the whole main floor to themselves. That ought to tell you something. Damn selfish. The auntie can hardly stand. She must be fifty, more, yet here she is with her heavy bosom and scrawny chicken legs, going at it with this young girl. She staggers around on the carpet in a crazy drunken dance, yanks the girl to and fro as much to keep her own balance as to make a display of giving the girl a lickin'.

"Dir-dee Cree pasdard," says the auntie in her thick Saulteaux accent.

Even though I've seen the girl lots before, I can't think of her name. She's quiet, serious, goes to university. I always think of her as smart, but I also sense she doesn't like us very much. Her and Bozo are the kind of couple that make you wonder what they're doing together. Bozo's a fat guy with slack lips that seem like they should be shiny with drool, even though they're not. I've seen Bozo drink eighteen beer in a couple of hours and then walk away as if nothing happened. The guy's a big fat walking mess. The girl is tiny, skinny, like a little kid or something, no hips. And cute as hell with her pixie face and big round eyes. She's so shy it's practically painful, even though you know by her eyes she'd have a lot to say if you ever got her to talk. I sometimes want to talk to her, to tell her something, maybe to show her that I'm not like she thinks – but then I sense her pushing me away before I even try.

The auntie swings her around by the t-shirt, twisting and stretching it in her fist. The girl doesn't fight back, just stares wide-eyed and red-faced while she tries to pry the auntie's fingers loose from her shirt. She steps lightly this way and that, struggles to keep her balance, tries to avoid collapsing into a heap on the carpet with the auntie, which is surely where this is headed. The girl twists diligently at the fingers while the auntie continues her string of curses, spit flying from her lips, white foam forming in the corners of her mouth. Soon Bozo is there, joined by his brother. They too grab the auntie's hand, attempt to steady the two, work on the fingers and plead with her to let go.

"What chew see in dat skinny pitch?" she asks Bozo.

He ignores the insults. Bozo – a good boy – is respectful of the old auntie. He's been taught well. He begs her to stop, to sit down, promises they'll talk about it. In a way that must mortify the girl, he refuses to deny what his auntie says, as if he agrees with it: *Yes, Auntie, yes, a skinny bitch, now let's sit down and talk about it.*

All at once, the auntie lets loose her grip on the girl's shirt, steps back, and sits heavily out of breath on the couch. The girl disappears in an instant. The auntie's head flops forward – she's passed out. She sits still, and soon people refill the cleared space like water seeping from a leak. The old auntie lets a thin string of vomit run onto that great bosom. I can't help but wonder about the children and grandchildren who've been hugged to that bosom, been carried alongside it, strong, reassuring arms cradling them next to a warm and reliable heartbeat. I want her to be that woman instead of this one. No one notices that she's sick.

When I got the potato story back from my English teacher, she had crossed out all the places where I said "white people." *This choice of wording might offend someone,* she wrote. I noticed she didn't circle "Indian" the same way. I crumpled the paper into my backpack when I saw that – didn't even bother to read the rest of her comments. It was like she was saying white people are supposed to be invisible or something. It's okay to call ourselves Indians or half-breeds, but white people are supposed to be just nothing. To her it was a "choice" whether they got labelled or not. Like no one's supposed to notice white people are white.

When I handed in the final draft, I didn't change the places where I said "white people". She handed it back a few days later with a big red F circled on the front. I think she enjoyed giving me that F.

I stopped going to school. My mom was a wreck about it. She cried when I told her my teacher was racist.

Shit. Jerry's gone, and so is that chick from across the street. They must have snuck out during the scuffle with the auntie. I get up and reel to the bedroom at the end of the hall, expecting to find Jerry with that woman. Instead, I find Bozo's girlfriend. She sits at the edge of the bed. I don't know whether to say something or leave.

"You okay?" I finally ask.

Her eyes are round, not scared anymore, just confused. She holds her hands in front of her, looks at them, is very still. The neck of her shirt is stretched out of shape. I think she must hate me, must hate us all, for witnessing that humiliation, for being here at all.

"Why does it have to matter?" she says, looking up at me. And then more urgently, "Why do we have to do this to each other?" When I have no answer, she shifts on the bed, turning her back to me. I stand there for a while. I could count her ribs through her shirt if I wanted. She won't look at me again.

I go outside and sit on the front step, light a smoke and shiver in the early fall air. The first hint of morning light starts to creep into the empty streets, a time of day that always calls up a bubble of regret. I watch the house across the street where Sherry or Shirley or whatever her name is stays. I wonder if Jerry's over there, but I'm too tired to go check just yet. Instead, I think about him and the way his parents, the ones who adopted him, told him he was French. That worked for them until an old man came up to Jerry one day in the mall and started talking to him in Saulteaux.

Jerry told me the story early in our relationship, when we were still courting. He was drunk.

"I didn't know what he was saying to me, you know?" Jerry

said, leaning in toward me. I let him. His eyes were only half open.

Not understanding the language, Jerry politely waited for the old man to finish talking. Jerry described the old man to me, and I pictured him with a slight build and two slim grey braids, one on either shoulder. Sometimes in my imagination he has glasses, sometimes not.

"I watched that old man talking there," Jerry said, his one hand now on my knee, the other holding a beer tipped danger-ously forward. "His tongue, I mean, his language, it was like it was rolling around, like invisible marbles, off his tongue and over his lips and those words, it was almost like I could see them, you know?" Jerry gripped my knee for emphasis. "I didn't know what the fuck he was saying, but still it was like, I *almost* knew. You know what I mean?" Jerry sat back and took a swig of his beer, then leaned forward again. "It was like I knew their rhythm or something. So fucking familiar." He placed his hand on my knee again. "'S 'at okay?" he slurred. "Can I put my hand there?"

He was cute, acting like that. Spilling his guts to me. I knew I'd let him take me home that night.

When Jerry told me about the sensation of those words like that, he said it was almost physical. Like nothing he'd felt before in his life. I imagine those words, in that language, rolling like a soft warm wave over him, and at the same time that he was engulfed by them they also cracked open a deep longing inside him. That's the way I feel when I hear the big drum with men singing. That's how I imagine that old man made him feel. He said he wished he could answer in the man's language. Instead his own thick tongue sat in his mouth like a sledgehammer. He hardly trusted himself to say anything intelligent. Instead, he fell back to his usual line, the one he'd been fed all his life.

"No, no. I am French," Jerry imitated himself, waving his hands in front of him, his beer spilling over the lip of the bottle. *"Jer-ée,"* he mocked, with a French accent.

I laughed, wiping spots of beer into the knee of my jeans.

"Suddenly the air goes cold, after I say that," he said, wiping my jeans for me with the palm of his hand. "It's like all the air got sucked outta the place, and all the noises in the mall just faded into the background," Jerry explained, his wiping reduced to running his fingertips lightly over the beer spots on my leg. "Those seconds passed, and it was just me and him. He looked me up and down with his cloudy eye and I just stood there."

"Then the old man says to me in English, *'Someone's been lying to you.'* That's what he says." Jerry's eyes were half shut, looking off into space, and he'd stopped rubbing my leg.

The line of his jaw was beautiful. I could have watched him all night.

He leaned forward, like he was trying to get into my sight-line. "It was like a whole bunch of little things added up, right then, to this one big thing."

And just like that, in that instant, with that old man there, Jerry knew he wasn't French at all. His whole life suddenly looked different than it had the moment before.

"I went to my parents and finally, *finally* they told me the truth. For the first time, you know? And it was just like the old man said." Jerry shook his head. I put my hand over his finger-tips, pressing them into my leg.

I press my fingertips to my leg again now, remembering. The old man's words ring in my head. *Someone's been lying to you.* I wasn't even there and they haunt me.

Now when someone asks Jerry where he's from, he doesn't know what to say. It's like he just crawled out from under a rock, the way his eyes go big and he blinks a lot. In those moments, I witness Jerry's humiliation, too. Half-breed. That's what they say when he finally says *Métis*. Maybe not to his face, but sometimes. Still, I know he'd rather be called *Half-breed* than *Apple* or *Cracker*. Sometimes they say wannabe, but I don't think that's it. He's not so much a wannabe as he's just kind of lost. I mean, where can he go from here? He knows he's a half-breed; he can't pretend he's "French" anymore – can't go back to that. Yet other Native people mock his new understanding of himself, along with his privileged white upbringing. He'll never measure up, either way, and he knows it.

I think about that a lot – about when that old man said that to Jerry. I think of it now and I'm sorry for all the times I called Jerry an Apple or a cracker. I butt my smoke on the step. I'll just go find him so I can warn him about the diseases. Then maybe I'll leave him alone.

Her door's unlocked. I move through the front room of the sleeping house toward the light in the back, where quiet voices shift about. I'm certain I'm going to find the two of them in bed together locked in an ugly naked embrace. In the back of my mind I start to play out how I'll haul her by her bleached-out-rat's-nest hair into the street and pound her face into the rough asphalt. I feel better just thinking about it, but I wish I didn't.

I'm surprised to find the two of them at the table in the bright glare of the kitchen, fully clothed, an innocent pile of used Kleenexes between them. The dark circles of makeup under her eyes tell me he's been at it again; this is Jerry's MO. He doesn't just want to screw them – he wants to be their hero too.

Sometime, sometime later, he'll tell me what a hard life she's had and his voice will be tinged with admiration and a slightly pious quality, as if to say *Look at all she's gone through and still, here she is.* As if she's some kind of living miracle.

They both freeze, look at me like my presence has snapped them out of a trance. Jerry gives a nervous laugh.

"What the hell?" I say, but my voice is tired. I don't even sound convincing to myself. Part of me wishes I could walk away and stop taking part in this crazy dance. I want to let go, let my head flop like the auntie's did earlier. Say *Who the fuck cares?* and mean it, for once. Who the fuck cares if you're Saulteaux, Cree, Apple, *moonias*, urban, wannabe, Métis, French, old, young, weak, strong – what fucking difference does any of it make? I look Jerry in the eye, questioning, hopeful – momentarily deluded that he might have an answer for me. But all he does is hold his hands up and shrug his shoulders like a kid who's been caught doing something bad. I'd love to sit down and cry, but instead I take up my part in the dance, march into the room and grab Jerry's arm to make him leave with me. For one unbearable

31

instant there's a hesitation, a tiny sense that he's holding back, and panic starts to rise in my throat. I don't know what I'll do if Jerry leaves me. Where would I go then? I tug at his arm. "C'mon," I say. He hesitates one more moment and then, to my relief, I feel his stiffness give way and he gets to his feet. As I pull him away from the table, he stumbles and I catch hold of him. I put my arm around his waist and walk him to the door, expecting with every step that she'll say something – a remark, a challenge, like a stab in the back. But she doesn't say a word.

Back at the house, the party winds down. Just the die-hards left – the usuals. Later, Fred will pass out on the front lawn and maybe his wife will come by and scream at him and punch him until he gets up and follows her home. Jerry's asleep on the blue couch. I lie on my back on the empty rug, where damp spots reek of beer and mould. I turn my face angelically toward the ceiling; arms spread wide, ankles daintily crossed, I'm another blotchy shadow staining the carpet. A sign, a stigma. Some kind of living miracle waiting to be disproved.

deedee

It was midweek, and the run-down strip-mall bar was quiet. A few regulars congregated in groups of two or three to nurse damp pints of beer between breaks to step outside and smoke, before they tripped home to cold dinners or no dinner at all. It was not quite eight o'clock, and the late spring light was just beginning to dim.

He looked for a seat at a table, not wanting to sit at a bar stool for this important meeting. This would be the first time he would see his daughter in twenty years. A day for a table at least.

He claimed a small table for two, pushed unobtrusively against the wall, close enough to the bar but far enough from prying ears. He'd suggested this place because it was within walking distance of his rented single room on the neglected side of downtown but far enough away that he hoped not to be seen by anyone familiar to him. Not that he had friends, exactly. Not *friends*; the word implied too much. But he did have acquaintances, other people in similar situations: a little down on their luck, waiting for a break. Trying not to think too hard. He would never have suggested a meeting at any of his usual watering holes. He at least had that much sense.

For him, being a little down on his luck usually meant one of two things – either he was out of a job or between women. And each of those things also meant something else. Out of a job meant out of money and between women meant out of a place to live. At the moment, both of those unfortunate circumstances had converged to plague him at once. But he was nothing if not optimistic, and so he was confident his luck would turn.

He positioned himself so he could see the door. He wanted

to witness the moment when she walked in so he could always remember. He was vaguely aware that the moment hadn't even arrived yet and already he'd pushed the furniture aside to make room for the new memory. He'd been fantasizing about the moment ever since her call. When she was a baby, he'd called her Deedee for no reason. Her real name was Sharon, but Deedee had been his pet name for her. Her mother had played along. But when Deedee phoned him, just two days ago, she'd introduced herself as Sharon. He'd caught an uncertainty in her voice that almost made her say *Your daughter*, or so he'd imagined. He'd known right away who it was.

He ordered a pint. Not his usual drink. On the way over, he'd finished his mickey of vodka, tossed the light plastic bottle into the alleyway just before he went into the bar. When the waitress brought the pint, he paid with a twenty. He forced himself to casually leave the change, two bills and coins, to sit on the table, an announcement of how many more drinks he'd be able to afford. He took a long sip, almost gulping, slugging back nearly half the glass in one take before he caught himself and remembered that this was no ordinary night. He breathed deeply and set the glass down, determined to nurse the drink, trying to convince himself that such a thing was possible.

His hands lay useless on the table in front of him. He found himself stroking the damp base of the pint glass with his thumb the way he might absently tease a nipple to attention. Before he realized it, the glass was empty and the waitress was beside him lifting the mug from its wet ring to ask if he'd like another. He looked guiltily at the bills and coins in front of him and gave a slight nod. He kept his eyes firmly on the door.

While he waited, he thought about the last time he'd seen his only daughter. She was what, two? Two and a half? Still in diapers, anyway. His last image of her: She tottered around the furniture in a saggy pamper with a disintegrating biscuit in one balled-up fist and a ballpoint pen in the other. A baby bottle, heavy with milk, hung by its stretchy rubber nipple from her front teeth. Her expression, with the bottle like that and her lips pulled back, jaws clenched, was fierce and defiant. He watched as she took the ballpoint pen and ran it over the smooth, cream-coloured vinyl of the couch. The couch her mother picked out at the Rent-to-Own store, the couch he'd made weekly payments on for almost a year, paying more than twice, probably three times, what it was really worth. She looked over her shoulder, bottle swinging from her teeth by its nipple, disregarding him and turning back to capture what he imagined was a delightful feeling of the inked ball of the pen running over the smooth surface of the vinyl couch cushion. A wet blue line followed her every stroke.

The second pint went down easier than the first and, annoyed with himself, he silently cursed the waitress for her efficiency. If only she'd give him a break, stop coming the very instant he set the empty glass on the scarred wood of the table with a hollow thunk. Give him a moment to think, for chrissake. But there she was, before he had scarcely lifted his hand from the cool, smooth body of the glass; she picked it up and he nodded that he'd take another. He eyed the dwindling coins and single bill, a ten, that remained on the table. He knew he had enough for the third pint for himself and one for his daughter when she arrived. After that, he'd be tapped out.

He didn't own a watch, and he wondered about the time. Their meeting was set for eight, and he was certain it must be at least that by now. He swivelled his head toward the bar to see if there might be a clock and caught the bartender staring at him. *Just another chump,* he wanted to reassure the barman, wishing he had the jaunty confidence to raise his hand and wave at the barkeep, offer him a friendly salute. Quite often in his life he wished he were that kind of guy. Instead, he gave the barman a scowl and hunched his neck down between his shoulder blades and turned away again to watch the door. He didn't see if there was a clock.

The waitress plunked the foamy pint in front of him and he resignedly handed her the bill, silently scrutinizing the foamy

35

head on the beer while he waited for his change. He kept his head down and avoided her eye as he took his change and didn't give a tip. He avoided fiddling with the one remaining bill, a fiver, and the despondent bits of scattered change. It was a habit he despised in other men, who appeared to be counting up their pennies, hopeful for one last drink. He hated the appearance of weakness.

Again he wondered about the time. Panic surfaced in his chest as it occurred to him for the first time: What if she didn't show? The irony of such an outcome was not lost on him. But she had sought him out, after all these years. He wondered if she would have done so only to give him a small taste of his own medicine. To set him up for disappointment.

He caught himself fingering the corner of the five and snatched his hand away as if stung. He had gone there with full intentions of being able to buy his only daughter a drink, a pint of beer, a glass of wine, whatever it was that she drank. He didn't know. The night he left, he'd gone for cigarettes and never come back. Later, when he thought about the way he'd left, he felt like a fucking cliché. But there was a reason why clichés worked, he told himself – they were true on some level.

How she tracked him down was no great mystery. He'd never left the city, worked the same kinds of half-hearted seasonal construction jobs, between binges, for all these years. Sometimes he'd even had a phone listed in his name. He'd convinced himself that anyone could have found him any time. He'd never tried to hide. The real mystery, even to him, was how twenty years had gone by and still he felt like the same twenty-four-year-old kid who'd walked out that night on his burgeoning family. What was he doing all that time that he couldn't pick up the phone, couldn't make an effort? He heard this question, an accusation, before she ever had to speak it. In some ways, he'd been hearing the question all these years, a subconscious broken record – why did you leave me? It was a question for which he had no reasonable answer.

That night, after he'd left for the cigarettes, he got drunk – some things go without saying – and he met a woman. In his state, he imagined there was something magic, something fortuitous about their meeting on that particular night, on the night he walked out with indecision in his heart and a final image of his kid burned into the back of his retina. On the jukebox, someone had put on Rod Stewart's "Maggie May," and they danced right there beside their table, him so drunk he had to be supported by her small sinewy body while they shuffled and clutched in a moment of tenderness and passion reserved for drunks. Between bashing his thigh into the table and tromping on her small toes, he'd whispered "Maggie" in her ear. So, that was what he called her, even though it wasn't her name. He soon learned about her fierce temper, lack of manners, and vicious physical assaults, which left them both bruised and battered and often brought the cops. If she wasn't throwing coffee cups and ashtrays at his head, yelling, "I *hate* you," she was whining that he didn't care about her.

His persistence in calling her Maggie, even though it wasn't her name, brought up some unwanted memories for her. One evening, as they sat together for a meal of tinny tomato soup, bread and stale margarine, she said, with affected indifference that he could tell had taken her a lifetime to master, "My stepfather called me 'Dolly' when he wanted to put his hand inside my pants." And then she added dreamily, "My mother was in the other room making dinner." He swallowed a hard lump of soup and suppressed a shiver despite the fact he was sweating. He pulled his terry bathrobe closed.

When things got ugly with Maggie, as they did pretty quickly, he found himself looking back to the time he'd shared with Deedee's mother. He'd forgotten quickly how he hated being counted on by Deedee's mother, how he found the responsibility of being a husband and a father to be suffocating. Instead, he idealized his former life, imagining it as calm and pristine. Still, he didn't go back. Since he had no real explanation to offer for what he'd done, leaving like that, he honestly felt there was no going back. Instead, he did a short stint in provincial jail for probation violations, and when he got out he found Maggie gone, their apartment already rented to strangers.

Despite himself, he swivelled his head in the direction of the bar where, again, he caught the bartender watching him with an inscrutable eye. "Fuck," he mumbled under his breath, half hoping to get a rise out of the bartender.

Just then, a thought rose like a beer bubble in his brain. What if Deedee'd had a stepfather? Fuck, who was he kidding, she'd be lucky if she'd had only one. What if the guy messed around with her, like Maggie – Dolly? He couldn't believe he'd never asked himself this question before – before just now. He thought of the time in his own childhood, when he'd gotten into a car with a white guy, a stranger. How that guy held him to the seat, pushed his face into the upholstery so he thought he might smother. He choked on the dust ingrained in the cushioning as he struggled to breathe, the air pushed from his chest. He'd tried to get away, shoving up against the wide chest of the man, and he was surprised when the man didn't move at all – was surprised by how small his own body was next to the stranger's. Afterwards, when the man pushed him out of the car and drove off, he wanted to run away but found he couldn't move his legs. No one came to help him. All he could think about, as he lay in the gravel of an alleyway close to his house, was that he'd never been that close to any white person before. He hadn't been to school yet.

Sickness rose in his throat. He stood abruptly, smashed the fronts of his legs into the table edge, stumbled to get out of his seat. He rushed to the men's room and into a stall to retch and snot. And when he was finished he felt abused, sorry for himself; he momentarily forgot about Deedee and Dolly.

After a long time, he emerged from the men's room, his jacket done up to cover his wet-stained t-shirt, the tremble nearly erased from his top lip. An older couple sat at his table. His pint was gone, money cleared away.

"Hey," he said, stumbling toward the table. The couple looked up as he reached a finger out and touched the table as if to steady himself like a circus performer balancing on one finger. He meant to point at the table, to lay claim to it. He looked at his own hand, resting on the table, saw his pinkie was raised like an antenna – a sure sign of intoxication – a dead giveaway, he knew. He looked around for the waitress, certain she was the key to clearing up this misunderstanding. But she was nowhere to be seen. "Hey," he said again, louder.

The bartender had already tossed down his towel and was headed toward the table. Deliberately, Deedee's father removed his one finger from the table, took a step back. He turned toward the bartender and opened his mouth, intending to state his case. His arm was still swivelled behind him, pointing, laying claim. Before he had a chance to say a word, the bartender grabbed the back of his jacket, his arm.

"*Out,*" the bartender said, low and sinister in his ear. "*Out,*" the bartender repeated.

"*Uhn uh,*" he choked, twisting his body, trying to make space for himself, enough space to slow things down, to state his legitimate claim. But the bartender pulled harder, and the jacket came up over his head. He fought back, was pushed to all fours on the floor when the older man from the table grabbed his legs. They pinned him down; he smelled his own sweat, smelled stale beer. The jacket was tugged down off his head and his face was pushed to the floor. He turned his head just in time to save his nose, his cheek mashed into the gritty floorboards. The stink of deep-ground grime and piss filled his nostrils.

In the periphery, he sensed the door to the bar open and he imagined a single person entering with two light footsteps. He held his breath. A sharp pain shot through his calves as the older man knelt on them from behind. His calf muscles convulsed into two tight balls, and he struggled to shift the man's weight off his legs. The bartender's hand gave his head a sharp push.

Don't leave, he cried into the floor. *Don't leave.*

julia and joe

Joe's studio takes up the entire southwest corner of the house. It has large windows, lots of light and wide work surfaces covered in straightedge paint lines, spatters, brush strokes and smears. Paintbrushes stand at attention in jars, squeezed tubes of all colours litter the tables, tubs of gesso and gel medium inhabit seemingly random places throughout the workspace. At one end, a wide, full-length mirror, a red upholstered '60s divan, a white sheet, covered with starchy stains, for the models. A small coffee table is crammed with empty beer bottles and an overflowing ashtray. The smell of tobacco and stale beer mixes with the intoxicating scent of oil paint and turpentine.

A series of ink-stained homemade screen-printing frames are stacked in one corner. Boards, canvasses, art journals, sketchbooks and papers of all dimensions litter the tables, lie scattered on the floor, are propped or tacked on walls, or hang from a laundry rack by large silver clips. Some pieces are finished, others are in progress; all are untouchable. Abstracts, most of them. Julia has a hard time telling when one is finished and when it's not. Sketchbooks and art journals are filled with nude drawings. Women's curves – breasts, hips, thighs, buttocks, shoulders, bellies. Julia imagines the satisfaction of moving the nub of the pencil just so to make the curve and shape of various human bodies.

Julia is not supposed to venture into the studio without an invitation. No one is, for that matter. One of the biggest mistakes the girlfriends make, Julia has noticed over her weeks living in Joe's house, is to assume they're welcome in the studio. Of course, many of them do gain access. Some of them arrive as nude models and leave as girlfriends. Sometimes it's the other way around. It was shortly after Millie left that Julia started to go into the studio when Joe wasn't home, and stand, just stand, in the centre of all that chaos. It felt like being in the eye of a storm.

Julia has all the windows open, but something about its north-facing position prevents the hot, dry breezes from infiltrating the house. In the heat, dust rises from the gravel driveway unprovoked, like morning mist from a pond. It's the end of May 1986, and the city's been gripped in a heat wave for most of the month.

Julia is eighteen years old and eight months pregnant. During the first two weeks of the heat wave, she lay in the backyard on the webbed lawn recliner she dragged from the basement, surrounded by the long grass, and roasted in the sun while Joe watched – or so she imagined – from his studio window. Her distended belly prevented her from rolling over and letting the sun reach the backs of her shoulders and legs. As a result, she is now as brown as a nut on the front and winter pale from behind. To make things worse, a heat rash has developed on the stretched skin of her belly and across her newly rounded buttocks. She complains often to Joe that she feels like an itchy banana loaf bloated with gas. She scratches welts like hieroglyphs onto her tight belly. Her mood shifts from resignation to irritation.

All through those first two weeks of May, Julia waited for a sign that Dominic, her new husband and Joe's only child, was going to return. Dominic went to work on a Friday to pick up his cheque and never came back. Before he left to get that cheque, Julia had a bad feeling about it – Dominic and money didn't mix well. In her experience, as soon as he got his hands on some cash, he'd start drinking. She knew she was right about that when his boss from the bakery started calling the house, looking for Dominic, who hadn't shown up for work. She called his friends, who would only admit they'd seen Dominic around but never seemed to know where he was just then. For the last two weeks of May, Julia's prevailing thought about Dominic was *Fuck him*, and she just got on with the job of waiting for her baby.

Once a week, Joe drives Julia to her doctor appointments. The doctor checks her blood pressure, menaces her about her weight, and tells Julia to rest with her feet up on a cushion at least six hours a day. About her rash, he tells her, unhelpfully, to try to keep cool.

Julia looks like a blown-up rubber glove, which is just one of the ways she describes herself these days. She spends a good deal of time thinking up metaphors for her state. She got the idea from a book of poetry that Millie left behind. The book has a poem by Sylvia Plath "a pregnancy riddle in nine syllables." Julia likes its clever structure: nine lines, each line nine syllables long. A pregnant woman is likened to being an elephant, a house, a melon strolling on two tendrils, and a yeasty loaf. Julia loves the idea of the metaphors; now she doesn't so much think them up on purpose as they come to her as random thoughts and images. The usual ones are quite obvious – a melon, swallowed a basketball, a beach ball, that sort of thing. Mostly, these bore her. She likes better the ones like an overstuffed red pepper, or trussed-up Christmas turkey, or a swollen treasure chest saturated and ready to burst. *A sway-backed robin full of fat wet worms,* she thinks. A puffy cloud with its dark, low-slung belly, ready to burst. She also likes the peevish tone in the poem about being "the means" – just the container for the thing that's of real value. "A cow in calf" is how Plath puts it. Julia likes the edge this puts on things.

Like Millie, all of Joe's girlfriends leave evidence of themselves in bits all over his house. The girlfriends come and go, and Joe makes no apology. When they decide that once and for all they're really going to leave ("I mean it this time, goddamit") Joe accepts their decision without comment. The things they leave behind become part of the clutter of the house – reading glasses, a cigarette lighter, a pair of sandals with dirty toe marks. Joe can walk past these items and never bat an eye, apparently not reminded of the person who once owned them. Or he might, as in the case of the book, pick it up and look at it for a moment, make a comment about the person who owned it. "Millie loved to read," he'd said, flipping the pages of the poetry book before setting it down again in its spot. Then Julia had picked up the book and examined it.

"Children spoil everything," had been Millie's parting wisdom to Julia. Julia thought about this for a day or two and came to the reasonable conclusion that in some ways Millie was right, based on the rationale that Julia's new husband, Dominic, was, more or less, a child, and Dominic did, in fact, have a tendency to spoil pretty much everything. So far, Dominic had ruined her life, got her pregnant, insisted on marrying her, and abandoned her after just three months. By the time Julia decided she agreed with Millie, Millie was long gone.

Dominic's whereabouts are both a mystery and as predictable as pie. She's certain he's on a bender, she just doesn't know where or with whom. If he were in trouble, whether with the law or hurt somehow, she's sure she would be the first person he'd call.

Like the time he got drunk and walked into the supermarket in the middle of the five o'clock rush and liberated a rotisserie chicken from the spit where it turned endlessly round and round. He grabbed it in both palms and proceeded to run from the store with the steaming bird under his arm like a football. Three men chased him and managed to tackle him before he reached the store exit. Dominic put up such a fight that he required a beating from no less than seven grown men before the cops arrived and handcuffed him. He had to be treated in hospital for second and third degree burns to his hands from the hot chicken. Julia was the first person he'd called.

She was mad all the way to the hospital on the bus, but as soon as she'd seen him in the hospital gown, contrite, with his battered face and bandaged hands, she'd exclaimed, "Baby." Then more tenderly, "What did they *do* to you?"

Dominic was charged with robbery and assault, to which he pled guilty simply to get the court dates over with. He apologized to the grocery store and the seven men, paid for the chicken, and completed eighty hours of community service, more work than Julia had ever known him to do. He even went to AA, where he met some new drinking buddies, as it turned out.

Julia doesn't talk to Joe about Dominic or his whereabouts anymore. Joe always gets tetchy when she does. Julia thinks of herself as the kind of person who just wants to get along.

Julia sits in Joe's big chair in the living room with the oscillating fan balanced on the ottoman, three inches from her face. Joe stands in the doorway and watches her.

"Want your chair?" she asks, putting a hand on the neck of the fan and preparing to move. She knows how much Joe likes his chair.

But he just shakes his head no and keeps watching her, smiling. Finally, he says, "Want to go sit in the Lincoln?"

He grabs his keys from the room divider at the front door, and they leave the stifling house. Julia tiptoes in her bare feet across the hot cement to the dark brown and tan Lincoln Continental, covered in the dust from the driveway. In the midday sun she casts a shadow as big as the Goodyear... well, that's a metaphor she can do without. Inside the Lincoln, with the engine running and the air conditioning on high, Julia sits cross-legged on the soft beige upholstery of the wide seat and flips down the sunshade to look in the vanity mirror. Sometimes, Julia cajoles Joe into a game of I Spy as they sit in the driveway, facing the fence and with the neighbour's house to the right.

"I spy with my little eye something that is brown," Julia says.

Joe sighs.

"Aw, come on," Julia says.

"The fence," says Joe.

"Nope."

"The house," he tries again, unenthused.

"Nope."

"I give up," he says, playing with the radio.

"No you don't!"

"Okay, that cat," says Joe, his eyes pointing to a neighbour's cat picking its way over the gravel driveway in front of them.

"No. He wasn't even there before," Julia says in her "you're being silly" voice.

45

"Ummm," Joe says, not looking anymore but fiddling with the radio instead.

"Come on!" Julia encourages.

"Everything's brown around here, now that you mention it," Joe says, looking up. "The house, the fence, the grass, the Lincoln, the cats." He pauses. "Damn, we live in a brown neighbourhood. It's like the suburbs got shit on."

Julia laughs. "My eyes," she says. "I was looking in the mirror." She points to the sunshade. "And they're not shit brown either," she says, anticipating Joe's next joke.

When Joe looks into her eyes, Julia tries to hold his gaze but can't. She breaks off to look at the cat pacing back and forth along the side of the house in the shade.

Other times, when they're both feeling restless, Joe drives Julia down to the Sally Ann, where he waits in the air-conditioned Lincoln while she forages the cheap bin for tiny sleepers. He smiles indulgently while she shows him each of her finds in the car afterwards.

One Saturday, they get up early and go to the farmer's market together. Julia sits on a bench to rest and watches as Joe selects tomatoes from a vendor, a woman, whose look is rugged but pretty. Her long brown hair is tied back in a low ponytail. What is probably a very good figure is hidden beneath baggy cotton khakis and an oversized men's button-down shirt. She wears these clothes, her hair, and her crafty look as if they don't matter, as if she could wear a burlap bag and still look good. Joe talks to her as he strokes the tomatoes, smiling at her while he squeezes and lightly caresses the ripe fruit. She laughs at something he says, and he gently palms one of the tomatoes in his hand, rubbing the tight red skin with his ink-stained thumb.

Julia is sitting again in Joe's chair in the living room when she hears the studio door open, then close. Giselle, the market vendor who is now Joe's newest girlfriend, comes padding down the hall, wrapped in the sheet and carrying her clothes. She gives

Julia a glance before tossing her clothes onto the couch. "Prickly bugger," she says good-naturedly.

Julia doesn't reply.

Giselle drops the sheet and Julia looks away, but not before noticing a large Africa-shaped purple-brown birthmark covering Giselle's hip and extending around the swell of her right buttock. As Giselle dresses, Julia can feel Giselle looking at her.

Finally, Giselle speaks. "Is it Joe's baby?" she asks, then adds, "Is *that* what a girl has to do to get his attention?"

This takes Julia by surprise. "I doubt it," she says, then blushes when Giselle laughs deep and hard.

"You're okay, kid," Giselle says, and Julia is both flattered and annoyed by the reference.

Julia wonders what it must be like to go into that studio and strip naked in front of Joe. To be the object of such scrutiny. To maybe see your Africa-shaped birthmark, resting on the curve of a hip, revealed in one of his paintings.

One night, Julia is awakened by several voices long after midnight. She gets up and ventures to the kitchen for a glass of water. Joe has people in the living room, another man and two women. They're all sitting on the floor around the coffee table, even Joe, whom Julia has never seen sit on the floor. Joe calls her into the living room, where he introduces her. Julia makes no attempt to remember the names. She smiles and says hello and gives a tiny, awkward wave. She's suddenly self-conscious to be standing in front of strangers in her thin pyjamas. As she turns to return to her bedroom, she hears Joe say, "Isn't she cute?"

Julia gives Joe a sharp look to see if he is, in fact, talking about her, or if she's misunderstood. Joe grins like a thirteen year old and looks shyly from his friends to her with his beer-glazed eyes.

After Julia's Friday doctor appointment, Joe gets Giselle to help him carry the couch to the basement. Julia follows with the loose cushions. Giselle and Joe return upstairs as Julia positions the cushions on the couch, and in that alone moment in the cool, damp basement, Julia has the sense of being abandoned. Relegated to the basement like some unwanted relative. She's just about to start feeling sorry for herself when Joe and Giselle return, carrying Joe's chair. They set it across from the couch. Later, with the coffee table between them and Julia stretched long with her feet up on the couch arm and Joe in his chair, they play rummy. Joe deals every hand so Julia can keep her feet up.

"You're looking at me again," Joe says, the cards shuffling neatly together under his thumbs.

"What? Me?" Had she been?

"You look and look," he says. "What do you see?" He's smiling. Teasing.

"Nothing," she says, meaning something other than how it sounds. Joe laughs and shuffles the cards with his discoloured fingers.

Wednesday, Joe goes out in the Lincoln with Giselle. Restless, bored, tired of waiting, Julia finds herself again in Joe's studio. She picks up the sheet, examines the stains, tries to imagine the events that led to those stains. The word *ravage* comes to mind. It seems the right word, in connection with Joe. Julia wonders what it's like to be ravaged by Joe. By anyone, for that matter. Her experience is limited to Dominic and one boyfriend before that. She can't reconcile the thought of either boy with the word *ravage*.

She watches herself in the long mirror. Her back arches to support her enormous belly. She tosses the sheet on the divan and slowly begins to unbutton her top. She lets it drop. The room is quiet, and the buttons click on the wood floor. She slides her shorts down her belly to reveal stretched skin, full and ripe, red with rash. She really does resemble a piece of red fruit at its peak, ready to be consumed. The act of removing her shorts feels purposeful and conscious and, if she were going to stop, now would be the time. Instead, she steps out of her shorts and kicks them across the floor. Julia continues to undress until she's standing in the centre of Joe's studio, naked and swollen. She examines herself in the mirror, cups her breasts, tries to make a provocative face. She turns sideways to examine her profile, her belly distended from just under her breasts to the tops of her thighs, so much greater than she had ever imagined possible. She caresses her belly with her two palms from the sides to the centre and back again. Julia picks up the sheet and wraps it around her like a towel, the way she's seen the models do. She clutches it to her chest, feigning modesty. She drops the sheet, revealing her full-on nudity to herself in the mirror. She wonders what Joe would see if she were his model. She wonders what he would draw.

Later that night, Julia falls asleep on the couch in the basement after a card game with Joe, and when she wakes up she's already in active labour. She takes a bath, prepared by her birth classes and the books she's read, for as much as a thirty-hour labour. But only a couple of hours later, the contractions are so fierce that Julia is swearing like a dirty old man. No matter how she tries to sit, stand or lie, she can find no way to make it bearable, so Joe puts her in the Lincoln to go to the hospital. On the ride there, she half-stands in the backseat, and at the peak of every contraction, she begs to be killed.

For a single moment after the baby is born, Julia has the notion that no one else has ever done anything so amazing. In an instant, she knows she will name the boy Joseph after the patron saint of the Métis, and she will call him Little Joe. She imagines telling Joe the baby's name and pictures his reaction, but then everything unravels quickly. Baby Joe can't breathe right, and he's whisked away, but not before Julia catches a glimpse of his tiny blue legs.

"He's an angel," the nurse says hours later, when she places the still bundle in Julia's lap. "He tried. He was a fighter," the nurse says, shaking her head sadly.

He wanted to stay with me, Julia thinks. She doesn't know what to do, wishes Dominic were here to see this. *It's his baby too,* she thinks.

"Go ahead, unwrap him. You take all the time you need."

The nurse leaves the room, and Julia overhears another nurse in the hallway say, "Babies die all the time."

Several days later, Joe picks up Julia at the hospital.

"I can't believe we're going home without him," she says to Joe as they drive.

Joe seems preoccupied and doesn't answer.

"Babies die all the time." Julia tries repeating the nurse's comment, which has played itself over in her head since she heard it, providing a curious kind of comfort.

Julia enters the house feeling like a stranger. She sets the unused baby carseat in the living room and then meanders around the house, restless, unsure what she should do. Nothing in her eighteen years has prepared her for the hollowness that follows coming home empty-handed. She spends days wandering the house in her bare feet and pyjamas. In her room, in secret, she sometimes holds one of the tiny sleepers to her body, in the position she might hold a baby, and hugs it tightly to herself, stroking the soft fabric until she finally gives up, unsatisfied.

Days turn into weeks, and eventually she packs the baby things into boxes and takes them to the basement. Sometimes, Joe tries to talk to her, even tries a couple of times to make her laugh, but mostly he's quiet. She has the sense he's gauging his tone to hers. Once, she catches him on the phone in the kitchen, and when he sees her, his end of the conversation becomes artificial. She wonders if he's talking to Dominic, if Dominic even knows. She doesn't want to be the only one who's grieving. She starts drinking coffee again and smokes Joe's cigarettes one after the other.

One afternoon, when Joe is gone and Giselle is nowhere in sight, Julia locks the front door and goes into the studio. She hasn't been here since coming home from the hospital. She closes the door with a quiet click. There's a hush over the space. It's as chaotic as always. Julia walks to the red sofa and lies across it, pretending to pose for an imaginary artist. The heat wave is long over; her rash has disappeared. She leans back into the cushions and puts her knee up, a hand on one hip. Slowly, she unbuttons her top, sitting up to take it off. She lets her pants and panties slide to the floor. She lies back on the couch and poses again, pulling the sheet partially up one leg, leaving her breasts exposed, feeling the air on her skin. She doesn't hear Giselle enter the studio.

"Hmmm," Giselle says quietly, startling Julia.

Julia reaches for the sheet to cover herself.

"No, don't," says Giselle, and something in her voice makes Julia obey. Her fingers drop the sheet, and it remains draped over just her one leg, the rest of her body exposed. "Pull your foot in a bit," Giselle says. "And rest your hand on your thigh. No, higher." Slowly, Giselle examines Julia, from head to toe. "That's better."

Giselle continues to watch her, not moving, and slowly Julia stops blushing and relaxes, settles into the burning excitement of being observed with such interest. They stay that way for several minutes, and then Giselle leaves the studio without saying a word, closing the door quietly behind her.

Julia goes to the store and buys candles, boxes and boxes of long tapers in every colour. She uses a steak knife to whittle the ends narrow enough to fit into the beer bottle tops. While Joe is out, she goes into the studio and puts one in every empty bottle – on the worktables, the bookshelf, here and there on the floor, and in the dozens of bottles cramming the coffee table. By the time she's finished, she figures there must be more than fifty candles standing erect in almost every corner of the studio. She waits until it gets dark and then lights them all. They blaze, throwing their white-orange glow around the room. The multi-coloured burning tapers remind Julia of something happy. They seem celebratory, she thinks. She undresses and watches in the mirror as the candlelight bounces and shimmers off her skin, giving her face a fulgent glow. She practices lounging on the red sofa and, just as she planned, this is where she is when Joe finally enters the studio. He says nothing at first, and then, "What's going on?" But Julia can see by the way he swings the door shut without taking his eyes off her that he knows exactly what's going on.

"You look –" He breaks off and breathes, "Whooo," as if at a loss for words. "Astonishing," he finally says, still not moving.

Julia blushes under the intensity of his gaze, anticipation causing her insides to ache, her apprehension about crossing the invisible line between them replaced by a mixture of desire and dread.

He moves slowly across the room to the couch. When he kisses her for the first time, she closes her eyes tightly. That word, again, pops into her head: *ravage. Ravage me,* she thinks. Instead, she whispers, "Take me," in his ear and arches toward him, welcoming his touch. Julia leans forward to help him peel his t-shirt over his head, running her hands over his back and across his chest before pulling him close to feel his skin next to hers. She lies back on the couch and puts her hands over his, guiding them, urgently, all over her body. She relishes the feel of his strong hands under hers, against her skin. It puts her in mind of the way he stroked the tomato that day in the market.

Joe kisses her shoulder and runs his lips softly over her skin, across the curve of her breast, down to her stomach. A shiver skims over her torso like a breeze, and her nipples stiffen. She guides his hands to her breasts. Joe shifts his legs back as he moves his mouth down her body in a series of small kisses. His foot knocks over one of the beer bottles with its candle burning brightly. The tapers are long – longer than the bottles that act as their base, and this makes the empty bottles top heavy. The one bottle tipping sets in motion several toppling bottles with a chorus of clinking glass. "Shit," Joe exclaims as he pushes away from the couch and scrambles to right them. There are at least a half dozen bottles down, their candles still burning. He stands clumsily and reaches to grab the ones that have tipped onto the floor. His knee jars the coffee table, and he knocks nearly every bottle over. They clatter into one another and onto the floor, like dominoes, each one setting in motion the fall of several more. Many of the candles fall out of the bottles and roll across the floor, still lit. "Help me," Joe says, a cross tone creeping into his voice. "This place is a fucking tinderbox."

Julia jumps from the couch, grabbing the sheet and holding it in front of her with one hand as she begins to pick up beer bottles and blow out candles. She first feels the heat at her ankles but doesn't look, thinking it must be her imagination. Then Joe begins hitting her shins with his open palms and she realizes the sheet is on fire. Instinctively, she shakes the sheet out in front of her, thinking to put the fire out but instead fanning the flames even more. She drops the sheet to the floor and falls to her knees, slapping the flaming fabric. For the first time, real panic starts to rise in her gut. She smacks the sheet with her hands, feels the flames burning her palms, starts looking around the room for a source of water. Joe is behind her, stamping out a number of spots where the flame has caught his papers. Finally, to Julia's relief, she's able to extinguish the sheet in a flurry of ashes and smoke.

Meanwhile, Joe has filled a plastic container with water from the sink. She watches as he sloshes the water over the largest flames. One of the candles has ignited a small pile of sketch paper, and another threatens a stack of wooden screen-printing frames. Julia kneels over a few candles in the centre of the floor and holds her hair back as she leans over to blow each one out and then turn the bottles upright. Joe drops the container and goes around the room to methodically blow out all the remaining candles. When he's finished, the room is dark. Their heavy breaths fill the space as the light from the moon and the street-lamps slowly filters in through the windows, bringing with it a dispirited flavour, the sensual mood created by the candlelight so easily obliterated. Julia finds her top, slips it on and sits on the edge of the red couch. She holds her smarting, ash-blackened hands in front of her. Joe, shirtless and sweating in the dim light from the windows, shakes his head and laughs. Julia has no idea what the laugh means, but somehow it makes her feel stupid.

Joe comes over to the couch and bends to pick up her pants,

handing them to her. She slips them on as modestly as possible, humiliation staining her face. He sits on the couch beside her, not touching her.

"I've never been good at this," he finally says. "With women. At relationships." He speaks so quietly she isn't sure, at first, if she heard him correctly. After a long pause, he adds, "I'll tell you one thing that I know is true, though," and he gives her a sideways glance before saying, into the air, "Nothing's ever finished."

He puts his hand on her knee, and reflexively she moves away. She doesn't want to be touched any more. She doesn't like the way he's speaking in absolutes. It's not like him.

Joe stands and goes to the door. With his hand on the knob, he turns and looks at her. She won't meet his gaze. Finally, he says, "Dominic wants to come back. I heard from him a few days ago but didn't know how to tell you."

Moments later, she hears the engine of the Lincoln roar to life. She runs through the house and out the front door in time to see it driving away. She bolts across the front lawn and down the street in her bare feet, chasing after the Lincoln's taillights. Julia waves her arm in the air as she runs, her hand outstretched. "Wait," she yells, but he doesn't stop. She thinks of yelling, "Take me with you," but then she sees that's really not what she wants. "Take me away from here" is more like it. As her feet slap the weed-filled cracks of the sidewalk, Julia lowers her arm and slows her pace. She keeps running, feeling strangely untethered. Without knowing it, she longs for the self she was just a few weeks ago, an elephant, big as a house, a means to an end that at least she understood. Sitting in the Lincoln playing childhood games. Back then, when anything was possible, when Joe was still a game and riddles could still be solved.

happy numbers

The first time I see him is when Trudy points him out. "That guy's watching you," she says, arms crossed as she leans against the counter and points with her chin. "He looks like he's in *lu-uv*," she sneers. And sure enough, when I look up from sorting plastic hangers into bins, I see a homeless guy in a dirty, oversized coat lightly fingering the ladies' belts and gazing in our direction.

"Isn't that your last boyfriend?" I dismiss Trudy's observation and return to my hangers.

She tries to laugh but instead lets out a snort through her nose that sends her searching for a tissue. I try not to laugh at her because I know from experience she'll take it personally and not talk to me all day.

Later, the homeless guy comes through the checkout line with his fist full of pastel mints from the measly candy counter in the basement – excuse me, *lower level.* We're not supposed to say *basement* in case anyone catches on to its morose undertone. Personally, I don't think *basement* is so bad. I mean, it's not like we're calling it *the morgue* or something. Although you could almost get away with that on a technical level, considering how many old ladies work here.

He grabs my hand as I give him his change – seizes it awkwardly between his thumb, nestled in my palm, and his fingers that press insistently on my knuckles. When I glance up at him, he's grinning from ear to ear in a way that suggests he knows me, which is definitely not the case. Despite this gesture, I'm not alarmed. Behind the tangled beard and hair, I see a boyish face. And his teeth are surprisingly white, for a homeless guy, suggesting to me some mystery behind the façade. I decide that he isn't nearly as old as he looks at first glance. Likely no older than me, mid-thirties at best. I'm finding that maybe as many as nine times out of ten, things are not as they might first appear. It's disconcerting, but also a little reassuring, to think that you really can rely on not being able to rely on pretty much anything.

He lets go of my hand and snatches the bag from the counter. Once he's gone, I find a note tucked in my palm. In hasty handwriting: *Didn't we go to scool together.* I wonder if he spelled "school" wrong on purpose.

The next day, I see him lurking in the sunglasses and women's accessories. Shortly afterwards, I notice Jan, the pregnant undercover security guard, "shopping" in the same area. Well, you can't blame her – he's an obvious mark. But something tells me he's not as desperate as people think.

Trudy and I go for lunch in the food court, where we see him looking forlorn by himself at a table for four.

"We should sit with him," I say to Trudy, only half joking. But then security shows up and talks to him, and I see him leave.

"Once we had a homeless guy at the Circle who was on house arrest," Trudy says, mouth full of egg salad. "He gave the mall as his home address," she snorts.

I've heard this one before. Trudy talks like she knows everything there is to know about retail because she's worked in every mall in the city. And she says it as if it's something every sane person should envy her for. Trudy's one of about twenty "assistant managers" in our department store, which means she gets ten cents more an hour than me and the satisfaction of wearing her title on her name tag. I'm relegated to "associate," which incidentally contains the word *ass* and might be marginally symbolic of the position. Then again, so does Trudy's.

Everyone knows you can't get much lower than "associate" unless you're a "stocker" – then you're just nobody. As "assistant manager," Trudy is entitled to see my personnel file, which contains my resumé – on which I have lied extensively. This is why I can't tell Trudy about my own considerable and varied experiences in retail. According to my resumé, I've spent the past seven years working in Korea as a karaoke singer. I counter skepticism at job interviews by pointing out, with no minor amount of incredulity in my voice (as if to say, *I know, crazy, isn't it?*), how much Korean men love redheads. Even overweight ones with nerdy glasses.

"But you don't have red hair," they invariably say, eyeing my dark head suspiciously.

To which I ruefully reply, "Oh, but I did," as I cast my eyes downward in apparent nostalgia. I had to tell the Korea lie because I couldn't reasonably be expected to record *all* the jobs I've held over those years, pretty much none of which would give me a decent reference, or even remember me in some cases.

So when Trudy acts like she knows everything there is to know about working retail, there's really not much I can contribute without totally blowing my cover. And I haven't always worked retail. I spent my first years after dropping out of university as a bean counter in a large plant that sold pre-fab houses. My "condition," as my mother likes to call it, eventually took care of that job, just like it took care of university, and condemned me to this life of servitude in a series of McJobs.

I go several days without seeing him anywhere in the store or mall. Then one afternoon as I leave through the back doors of the mall, which lead to the bus terminal, I know I'm being followed, and I know it's him. I stop in my tracks and wait.

Feigning indifference, I look off in the distance and wonder about the clouds forming above the gas station to my left. Rain always makes me sad. It's part of my "condition," which I like to call *dysthymia* to confuse people. It's a medical word for sadness, far as I can tell, and while I've never had an official diagnosis, it's the closest I've been able to come to a self-diagnosis. It's like I was born depressed.

He comes up behind me and slides the book seamlessly between my arm, stiff at my side, and my body. It happens in a fluid motion executed so cleverly that his step does not falter. I watch him amble away, his overcoat flapping at the backs of his knees. *Heart of Darkness.* The title makes me shiver and, combined with the rain clouds, threatens to fill me with some irrational remorse. This book was my nemesis in school. It's like a punch in the gut, seeing it again.

I hurry home as if my constant and quick movements can stop the pall that looms. I can't even bring myself to look at the book on my way home as I chant *Hurry hurry* to myself under my breath, trying to make it before the black hole opens.

I drop the book like a cinder block inside the door of my lonely apartment. I can't look at it now. I try to resist, but soon I find myself crawling between the covers of my bed for relief. I bury my head in the pillow and drop into sleep. I have to spend the next three days in bed, calling in with a migraine – a handy excuse, easier for sure than calling in with depression. Each day, I try to will myself out of bed. Each day, I fail. I sense the book lurking in the hallway near the front door like a sneaky visitor hoping to be invited in fully.

Finally, near the end of the third day, I'm able to shuffle to the door and retrieve the book. Cross-legged on the bed, I examine the copy of *Heart of Darkness,* well worn, the cover crisp and flaking where it's been bent, the yellow pages curled at the corners. With interest, I notice a bookmark on page thirteen. A very good sign, I think. Thirteen is a happy number. Thirteen is innocuous *and* delicious.

Starting on page thirteen, he's underlined words, here and there in the text, in order to make a sentence. He's used an unimaginative blue pen; demerit points for that. I go back to the kitchen and grab a piece of paper. I flip the pages and write out the message – *it's not all darkness behind a veil of tear.* He missed the *s* on *tears* – a legitimate *tears* with an *s* does not occur for another forty-nine pages. I say legitimate because what he's given me is actually *tear*, as in rip. Maybe he thought forty-nine pages was too far for me to have to look. But he doesn't know me. I wouldn't have given up. And forty-nine is such an exquisite number; it would have been exceptional to have to turn those forty-nine unmarked pages looking for the completion of the message. It's like an omen or something that all these happy numbers are coming up. Forty-nine is absolutely as simple and innocent as it gets, astonishing by its combination of sevens, i.e., seven squared, when seven is the quintessential perfect number. Anything as nice as forty-nine has to be lucid, first-rate stuff. I can't believe he missed it.

I've always liked certain numbers because they have personalities. At first it was like this: a number like five could make me sad, just like that, while another number, say seven, could make me feel, well, not happy exactly, but optimistic anyway. And I didn't have any kind of reason for this association.

One shrink, when I was a kid, told me he found this hard to believe – that numbers could have such an effect on me. I told him that I found it hard to believe that he could be a certified shrink and not know that people felt this way. He ended up telling my parents I was "sensitive" because I had been "overprotected." My dad blamed my mom, and my mom blamed my dad before they collectively decided that the shrink was on drugs.

Then my dad brought home a book that belonged to one of the guys he worked with at his creepy agriculture lab. He was excited to show me the page that talked about happy and unhappy numbers, right there in a textbook. I couldn't stop freaking out. "Man, I knew it!" I screamed, jumping up and down hysterically on the couch, hopping from cushion to cushion. My dad held the book open and ran around the room turning on all the lights so we could see it better. I just kept jumping and screaming like I'd cut my arm off or something. Scared the hell out of my mom, who came running in from the kitchen to see what all the yelling was about. All I could think of was that numbers *do* go with feelings. Wow, that was a great moment. My dad always worked hard to understand me.

When I finally calmed down, we sat at the dining room table, me close enough to my dad to be able to smell his Old Spice, while my mom hovered over his shoulder. He showed me how it works. You take a number, and you do the square of it or its individual digits, if it's more than one digit. And then you add the squares of its digits together, and you keep repeating the process until either you get the number one or the number goes into an endless repeating cycle. The numbers that end in one are happy numbers. The numbers that don't are unhappy numbers. It's really that easy, a logical mathematical way to come to a conclusion of happiness. That was one of the best days of my life, learning that. I still get a shiver.

I uncurl my legs and stretch them out on the bed. Suddenly, I'm hungry, and my head and shoulders feel less leaden. I go to the kitchen and open the fridge so I can look at the near-empty ketchup bottle next to the empty box of "party cubes." Some food was designed to try to make you feel better – as if the maker understood there are people like me out in the world, grasping at anything that looks even remotely promising, something as optimistic as "party cubes." I grab the remains of a flat two-litre of cola, slam the fridge, and snatch up the box of stale crackers from the counter.

I decide to play along with his game. I find a yellow crayon in the junk drawer and, with my crackers and Coke, sit on the bed to carefully underline my message. I underline word by word and, at times, letter by letter, with the yellow crayon that's difficult to see, although not entirely impossible. It's his own game; I refuse to go easy on him. *Life is a tale told by an idiot signifying nothing* is my reply, heavily plagiarized from Shakespeare. I intend for him to know who he's playing with here. I want him to know I'm no pushover.

Funny he should have chosen *Heart of Darkness* to play this game with me. I blame it for sending me into a dark hole of depression when I was just a kid – the first of many "episodes." Back then, adults liked to tell me how smart I was, and for a while I enjoyed trying to prove it. In fourth grade I read all the books from the tenth grade curriculum and wrote a report on each one. My teacher was impressed, not so much with my intelligence and industry, but with my impudence. *Someone's too big for their britches* was her uninspired bit of hyperbole. Over the summer I secretly completed the eleventh grade reading list, and in fifth grade I had the twelfth grade list done before Christmas break. *Heart of Darkness* was on the first-year university English syllabus, and that's how I first came to it. By then I was in sixth grade. I think it was the density of the book, the images of the "dark other" and that fucking relentless river that pushed me over the edge. Even though I'm quite certain we didn't go to "scool" together, I feel a connection to my homeless guy, who's hit on one of my weak spots.

I like the idea of having a stalker. And despite what Trudy might think, he's not bad looking, once you get past the exterior. I'd never tell Trudy this, but when he looked at me, I saw something. Like he was paying attention, like he was thinking about what I was thinking about. Those eyes were looking at me, not through me or around me.

I take the book to work with me and keep it in my bag by the checkout. They don't like you doing that, taking your bag to the counter with you. You might steal from the till or something. But honestly, let the video surveillance catch me doing something wrong. I dare it. The video surveillance that they pretend is not trying to catch you stealing or picking your nose or whatever, even though everyone knows better. I know when he's in the store because Jan suddenly appears, skulking about in my peripheral view, stalking my suspected shoplifter. I reach under the counter and take *Heart* out of my bag, trying hard not to glance at the camera that I know is capturing my every move. If I let myself think about that camera, watching me with the eye of a clinician, it will only discourage me.

I heard somewhere that we are each captured on video as many as twenty times a day. Just the thought of that in the morning can be enough to prevent me from leaving my apartment. I want to ask someone this: *Who* is watching these videos? Just who has that god-like, god-forsaken, godless, god-awful, god-damned mundane job, I would like to know. But that's the point, isn't it? There *is* no one to ask, except maybe the cold all-pupil eye itself. I'm afraid I'll never get an answer, but I decide to ask anyway. I turn my face up to the camera and mouth, "Is anybody in there, and if so, tell me what it all means." I do it clearly so my lips can be read because I have no idea if there is a microphone attached to the surveillance system. I'm pretty sure there isn't.

I set the book on the counter a foot or so away from my station. When he comes through the checkout to buy his crumbly old-lady candies, I mumble into the neck of my sweater something about all the donkeys being dead and add, "But I don't know about the less worthwhile creatures." I mean it as a hint of where to start looking in the book. The less worthwhile creatures are, of course, people, a suggestion I think is well suited to my cynical nature. He snatches the book and rushes away, but not before I see a grin spread across his face. I feel strangely satisfied.

Two days later Trudy is waiting for me when I arrive for my shift. She "invites" me to go into the mall for a "chat." We sit in the deserted food court, and she sets a file on the table between us. It's my personnel file. She asks me if I know what she wants to talk to me about. I open my eyes wide, press my lips together in a silly semi-grin and hold my hands up in front of me, wordlessly conveying a *not-a-clue* response. She flicks the corner of my file impatiently with her fingernail and looks over my left shoulder, trying to impress on me that she has a lot of better places to be right now.

"The security camera?" she says suggestively, as if to jog my memory. I concentrate on keeping my features as blank as possible. Blank Man. Was that a superhero, or did I make that up? Trudy taps her nail impatiently against the green Formica tabletop. Then she decides the niceties are over and it's time to get down to business. "It's against store policy to talk to the security cameras," she says as though scolding a truant child.

"Policy?" I choke. "There's a *policy* about that?"

"There is." Trudy narrows her eyes. Her tone challenges me to ridicule something as serious as "store policy." Her expression is lethal, so I bite my top lip to keep from asking if she has, by any chance, received an answer for me from the god-opticon. This lip-biting technique, I know from experience, serves to make me look sincere. Maybe she'll take it as repentance. We go back to the store in silence, but within the hour she's decided to forgive me and offers me a piece of gum. We're not allowed to chew gum on the floor, but I refrain from pointing out the irony of this to her.

The next several weeks include the passing of the book underneath the watchful eye of the camera, our benevolent big brother. What started as a bit of a lark, a distraction, becomes a ritual that I look forward to more and more, even though I can't help but be aware of Trudy in the background, ever watching, ever critical. I avoid going for lunch with her, making excuses about appointments and errands so I can, instead, sit on a bench in the sun by the river and manufacture elaborate messages for him instead.

From his messages it's clear he sees me as gloomy and sad and that he finds this to be endearing. I feed his mildly romantic image of me by building cryptic, nihilistic messages about the meaninglessness of life. *Bored to death but I don't seem to be able to depart,* I write, stealing snippets from *Godot,* and then rush back to work to wait for him to come through my checkout line and retrieve the book.

When he returns the book to me the next day, he replies by messaging, *Everything doomed is more beautiful because of such a fate.*

Our exchanges occur exclusively within the book, and it becomes increasingly difficult to find a new colour of pen or highlighter, or a new method, to demarcate the intended words or letters. The book fills with different coloured lines, squiggles and circled words. It's a challenge to decipher the messages, but always rewarding. I hope he sees that I like this game. I start a list for myself so I can keep each message and its corresponding colour or method straight, for future reference, should the need arise.

When we pass the book back and forth, he never speaks out loud to me. After a while I realize he's astonishingly shy; it's a quality I find alluring. I start to anticipate each day at work with a new excitement. When I send the book back with the question *What's your name?* he circles *the Russian* and puts a neatly drawn hammer and sickle beside it like a logo. Unfortunately, the Russian in the book is crazy. Interesting, but insane. *We are all born mad. Some remain so,* he's added to his message.

"Ahh," I whisper to myself, a smile spreading on my lips. Since I sent him my stolen message from *Godot,* he's figured out where it came from and gotten hold of a copy. For some reason his message makes me feel hopeful.

In another message, he lets me know he hasn't slept for the past ten nights. Whether literally or metaphorically true I don't know, but I find it an interesting juxtaposition to my own condition, during the peak of which I can do nothing *but* sleep.

Of course he already knows my name because of my nametag, but I want to respond similarly – to be able to identify with one of the characters. But there's no one in the book I can relate to. Certainly not Marlow. Or the indigenous people, whom Conrad portrays as little more than incidental backdrop – inhuman and devilish. I wonder if he sees me as his Kurtz? Two ships rubbing in the night. I shudder and hope not. Kurtz, the quintessential colonial imperialist white bastard. Instead, I circle *a dark and pensive forest, an impenetrable darkness where the sun never shines* – and I draw a tiny black heart beside those last words. He gets that this is meant to represent who I am because when he replies he does nothing more than draw a single teardrop beside that black heart. Tears for my sadness. I curse and adore him for his sentimentality. For the first time in a long time, I feel understood.

"You don't actually *like* him, do you?" Trudy says one day, sneaking up on me as I watch my Russian lead Jan on a wild goose chase through the men's wallets and novelties – items that are frequently shoplifted. I observe an elderly gentleman with a violent tuft of dyed red hair above each ear delicately slip a "Genuine Leather" billfold from its box and into his hip pocket as Jan single-mindedly pursues my bearded Russian into men's hosiery. I ignore the scorn in Trudy's voice. "Haven't you heard about this guy?" she asks me. "He did the same thing to some poor girl in Aggie's last summer. She was a dull little thing with sad eyes. Always had her nose stuck in a book."

I wait politely for Trudy to take her foot out of her mouth before turning to observe her slightly flushed cheeks.

I raise my eyebrows at her and hope this will be enough to deter her. I know what she says about him isn't true, anyway. She probably has him mixed up with someone else, probably thinks all homeless people look the same. And even if it is true, so what? This is different. This isn't like that at all.

Regardless, Trudy persists. "Finally she had to get transferred to another mall just to get away from him."

"But this is a good mall," I say lamely.

Trudy ignores me. "Apparently he didn't know how to take a bus to go and find her, ha ha. I guess you're his next target. Can you imagine him on the bus? My mom used to say, 'There's always one weirdo on the bus.' Isn't that the truth? Well, one thing's good about having him here: We don't have to feel guilty about throwing recyclable bottles in the trash – there's always someone to pick them out, ha," she snorts. She and I both know she's stereotyping. After a moment she sighs philosophically. "Ah well, I guess every mall's got one."

I don't tell Trudy that pretty much every mall's got one of her kind too.

I exit through the back door and wait. The clouds are building again over the gas station, and I can see we're in for another good rain. He's no more than one minute behind me, a good sign – a happy number. When he puts the book in my hand, he lingers, and we both stand steady in that awkward embrace, each of our hands clutching different ends of the book. He leans toward me and I don't move away. He leans in slightly more, and when it seems apparent that we will, he says, in a voice that's soft and kind, "I've never kissed a girl with glasses before," as though this is the most important point to be made at this moment. He has the tiniest bit of a lisp.

"I've never kissed a boy with a beard before," I reply, although neither of us qualifies as the child that "boy" and "girl" suggest. I notice light freckles on his cheeks, under his eyes. He plunges toward me headlong, mashing unpredictably soft lips against mine. Rationally, I think he should smell of pastel mints, since that's all he's ever bought, but he doesn't. Just as I twig to the taste of salt and the smell of stale tobacco, the hopeful tip of his tongue and the long-forgotten electric shiver up my spine, the back door bursts open with a clack like a shot, and Trudy lunges through with an unlit smoke between the fingers of one hand, flinging a laugh over her shoulder. She's followed by the girl from the Orange Julius. Both of their expressions freeze for a split second, and I see Trudy's tiny wheels turning as she grasps what's transpired between me and the Russian. Before Trudy can twist her mouth into her tell-tale sneer, I pivot on the ball of my right foot and run like I'm in the hundred-metre dash through the nearby bus terminal and down the street. I've left the book behind.

For the next three mornings, I manage to drag myself out of my black pit and call in sick. For two more I let the phone ring itself silly before it finally stops. For two days after that, I stay in my bed eating potato chips and watching the Shopping Channel. When I do rise on the seventh day, determined to leave my apartment, I shower lethargically and consider my options. I think about running away like that, how silly it must have looked. I think I'll probably just add the past seven months to my time in Korea and go out to look for another McJob.

I dress and put my glasses on. It's then that I see the mark. One lens bears the residue of a greasy nose print, testament to what's evolved over the past weeks with my Russian, culminating in that one awkward kiss.

I remove the glasses and hold them up in the window where the sun shines in so I can get a better look.

The book, I think, rubbing my glasses clean with my shirt. The book. Whoever has the book holds the key to the next interaction. It's occurred to me before, during this game, that at any time I might pass the book back to him, with my carefully coded message, and never see him again. He could take the book and not reply – and wouldn't that be the height of loss, in this game? If it is a game, which all along is how I've thought of it, then doesn't a game need a winner and a loser? And now, with what I've done, running away like that, I'm not sure if I've made him the winner or the loser. I've left the book behind with his last message unseen by me, as if I didn't want it. I've left him with his own unsent message.

I go back to the mall, sit in the food court for more than two hours, waiting to see if he'll show. I stay on the lookout for Trudy, hoping to avoid her. Later, I sit outside the entrance to the store. The store is at the end of the mall – it's what's known as an anchor – holding the mall down, one big department store at either end. I stay as long as I can without risking Trudy coming by for her break. Finally, I spend a small amount of time in the parking lot outside the back door before I go home on the bus.

The next day I rise early. This time, I put on my work clothes and clip my nametag to my vest. I sit in the food court, waiting. I wait throughout the morning. I wait so long I start to wonder if I've been the object of my own elaborate delusion. Perhaps I made him up, my Russian with his book – imagined the whole crazy thing.

The lunch rush starts to arrive. Trudy and one of the clerks from the CD store show up and sit near the taco vendor. I'm frozen, waiting to see what will happen next. I know hot sauce gives Trudy heartburn, but I see her eating it anyway. She doesn't notice me at first. Only as she's squeezing her little white cup of sour cream in half to lick the remaining line from its collapsed rim do her eyes search the food court and meet mine. She stops with her tongue out, white cream on its tip, and eyes me suspiciously. She puts the cup down and says something to her lunch mate, who immediately turns to look in my direction.

I look away and grab my bag, hear Trudy's laugh. I walk quickly across the food court to the narrow hallway that leads to the back door, my quickest escape. I imagine Trudy in hot pursuit, and I begin to run. Clack goes the handle, and I burst into the sunlight, still running. I imagine the Russian at my side, him and me, sprinting through the bus terminal. I see the number seven just pulling away, and I wave my arms to flag it down. All I can think is that at least seven is a happy number. I run up the steps, and from the top one I turn and shout at my pursuer through the still open door, "Love is a dark devil!" One of the Russian's early coded messages to me.

But instead of Trudy at the back door of the mall, I see the Russian, in his long coat, holding the book abreast in one hand like a gift, his other arm raised in an open palmed salute.

the visit

After being spit-polished and having his cheeks rubbed hard enough to make his eyes water, the boy retreated to the window to avoid his brothers thinking he was crying and calling him a baby for it. His dad had left the house early enough that the boy had not even stirred, else he would've begged to be taken along to Toronto for the day. He knew from experience that his daddy would not return until long after the women had cleared the house, leaving only the aroma of succulent meats and cheeses to linger in the still air. In spite of the fact that these were his dad's own relatives, obvious by the way they all talked alike, with their Irish accents, even his dad couldn't stand to stay for the visit. Likewise, the boy longed to be anywhere else.

He knew the Aunties and the old Gran would arrive sometime shortly before the sun shone its brightest beams from between the clouds – arrive just in time to obliterate it all, their hulking, corseted, crisp-rustling figures like battleships, inevitably coming between him and the best part of the day. Then, instead of running off to catch up with his friends and down to the quarry with its crumbling edges, he'd be forced to watch as the women invaded the family house, their legs like fat hams wrapped in scratchy nylon whispering *gzwee, gzwee, gzwee* as they marched through the gate and up the walk, leaving his mom to haul the boxes of food in by herself. Then the Aunties would assemble themselves in the living room to complain of the humidity and stale air of the house.

"Can't even catch a breeze off the lake, it's so close in here," one of them would say, fanning her plump, red face.

Another would be bound to reply, "It's a hothouse in here, it is." And then, leaning conspiratorially in, although the volume of her voice wouldn't change a bit, she'd add, "And what about the odour, hmm?" then sit back, *tsking* between her teeth. This despite the fact that his mother had done nothing but scour and clean since she'd heard of the impending visit. If you asked the boy, he'd tell you he was sick with the smell of ammonia and disinfectant.

Each of the Aunties would have her thick torso encased in a pastel-coloured suit – a uniform involving a skirt, a jacket, a perfumed silk blouse and an ornate golden brooch, all topped off with a perfectly matched hat that often included a small, finely woven net veil. Pristine white gloves polished the outfit off. The physiques of the women, combined with the suits and hats, were all so similar in shape, texture and tone as to render one aunt hopelessly indistinguishable from another.

On the occasion of the Aunties and Gran's visit to his house, the boy knew that three things would happen. First, he'd be paraded into the living room to be asked such questions as "Do you say your prayers now, do you?" and "Are you a good lad?" to which there was no possible answer but "Yes'm." During these inquisitions, the boy would do his best to focus on the brilliantly patterned carpet of the living room, concentrating on moving his eyes rhythmically up, down and around the black curlicues, memorizing their shapes and graceful movements. The living room was where he and his brothers and sisters were not allowed, these visits and Christmas being the two exceptions to the rule.

During these sessions, each of the children would be interrogated and then a judgement cast upon them like a blessing or a curse before the child was mercifully dismissed. His older brother, the eldest boy and therefore the favourite, received the highest blessing possible, as was to be expected. "Well, he's no Einstein, but he'll do, won't he, Mum?" one of the Aunties would shout across the room at the Gran, who would scowl in response. Then the boy, quite inferior to his brother, as he had naturally been led to believe, usually received a mixed review, garnering such responses as, "That one, he's a black sheep, now isn't he?"

"Sure he is, now," the others would concur. After he was per-
mitted to step off the holy shrine of the carpet, the Aunties' words
would resonate, giving the boy cause to wonder about his "look,"
which he had been told, in times past, was "dark." He'd imagine
the natives pictured in his brother's schoolbooks, half naked and
dancing with spears, and become afraid that this was where he was
headed (for he knew from the words of the priest that these were
HEATHENS and so, sadly, would not be going to heaven).
Sometimes, in bed at night, he had to cry – silently, so as not to
wake his brothers, one on either side, lest they call him a sissy and
clobber him for it – because he was sad about the idea of maybe
not going to heaven, where Jesus would surely be. He also took to
looking up "sheep" in his father's set of encyclopaedias, wondering
how his demeanour or look could lead anyone to mistake him for
one of those stupid animals. These sorts of worries might preoc-
cupy his little mind for several days after each visit before finally
giving way to less troublesome thoughts.

Even though the meats and cheeses and cakes and biscuits
and bottles of currant juice would be brought into the house and
laid out on the table in such a manner as to make his small, tight
stomach rumble and groan, the boy knew as sure as it was
Sunday that those same meats and cheeses and so on would be
packed up into the boxes again and hustled out to the car to go
back from where they came – along with the Aunties and the
Gran, of course. This was the second thing he knew for sure –
that the food would drive him mad with desire and that despite
this, he'd not be able to steal even a single scrap. He knew he'd
see the chubby pink fingers of his Aunts popping bits of Sunday
ham, creamy orange cheese, and glistening Irish sausages between
their thick lips, and it would be all he could do to keep from beg-
ging for a taste. He tried to, but couldn't, remember the last time
his family had meat on the table, even on a Sunday.

All that food, more than their whole family would see in a
week, in and out of the house, without even a nibble to be gotten
by himself or his siblings. He also did not know it then, but
would in coming years, that his mother, although she served the

food to her in-laws, refused to touch a morsel of it herself, even though her stomach too knotted in anticipation as she set out the feast. As long as her children were not welcome to eat, she would not bring herself to do so either. When he was older, at least eleven, the boy would think this was the reason behind his father's words, "Your mother's a saint, that she is."

The other person who would not eat at these gatherings was the old Gran. Her role was to sit propped in the large wing-backed chair in the corner, covered with the plaid wool blanket that accompanied her everywhere and gave off a smell like damp dogs and farts, and clutch a narrow glass of amber liquid in her bony claw. The boy was terrified of the Gran, because she never talked except to shout "More!" at his mom, who refilled the tumbler from time to time. He could vaguely recall a time past when he was taken to the old woman's house for a visit. Before they left to return home, his mother had tucked the old woman into her covers with a bottle of Southern Comfort clutched tight to her bony chest, where it remained lodged between her deflated breasts.

And this led to the third thing that the boy knew – that at some point during the visit, he would be pressed to approach the old Gran, with her smelly blanket and festering breath, and plant a kiss on her withered cheek. "Stop lurking around that doorway now, and come say a proper hello to your Granny," one of the Aunties would inevitably command, and the boy would be obliged once again to lay his freshly polished second-hand shoes on the good carpet and make his way to the chair in the far corner. The expanse between him and the old woman would seem to grow once he stepped onto the carpet, as though magic had infused the room with a shape-shifting expanding floor like something he might read about in one of his brother's comic books. In the eternity it took him to cross the room, the boy would try not to think about what he was expected to do once he arrived. He would keep his eyes cast down, monitoring the progress of his small steps across the wilderness of carpet, afraid to look up lest the old woman cast an evil milky eye upon him and command him to do something even more hideous than what was already expected.

Upon finally arriving, the boy would lift his barely dry eyes as far as the old crone's gnarly fingers, clasped in their death grip around the slender glass, and wait. Eventually, one of the Aunts would throw out a prompt like a barb: "Go on then. Give your Granny a kiss." The boy, not tall enough to reach the Granny's cheek without serious effort, would have to stand on tip-toes and lean deep into the farty odour, grasping the arm of the chair for balance until his baby-plump lips grazed the folds of her cheek, after which he would release himself from his contortions to land back on the flats of his feet and hustle from the room, sneakily wiping his lips with the back of his hand.

These were the things he knew, but it didn't stop him from wishing for something to change.

Standing at the window, waiting for his eyes to dry, the boy saw the car pull up the road and park in front of the house. His mother flew to the front door, smacking him lightly on the back of the head as she passed. "Stop daydreaming, will you? Come and say hello to your Aunties, for heaven's sake." The boy had to stay an extra moment to allow his eyes to dry out again. Then he trundled over the doorstep in hopeful expectation. Maybe this time, things would be different.

And just as he was brightly optimistic for something new, he saw that already his wish was coming true, for the Aunties had opened the rear door of the car and were working bodily to haul the old woman from the back seat. Her head flopped from shoulder to shoulder as the Aunties struggled, bumping one another and mashing each other's toes underfoot in the manner of a sideshow. "Ah, no," he heard one of the Aunties, the one in pink, say to his mother. "She's only a bit wilted from the heat. Let's get her indoors, and I'm sure she'll be fine," although it was clear, even to the boy, that she was less than fine.

The Aunties and his mommy worked to get the Granny's limp legs out of the car and to get her to the edge of the seat.

As they did, the old woman tumbled forward as though pitched and landed with a thud on the gravel lane at their feet. His mother let out a small cry, but the Aunties seemed unable to respond. Instead, they avoided looking at the crumpled body in front of them and passed a linen handkerchief amongst themselves, dabbing drops of perspiration from tops of lips and napes of necks.

One of the Aunties turned and saw the boy in the doorway. "What're you gawking at, you little sod? Go on." She flicked her hankie at him as if he were an annoying bug. He slunk back into the shadow of the door but went no further. He heard the voices of the Aunties whispering all at once, which made it especially hard to understand what was being said. He imagined they were picking up the Gran and propping her in the car, but he dared not peek around the doorway for fear of being scolded again.

When he did finally look, he saw the Granny in the same spot on the ground, motionless, one of the Aunties fanning her with the handkerchief. His mom was walking toward the side of the house. He ran through the house to the kitchen door, opened it quietly and slipped out. Staying in the shadows, he watched while she went to the neighbour's house and rapped on the side door. He wondered what she could possibly want from the old bachelor. He observed them talk for a moment; the man pointed in the direction of his sheds, nodded a curt goodbye and closed his door. His mom went to the sheds and soon emerged with an enormous wheelbarrow balanced on a tipsy front wheel. Her skinny arms had a time of keeping the contraption in line.

Not for one moment had the boy imagined what would happen after his mom wrestled the wheelbarrow back to the front of the house and parked it next to the car. He was about to emerge from his hiding spot behind the short wall that separated their property from their neighbours when the Aunties began to haul the Gran's limp body into the barrow. They spent considerable time wrestling with non-compliant limbs that, with a mind of their own, pitched themselves over the sides of the wheelbarrow one after another.

Finally, all the limbs were contained. The Aunties sent his mommy away again, but the boy could not take his eyes from the sight of the Granny's body folded into the wheelbarrow. Soon, his mother returned with an old rope from the back shed, and together with the Aunties, they tied it carefully over the load. Once the rope had been secured to the Aunties' satisfaction, the boy's mouth fell agape as he understood that their intention was to wheel the barrow and its load *into the house*. But not before an argument ensued as to who would do the actual pushing. As the deliberations took place, the Aunties were seen to pass the linen handkerchief from gloved hand to gloved hand; the boy noticed this time that it was not offered to his mother, who, unlike the Aunties, was wearing a flowered cotton dress and no gloves.

Finally, it was the Auntie in the peach-coloured suit who grimaced and, with a resolve worthy of Job, took the wooden handles in her grasp and lifted the load. Immediately, the wheelbarrow tipped sharply to one side and the boy was sure the Gran would tumble out and potentially begin an uneven roll down the dusty hill, gradually picking up steam. Instead, the other Aunties and his mom rushed to steady the wheelbarrow, one flanking each side while the other assisted with the handles. And so they proceeded up the walk to the house to navigate the doorstep. From his hiding spot, the boy lost sight of them as they entered the house, but he could hear them bickering before peach Auntie exclaimed, "For the love of God, will you just let me do it?" Their voices got slightly fainter as they receded further into the house. He imagined them perching the old woman on her chair in the living room, perhaps even tying her in with the rope.

All at once, the boy wondered about the food. In the excitement, the food hadn't been brought into the house and was still sitting in the car. The door of the car remained open, forgotten. Cautiously, he approached the car, where he could see boxes of food stacked neatly on the back seat. He was certain there would be more in the trunk. The box nearest the open door beckoned; he imagined a fat pink ham inside, wrapped in paper and marbled with bits of glistening pork fat. The temptation was too much for him, and he laid a small foot on the edge of the car's doorframe. He couldn't bring himself to look over his shoulder to check if anyone was watching – his ears rang with fear and anticipation. He grabbed the top box from the pile and stepped backwards out of the car with the prize cradled in his arms. It was heavy and difficult for him to balance. Just as he considered bolting down the roadway to hide in the ravine with his treasure, one of the Aunties appeared on the doorstep.

"Be careful, lad – bring them boxes in, will you now. Come on, hurry up!"

So the boy was forced to bring the food in from the car, his small arms rubbery and worn out by the time the last box was placed on the table.

When he looked into the living room, he found that the Gran had not been placed in her chair as he had expected. Instead, the Aunties, his mom, and the empty wheelbarrow filled the narrow hallway that led to the bedrooms. He wondered what that could mean. The women were arguing, and the boy decided to sneak away before he was noticed.

He returned to the kitchen, where his brothers and sisters had appeared as if alerted by a silent alarm. They poked about in the food boxes now so cavalierly abandoned by the adults. His oldest brother removed a small, foil-wrapped cooked chicken and tucked it beneath his sweater. His sister, the one his dad locked in her room at night for being too wild, carefully slid a small block of cheese and a small, hard-shelled loaf of bread inside the sleeves of her blouse. Without a word, they all disappeared from the kitchen through the side door, as if a silent signal had been sounded to which the boy alone was deaf.

The argument in the hall went on for some time, and the boy was able to lift the corner of a box several times and sneak a pinch of ham from a cooked shank. Finally, his mother came through the kitchen and headed for the side door, her face drawn and tight. She passed the boy, seemed not to notice him, but then absently issued a command to "Go outside and play now. You stay out from underfoot. *Kinisitohten nâ?*" Then she was gone. He waited a moment, torn between the food, the unfolding drama in the hallway, and a mix of curiosity and fear that his mother was leaving him behind forever. Her slipping the Cree word into her sentence alarmed him, something she usually did only in secret, when they were alone. He knew, without being told, that it was forbidden. He followed her out the door but saw that she was only retrieving sheets off the line, so he ducked back inside.

His mother took the clean linen to the hallway, and the Aunties murmured with satisfaction. The boy remained in the kitchen, stealing ham from the box until he heard them returning to the main part of the house. Peach Auntie expertly rolled the empty wheelbarrow through the front door, down the walk and onto the road, where she parked it. The Aunties and his mom followed.

Curious where the Gran was, the boy approached the now quiet hallway. Something about the house in midday, with its dim light and unusual silence, made the boy feel as if he were trespassing, as if he were entering a forbidden place. His shoes made no sound on the hallway carpet. He looked into his mommy and daddy's bedroom, with its drawn drapes and large, heavy dressers, but there was nothing out of place. The two rooms at the end of the hall were the boys' room and the girls' room. The door to the girls' room was open, and all was as it should be. The door to the bedroom that he shared with his brothers, all three of them in the one large bed, was closed tight. The boy approached the room with dread. Still, he forced his small legs to advance toward the door, watched as his hand reached out and turned the knob and let his fingertips give a small push so that the door swung slowly open.

The Granny lay in the centre of the big bed, in the spot that was his, with her head on his very own pillow. Her moist eye glistened in the shadows, and she watched him silently.

She was here to stay. He knew this suddenly. He also knew that the boys' room, and his place in it, would never be the same. Even his older brother's coveted pile of comic books, sitting in their off-limits place on the centre shelf, seemed defenseless and inconsequential in the presence of the Granny. Even though he knew the Aunties were outside in the yard, the boy couldn't help but feel their heavy presence, like a dreadful shadow, hovering in the boys' room.

A scratchy noise in the back of Gran's throat brought him to his senses. She spoke to him in a voice both demanding and delicate. "Come over here, boy. Give us a kiss," she said, her one watery eye firmly pinning him into place. He made a small choking sound, and the Gran repeated, "Give us a kiss."

oldest sons

Your house is filled with his artwork. Every week, you dust family pictures from which he smiles at you, genuine and not cynical. In the photos he looks like a little boy, grinning, showing his teeth. You don't even know what he looks like now, but you've heard he's gotten very thin as he tries out one new diet after another. You've heard he's gone from kosher (none of you are Jewish), to vegetarian, to organic-fooditarian, to raw-fooditarian. Also, that he's let his hair grow into long curls. That he wants to start a commune out in BC, far from his prairie upbringing in a small Saskatchewan city. Another world, Vancouver.

He still allows his little sister Wanda to contact him, and in turn she passes on the tiniest tidbits of information quietly, quickly, with a neutral tone, her voice free of judgement.

"Sal got a new job," she says. "In a theatre. He takes the tickets." You comment that this is funny, since Sal hates movies. She doesn't answer. The whole situation is painful. She doesn't want to be in the middle, but she is anyway. You long to ask Wanda what Sal has said about you, "the stepmother," or about your husband, their dad. You want to try to understand Sal's reasons, his resentments. But you know enough not to ask. Instead, you look at his emails, the short, crisp sentences: *Fuck off* and *Leave me alone*. The lines are so short you find it impossible to read between them. Neither you nor your husband "get it."

You've always been pleased to tell people you have seven children, learned to say their names like a chant: Sal, Jordan, Maria, Dez, Wanda, Aaron, Zach.

"Never mind it's a blended family," you sometimes say defensively. "We raised them all, full custody. All seven." Sal's the oldest, your husband's son. Your oldest, Jordan, is also a boy. Sons.

You suspect you know how your divorce, when he was seven, affected Jordan: the instability, the many many moves, the grinding poverty and vulnerability of a family headed by a single mother. You suspect you know because you have your own guilt, remorse, shame. Regret. You suspect oldest sons are destined to have it the hardest. You suspect your memories are suspect.

Sal too was devastated by his parents' divorce, but differently. You only know bits of the story, didn't have to live it like his dad.

"She kidnapped them," he's told you. "Right after the last family court decision, where she lost custody." They were taken to Montreal, where they hid out, didn't go to school. There were months of searching and uncertainty. You don't know all the details, but you've seen the aftermath, the anger and the tantrums. Insecurity all around. Your husband sometimes cries when he talks about that time in their lives. You know all you really need to know.

Sal accuses his dad of remanufacturing reality, which makes you laugh out loud. You know it's unwise, but you say anyway, "Don't we all? Isn't that what it's all about? Otherwise, how could we live with ourselves, in the end?" No one seems to appreciate your contribution.

Seven children, two of them artists. So far. Not surprising, the two artists are the two oldest sons, Sal and Jordan. Their artwork hangs in almost every room as if the whole house is a shrine to lost sons. You sense a future when the house will be like a shrine to all seven children, whom you know, in advance, you will miss with the dull ache of amputated limbs. You never want that day to arrive. This, now, with the oldest son, is hard enough.

Sal's work includes screen prints, drawings, oil pastels. Large pieces. Bold colours. You imagine the dark lines are angry, that the overarching theme of all the pieces is rebellion. The look of the artwork begins to change for you. It seems to look at you accusingly as you enter rooms, as you pass from room to room. This artwork that's been left behind, as if the son knew he ought to leave something before blowing you all off. More likely, you realize, he gave it no thought.

Your husband's office has artwork on the walls too. Artwork and photographs. All the artwork was made by Sal; all the pictures are family photos. And yet there's a certain irony to this because you suspect his father's business, money, work ethic, whatever you want to call it, is just the thing Sal is rejecting. You have a moment when you wish you could take Sal by the shoulders and shake him. You want to make him smarten up.

Part of you would be afraid to shake Sal. You imagine he could strike you, shouting, "Fuck off. Leave me alone." You wish you didn't have to live with that.

Sal's absence hovers. Increasingly, you and your husband find yourselves in various rooms of the house, questioning the air. As you gather laundry from the bedrooms together on a Saturday morning, he says, "Maybe I said something? The last time we talked?" Second guessing. First son. You listen, grateful that he doesn't shut you out. You're not sure why you think he might. His bewildered look prompts you to reach out and hold his hand. You listen. You want to say that time is likely the answer. That when Sal matures, when he experiences a big event – decides to get married, has a child, experiences grief, catastrophe or loss – he will come back. But you hold back on saying this because you know it's unsatisfactory and really just a guess, anyway.

"Jeff Shaw's getting married," Wanda tells you. Jeff is Sal's childhood friend.

"When?" you ask, calm.

"This weekend," she answers, careful to keep emotion out of her voice. "Sal's here for the wedding." They're getting to the age for that. Sal turned twenty-five this year. Later, you overhear her on the phone when she says the address out loud and you write it down, pocketing the scrap of paper. You want so badly to drive to the house, to park out front. You imagine surreptitiously taking his photo from your car when he opens the front door, not sure what this photo would prove. Better yet, you imagine boldly going to the door, ringing the bell, and asking to speak to him. Then you imagine hearing his voice from somewhere inside, "Fuck off."

Imagining standing in that doorway, you remember a time when you were first divorced and your little boys weren't returned to you after a visit with their dad. You went to where they were and politely rang the doorbell, no idea what you'd do next. Your brother-in-law answered, and when you asked for the boys, he looked guilty and embarrassed as he shook his head. You stepped into the doorway, past the brother-in-law, walked right through the house, down the stairs, found the boys happy, oblivious, playing video games in the basement. Your fake happy voice told them to get their shoes because it was time to go home. You all left together. It was that easy, that time.

So you imagine going to the door for Sal and hearing "Fuck off" from inside the house, then stepping anyway through the door, walking boldly into a stranger's house to command this oldest son to get his things and come home.

Later, you show your husband the address you wrote down, where Sal's staying, and ask him if he wants to go by the house. You're emboldened by your memories and imaginings. But your husband seems paralyzed. "I don't know," he says. "I don't know what to do." So you don't do anything, and then Sal is gone again, back to Vancouver and his raw-food diet and communistic ideals.

Partly you feel contempt for the poor-little-rich-boy game Sal is playing. You are staggered that he doesn't account for how lucky he's been, for all he's been given. You are tempted to make a list. Fortunately, you don't. Instead, you think of your hopes for these seven children, Sal, Jordan, Maria, Dez, Wanda, Aaron, Zach. From the beginning, your hopes were for the bunch of you as a family. You wanted the family home that you all built together to be their home for always – a soft place to fall, should they need it. You wanted them to come together in this home at Christmases and birthdays, for them to eventually marry, to bring their children, to find comfort here. You berate yourself for believing in this happy family, and you wonder if you could have ever done enough. You doubt that you did enough. Doubt even that you did your best.

"You can't escape your family," you tell your husband. "He'll be back." You're afraid of the consequences of being wrong about this – waiting for him to come to his senses when maybe you should do more. Afraid to make the wrong choice, you avoid making any move. You come to realize that inaction is a choice too.

Your husband looks for some sort of answer. Maybe there's someone to blame. He tells you his theories, one by one, like sweaters he tries on, then sheds. Soon, the sweater-reasons litter the floor around you until you're swamped by them. They go: Sal resents his dad for marrying you; Sal's mother said something bad about his dad; a family friend said something; Sal is suffering from a mental illness; Sal is acting out repressed anger about his parents' divorce; Sal believes his dad didn't support his art; Sal is angry about money; Sal rejects money. On it goes. Still, neither of you "get it." You want to tell your husband you think it's a mistake to look for a rational answer in an irrational situation. The only thing you know: Sal is not who you thought he was.

Sal is an articulate guy. He could simply tell you what his problem is. Instead he's chosen the most hurtful path he can find. *Fuck off. Leave me alone.*

You know things you are not supposed to know. You know there was a girlfriend, quite a few years ago now. Shortly after they broke up, he made a hasty move to Winnipeg. She had a baby boy. You've always been suspicious the baby was his, even though he denied it. You wish you had done more at the time. For Sal, you secretly fear the worst and hope for the best. Pray he doesn't turn up on Hastings Street someday.

You track down the ex-girlfriend's number, then use the reverse directory to find her address. The first time, you only drive by, quickly take in the small wartime house, painted a deep shade of blue. Curtains close every window, making the house look muffled and insular. You can hear the cars just half a block away speeding down one of the city's major traffic arteries. It appears no one is home.

The second time, you drive down the back alley more slowly, take a good look. The back lawn is overgrown. There is no rusty swing set planted in the long grass, no tipped ride-on toys scattering the cracked patio. Only a single plastic chair sits beside the back door. Butts litter the broken cement. You must have the wrong house; you think she must have moved.

The third time, you park two blocks away, pocket your car key and walk down the back alley. The day is warm and dry, and the gravel crunches under your sneakers. You feel out of place. Obvious. The alleyway is littered with garbage; ripped plastic grocery bags scatter bits of lives along the fence lines and amongst the weeds.

A child's voice makes nonsense singsong murmurs close to your right ear. You look over your right shoulder and see it's a trick of sound carried like a ventriloquist because the child is in his yard, behind his fence, isn't talking to you, hasn't noticed you at all. He sits on his shins, his legs doubled underneath him, plays in the gravel and weeds and says his incantation again.

"Doodee doodee doodee."

You stop to consider the boy. He must be three or four. He's tiny – fragile. He wears blue jeans and a Celtic green t-shirt that looks washer-soft. You imagine he smells like fabric softener and dust. The notion of *lonely* brushes past you like a cat and lingers for a moment afterward. On his nose, a spray of freckles. He's playing with something, a Barbie doll that's naked from the waist down. He dances her along the gravel on her tiptoes, her long blonde hair swinging. You watch him pull a plastic syringe from the dirt and jab at her leg.

"Doodee doodee doodee doo," he sings.

You're relieved to see there is no sharp needle in the syringe.

When you get home, you strip every piece of art from the walls, every picture from every room, until the house is naked and raw. You are sweating from the effort. When you're done, the framed pieces are piled like bones in the centre of the garage. The pile is immense, several bodies of evidence. Without thinking, you pick up the phone, call the real estate agent, leave an incoherent voice-mail about appraising the house for the market. You don't know what you're thinking. You find as many boxes in the basement as you can and begin to fill each one with the articles from the shelves of your house. Years of accumulation. Seven children worth of stuff. You find his first glass bowl. His dream was to make it as a glass blower. It's why he went to Vancouver. When your children ask you what you are doing, you say, *Cleaning up. Go play.*

You're sitting in the midst of boxes, tissue paper and the arti-facts of your lives together when your husband arrives home. The adrenaline has worn off, and you are in a quiet state of shock. He sits beside you on the floor in his business suit, and you tell him everything – about the blue house and the curtains and the over-grown yard and the busy street and the butts and the weeds and the doll and the needle.

"He has long hair," you say. "It's brown. And curly." You wait while the image settles in your husband's mind. Likely the image of Sal as a little boy, you think. You say that you think the boy has his mother's nose, pushed in at the eyes.

"His shoulders are very thin." You don't like the way your voice has started to sound like you're pleading.

When he asks, you tell your husband you think the boy looked happy enough.

Later, you lie in bed, spent but unable to sleep. Part of you wants to make demands, as if someone owes you something, some lost years that can be repaid. You can't stop thinking about the little boy. Left behind like the artwork, by accident. An oldest son. The window is open, and the street you live on is quiet. The cedar outside the bed-room window has grown over the years past the second-story window so that its branches scratch lightly at the glass. At times, you have the impression someone is outside the window, looking in, trying to get your attention. But really, it's only the cedar.

mister x

eate pulls her short, rabbit-fur jacket closed over a flat bead-board chest, crosses her arms. Her childlike fingers, hidden under her elbows, habitually stroke the soft, white fur. Honey-blonde hair, moments ago alive with winter static, now lies close to her scalp as though frightened. Her head resembles a tight, round melon. She peers over the counter at the nurse.

The nurse wrinkles her nose as if imagining white rabbit hairs floating in the air. She waves away an illusory bit of fluff.

"Name?"

"Wha...?"

The nurse puts her pencil down and leans forward to over-enunciate "Who are you here to see?" Beate, who's not stupid, knows the nurse thinks she is.

Inside Beate's head, Ivy whispers, *She doesn't think you're stupid. She thinks you're a retard.*

"I...don't..." Beate stammers. This was a mistake. She can't believe she skipped out on Rick and left him to run the shop, put one foot in front of the other, took the number eleven and transferred twice to come all the way out here.

Ivy says, *You gonna turn back now?*

Beate blocks the sneer in Ivy's voice and says, "Mister X. I'm here to see Mister X."

In a pile of comics in her room at home lies a first edition, in a plastic sleeve, where Mister X made his debut. Mister X: Marvel supervillain. Mister X can read his opponents' minds during a fight by using his powers of telepathy. He sees his opponents' moves in advance and can stay one step ahead at all times. Since his only superpower is telepathy and not strength, he's worked hard to master every form of combat and to build the strength he does have to the highest level possible. Even though he's a villain, Beate sees the possibility for good in him. She fantasizes that Mister X will use his powers of telepathy to see her and do just one act that will redeem him: save her. He is, by far, her favourite Mister X.

A faint tune plays in the shadows, and he can't quite put his finger on what it might be. The swirling vortex somewhere behind him blocks him from hearing it clearly. He cranes his neck first to the right and then to the left, and still the mystery remains a vague impression at the periphery of his perception. He imagines the vacuum-like sound coming from a huge, sucking black hole. He keeps his body tense to prevent falling in. A voice calls out out from the void one cryptic word: *misdirects.* He wonders if it's God.

He's in a private room. Beate can hardly look. She's seen a lot of things in her sixteen years, but nothing like this. She puts her hand to her face, smells the baby powder scent that reminds her of taking care of Momma. The smell makes her want to vomit.

This isn't him, Ivy declares. Ivy. I.V. Internal Voice. Beate hates her and yet can't get along without her.

Beate gazes at Mister X through squinted eyes. If he would open an eye, wink at her in his way that suggests they share a delicious secret, then she'd know. But his eyes are fluid-filled and swollen shut, purple. They remind her of cartoon black eyes, the kind Fred or Barney might slap an enormous red steak over. A respirator moves his chest up and down, tapping out a flat tuneless beat.

Blood is caked under his nails; the knuckles of his right hand are cut and scabbed over. Ivy laughs at Beate for trying to be quiet. *You can't wake him. He's in a COMA.* Beate stands close on his left side, afraid to touch him. She looks at his hands because she can't look at his face. *Closed head injury. Blunt trauma.* The nurse's words loop in her head. Tentatively she puts her hand out, softly traces the place on his wrist where she imagines a tan mark from his wristwatch lingers. She already knows the watch has been stolen along with all his other possessions: jacket, boots, wallet, ID, jewellery. She shivers to think of him alone and cold in the February night after he left her place. Her fingers dig into the fur of her jacket.

She read once about a spy called Mister X. He was an anonymous French agent in the XYZ Affair. Three agents – X, Y and Z – were sent by France's foreign minister to offer a cleverly veiled insult to American envoys attempting to resolve a diplomatic dispute. The anonymous French agents, X, Y and Z, were later vilified by the Americans. They went down in infamy. Beate prefers the idea of infamy, as a concept, over fame. It seems much more realistic.

He lies flat to anchor himself and plants his cheek next to earth as soft as black velvet. The faint liquorice scent reminds him of another time, twenty years earlier, a time when the sounds were similar, swirling patterned but indistinct, a time in the womb when his mother compulsively ate the fresh dug loam from beneath the poplar tree, searching for hidden deposits, nutrients, iron, elements from the mother of us all to nourish the life inside her belly. He's tasted dirt before and knows it to be scattered through with love. His fingers dig, and the velvet ground gives way.

Talk to him. He can hear you, Ivy prompts.
"I waited for you," Beate whispers, close to his ear.
She's close enough to see the individual black hairs pop out of his scalp as if they've been tidily sewn in. She remembers the dolls she owned when she was a girl and how one by one she cut their hair down to the scalp with the kitchen scissors, made them all ugly, the same as she felt. Their root-hole riddled heads were

like an accusation until she stuffed them under her bed, out of sight. When Momma found them, Beate blamed Ivy, but even so, she got the belt, Ivy reduced to a silent accomplice. Beate sees a crust of dried brown blood inside the rim of his ear as if he's a pie that's overflowed its dish.

She can't think of anything else to say, so she repeats, "I waited for you, Mister X."

Another Mister X, also known as Avenger X, is a first-rate thief – suave, daring and a master of disguise. In a classic B movie from the '60s, Mister X becomes Avenger X to clear his own name after he's set up for a murder he didn't commit. Avenger X takes on several disguises, uses lots of clever gadgets and encounters more than his share of action. Avenger X is in love with a beautiful woman, his sidekick in crime. Beate will force Momma to let her put on the tape tonight and watch it again. But Momma can be prickly about her TV.

Beate can see Rick is relieved when she returns to her post on the stool behind the glass counter at the pawn shop. He's uncomfortable dealing with what he calls "the riffraff" – the scammer who sells his girlfriend's stuff, the druggie who pawns grandma's wedding rings, the single mom whose kids scrap in the car while she pawns their TV for McDonalds and says she'll be back for it on "cheque day."

TV sets line up like rag-tag soldiers on the grey metal shelving, where they wait to be either retrieved or forsaken. One small television sits at Rick's end of the counter bleating out game show music, news and soap opera drama day after day.

Beate's not like Rick; she sees people differently, sees through the thick layer of crappy life chances and bad luck to the cores of the people they might have been once. She'd be the first to admit she has to scrape pretty hard to find even a glimmer of a long-forgotten innocence in some of them, but usually, eventually, she does.

She saw it right away in Mister X.

Each of his organs works inside his body. One by one, he enumerates them: lungs, heart, kidneys, spleen, stomach, brain. His organs work together as a whole in neat tandem with one another to contribute to the rhythm of the earth under his chest. Heart skips a beat to tell brain, *There's something about this girl, the soft one with the baby powder smell.* Brain's too busy now to listen. His breath slows to keep time, and the faint tune from the shadows is subsumed in the operation of his lungs and the deep inhale-exhale of Mother Earth. In his attempt to get closer to her, he stuffs his mouth with dirt.

The day after Beate's visit to the hospital, a young woman, no more than twenty, comes into the shop with a jangle of the door. The woman approaches Beate and slips a man's watch from her wrist and lets it clatter to the scarred counter. Of course, Beate recognizes it right away. It's a decent watch. Beate remembers selling it to Mister X – part of his careful dance around her. He wanted her to notice him, didn't want to scare her off. The woman handles the watch confidently, carelessly. Beate turns it over to make sure it's the same one. It's warm from the woman's skin. Iron brown specks like rust mark the stainless plate on the back. She scrapes one away with her nail. She avoids the girl's eyes. Ivy chides, *Stupid,* and Beate wonders if this girl heard Mister X's last words and, if so, what they were.

"Sell or pawn?" Beate asks.

"Sell."

"Got ID?"

The girl tosses a battered card onto the counter. Beate examines the picture, fills out a form.

Her least favourite Mister X: Vortex Comics' human quasi-hero. Gaunt, mysterious and trench-coated, he makes his "living," such as it is, working as a private eye. He takes sleep-restrictive drugs to stay awake twenty-four hours a day so he can stalk the streets of dystopia looking for answers. Beate gives him credit for trying.

When Beate finally agreed to go out with him, it was the end of summer. He took her to the fair, the exhibition. They rode the merry-go-round and he jumped from horse to horse; he rode backwards and looked into her face, trying to make her laugh while his eyes danced like shiny black coals. After, when he walked her home, all the way over the bridge and through the dark streets, he held her hand like it was the most natural thing to do, as though they did this every day. Beate wouldn't let Ivy say a thing.

They passed a group of boys, who called out "Chink," unprovoked, then, "Indian," as if they were guessing.

He laughed and said to Beate, "Yeah, *I'm* the missing link in the Bering Strait theory." Beate laughed too, partly because it was funny, what he said about the Bering Strait theory, and partly because it was true, he did look kind of ambiguous.

After that he swung her arm with his between them, still holding her hand, as though the encounter had put him in a good mood. His step was light.

Outside her house, she could tell he wanted her to invite him in. That's when Ivy finally piped up, alarmed. *You can't take him in there. Are you crazy?* Of course Ivy was right. He kissed her on the lips before she ran inside.

Misdirects. The word comes to him on a sweet platform of baby powder scent that makes him calm and happy inside, reminding him of a girl, *his* girl. Frustrated that he can't crack the code, the whispered word that comes to him through the sucking, humming, heart-beating noise, he reaches deeper into the reliable pocket of earth to bring her close in an extended bear hug. He puts out his hand to stop the noise, turn it down, but he has no effect. *It's broken,* he sobs inside his chest and knows he'll never escape the din. *Misdirects* comes the secret word again to remind him how his mother whispered comfort in his ear when all else raged around them, underneath the poplar tree, a sanctuary.

Beate's marked her calendar – it's been almost two weeks. They only ever did it the one time, out back, between the falling-down shed and the falling-down fence, where the overgrown autumn olive looked as if it would, any minute, push the fence clean over with a spindly finger. It was cold, February-cold, but the structures that surrounded them gave shelter from the wind and made it bearable. When he came close and kissed her, Beate held her breath.

"It's okay," he whispered in her ear.

She pressed her body into his and welcomed his warm hand, sliding up her back. His fingers left a trail of fire up her spine, over her ribs, across her belly and down her hip. She helped him undo her clothes, then his. With her back against the shed, he pushed inside her, still with his mouth on hers.

"It's okay," he breathed into her mouth.

"Okay," she repeated and bit his lip. The whole time she half expected to hear Momma's gravelly voice demand to know just what she thought she was doing. But Momma could never leave the house, could never haul herself over the doorstop, down the back porch steps and across the patchy weeds covered in snow. Momma couldn't even lug herself to the bathroom anymore. These were the things Beate thought about that one time.

Later, Ivy couldn't stop laughing at her.

He leaves the vortex behind to move closer to the earth. He sees through to the centre: a place within the musical hiss and click. No longer afraid of the rhythm, he instead seeks it out, the swirl and hum, the beat of life, the sound that's now a part of his existence here, in the dark, his cheek next to Mother Earth. He longs, to the point of tears, to fill himself with the sound and feel of the fluid heartbeat from the centre of the womb.

After that one time, Beate waited for him to come back. She waited at the pawnshop. She looked more often out the window at home. Momma's breathless voice scalded the back of her neck. "What the hell's (breathe) gotten into you (wheeze), girl? Didn't you hear (breathe) me say (wheeze) to bring the bucket?"

Ivy called her a retard and ran away.

The television is Momma's only friend in the same way Ivy is Beate's. One night, after ten days of waiting, the continuous background noise of the television broke into Beate's thoughts. Local newscast. The police – asking for public help to identify a man. Found. Unconscious but alive. Possibly Asian, said the reporter.

Chink. Indian, Ivy chided.

Missing link. Beate knew he was a half-breed. Métis.

Day after day, the news reported on the search for someone who could identify him, and Mister X took on a certain curious infamy. That was when she went to see him.

Mister X: In the Uniform Case Naming Guidelines, *Mister X* is a legal term used to refer to an unknown or anonymous person. The guidelines exist so that cases can be referred to and looked up with relative ease. A fictitious name or set of initials may be used, such as *Jane Doe* or *Mister X*. Mister X can also be referred to as *Personne anonyme.* Unnamed person. To her, he's not unnamed. To her, he *is* Mister X.

Earth runs through his fingers like fine beads, jewels, treasure. He's a little boy again discovering the rich black earth beneath the poplar tree where his mother looked into his eyes and shared the gift of sight. She is the precious dirt he caresses in his hands. His mother is earth. She speaks to him without words, and he listens without mortal ears. Her message soothes and humbles him. He takes her hand and steps into the circle.

As Beate fills out the form for the young woman to sell the watch, the local newscast from Rick's TV cuts through her thoughts.

"The man, known only as Mister X, has died." Beate's pen stops moving; she listens intently to the newscaster's thick voice.

His slight pause just before saying "has died" make his words sound at once both dramatic and sad. "Police continue to appeal to the public for clues to his identity. The coroner is expected to call an inquiry."

Beate doesn't look up, either at the girl or the TV. Time stands still as Beate pauses over the form. Her hand shakes. She wonders who this woman is in relation to Mister X, what she knows. Still, she can't bring herself to look into the woman's eyes and see.

What now? Ivy sneers. *You're not gonna cry, are you?* Beate's pen moves again.

"I'll give you fifty," Beate says without looking up. She feels the woman's posture brighten.

"Sixty," the woman demands. Beate knows the woman would be lucky to get thirty, max, at any other shop on the street. Beate sold it to Mister X for fifty. Reaching into her pocket for her own money, Beate steals a glance at the woman, who taps her fingers impatiently on the glass and checks on her ride parked by the curb.

Say something, Ivy hisses.

Beate hands over the money, watches through the window as the woman gets in the waiting car, a young man in a ballcap at the wheel.

Beate slips the watch into the front pocket of her jeans, where its heft spoons into the cleft under her hipbone. A transparent tadpole listens with a keen inner ear for a reliable *tick-tock* that comforts like a third heartbeat.

Now you've done it, Ivy says.

single native female

"Okay, fine," I say, slapping the table. "If I listen, will you stop pestering me?"

"Pestering? More like saving you from yourself." My sister Gloria has been at this since she arrived this morning to drink my coffee and eat Froot Loops from the box by the handful.

"Just read before I leave," I say. But I can't leave; it's my own damn house.

"Okay, okay. Jeez. Ahem." She rattles the loose-leaf paper, covered in pencil scratches, in front of her face as though preparing to give a speech. "SNF with good sense of humour..."

"Wait a minute. SNF? You make me sound like a bad cheque."

"Nooo. Silly, that's NSF." Gloria laughs and waves a hand at me to say *go on*. "You're not *non-sufficient funds*."

"I know what it means, Gloria. I'm just saying...."

"Everybody who reads these ads knows that *SNF* means 'Single Native Female'. At least the SNMs will, and that's what counts." Gloria cocks her head as though an idea has just occurred to her. She shakes her finger and looks annoyed. "You know, speaking of NSF, that reminds me – that damned Gilbert wrote me a bad cheque back in May, and now my bank put 'restrictions' on my account."

I ignore her. "There are no SNMs out there, anyway," I mutter half-heartedly, cupping my over-sized coffee mug in my hands and gazing out the window at the ragged carpet of chickweed that's taken over my front lawn. With the sun shining like it is, if I squint my eyes just so, my lawn becomes lush and green – the envy of the hood.

"I'm gonna hafta go over there and kick his ass. I can't believe I forgot about that cheque." Gloria taps her forehead with her middle finger, like this might be the magic touch that makes things stick in that head of hers.

Still thinking of the SNMs I say, "They're all married or hooked up, and anyone who answers this ad is just out being a dog."

"There you go again. How'd you expect me to be able to convince anyone you got 'a good sense of humour' when you keep that up?"

But I'm on a roll now. "And if they *are* single, there's a damned good reason for it," I say.

"Hey, you got any peanut butter?" Gloria asks, distracted. She heads for my cupboards.

"Men are like a box of chocolates," I say, trying to sound philosophical.

"Okay, Forest Gump," she shoots over her shoulder, her head buried in the cupboard.

"All the good ones are gone."

"Here we go again," I hear her mutter.

"And what's left turns out to be fruits or nuts."

"Chocolate. That'd go nice with the peanut butter. Where'd you say you keep it?" That Gloria, always with the food.

"I thought you said you were on a diet."

"I am. But I read somewhere that chocolate is good for you," she says.

"So is drinking your own piss, according to some people. Doesn't mean it's true."

Gloria ignores me. "And peanut butter has protein. Gotta keep up my strength."

"All that sugar's not bad for your diabetes?" I ask.

Gloria plops into her chair, peanut butter and a small spoon in hand, her eyes on the paper in front of her. "So you wanna hear the rest of it or what?"

"Not really." And then I say, trying not to look like I'm trying too hard to be casual, "Hey, speaking of Gilbert, where's he at these days?"

"You know he's shacked up with that Juicy what's-her-face," Gloria says, her voice taking on an accusatory tone, as if this were somehow my fault.

"You heard she won ten grand in the slots, hey?" I ask, trying to keep my voice light. I know Gloria's heard – everybody's heard.

"Yeah. Gilbert heard it too," she says.

"I thought you two were going to work things out?"

"He says we are, but that doesn't stop him from spending all day wallowing around in her big old smelly bed like a pig. You know she's got a king-size? Probably needs the space for all her acrobatics."

"King-size what?" I ask.

"Oh, you," Gloria says, waving her hand. She's smiling.

"See? I told you, men are dogs."

"Hey," Gloria changes the topic, "since we're catching up on missing people, have you heard from your boy lately?"

"Jeremy? I thought you didn't want to hear about that any more?"

"Well, I'm asking now, aren't I?" Gloria's voice takes on a pouty tone.

"Had a postcard from Jakarta a couple weeks ago," I say.

"Ja – *what?*" She doesn't let me answer. "I still don't know how you could just let him go off that way."

"How could I stop him? He's almost twenty years old, for heaven's sake. Besides, somebody's got to get out of this place."

"But it's all so unsafe," she says.

"An adventure. That's how he describes it," I say. "But it's keeping him clean. That's got to count for something."

"He'll need therapy," Gloria says, ignoring me. "Haven't you heard of PTSD?"

"Yeah, I think I feel it coming on right now," I say, holding my head. "Gloria, you've been watching too much TV."

"He'll have issues," she insists.

"Besides, therapy's overrated."

"Have you been? To therapy?" Gloria's question surprises me. What does she know, or think she knows? I wonder if Gilbert's been pillow-talking.

"Once," I quip. "It's all our mother's fault."

"I could've told you that," Gloria says, and we laugh.

"What's he doing in Ja – whatever, anyway?"

"Sandbagging. Peace work. Terrible flooding. I heard it on the news."

"That's not so bad. No fighting, at least."

"He told me they met up with a troop from the Foreign Legion. And those soldiers, they bite the heads off live chickens – a sort of initiation ritual."

"And you think he won't need therapy after that?"

"Could you do it?" I ask her.

"What? Bite the head off a chicken?" she asks, making a face.

"A *live* chicken," I say.

"Don't be absurd."

"To save your child's life," I press.

"That would be an unfair choice."

"Who said life was fair?" I don't know why I'm goading her. Except she's so aggravating, so blind. So uncritical.

"Okay. Enough. Listen to this – *SNF with good sense of humour loves fine dining...*"

"Mmm, chicken," I say.

"*...is honest...*"

"Meaning I'm not a convicted felon," I interject.

"*...and comes with no baggage.*"

"Am I suddenly going to develop long-term memory loss?"

"*Willing to meet and take it from there.*"

"Should we add *Bring your own bus fare, just in case?*" I ask.

"I think we should put in a hobby," Gloria says, ignoring me. "Tell me one of your hobbies."

"You mean besides the macroindianophilia?"

"I hate it when you use big words," she whines.

"I hate it when you write personal ads for me."

"Okay. Whatever. Just spell it for me."

"M-a-c..."

"Wait a minute. Are you pulling my leg?"

"I don't know. Does it seem longer than the other one?"

"Carmellll," Gloria says in a familiar whine.

"Sorry, sweetie. I'm just having some fun."

"I need to hurry up and get this done. I gotta pick up Junior from school." Gloria makes a face, clearly annoyed.

"Junior's in school?"

"Yeah, I finally convinced him to go."

"And it's your job to drive him there and pick him up?"

"How else is he going to get there? Hey can I borrow your car?"

"Gloria, Junior's twenty-three. You gotta make him grow up sometime."

"You know he's my baby."

"He's a baby, alright," I mutter.

"What's that supposed to mean?"

"Did you forget about last time he stole your bank card and cleaned out your account?"

"He can't help it. He's got addictions. He caught it from his father."

"Enough about his father. What about his mother? Did you ever hear of being an enabler?"

"I am not! How can you say that?"

"And why do you need my car? Where's yours?"

"Gilbert had an appointment today. I lent him."

"What's the matter, Juicy's got a big old king size, but no car for him?" I tease.

"Guess not," Gloria says quietly. She sniffs.

"Don't be getting all emotional, you. I'm just looking out for you. You're such a damn pushover."

Gloria sniffs again.

"Come on, sis. I'll let you have my car."

"You will?" She brightens.

"On one account."

"What's that?"

"You stop harassing me about this damned ad."

"But you didn't even finish hearing it."

I stand up and walk to the coffee pot, my back to Gloria, pretend I need a warm up. "Hey, Gloria, what would you do if you won ten grand like Juicy?"

"I dunno." She's still re-reading her ad.

"I know what I *wouldn't* do," I say.

"What's that?"

"I wouldn't let some man get his hands on it."

"All men aren't bad, you know," she says.

"Oh yeah. You mean like Gilbert." I bite my tongue before I say too much.

"That's not fair," Gloria whines. "Gilbert's the father of my children. I have an obligation to work things out."

"Gloria, your kids are grown. Cut the strings."

"That's easy for you to say." Gloria looks away as if she realizes what she's just said. On the record, Jeremy's an official case of *father unknown.*

When he was a toddler, Jeremy loved when Gilbert would come to the house. As soon as Gilbert walked in the door, Jeremy would waddle up to him and hold out his arms to be picked up. It was clear to me – Jeremy wanted a man in his life. Then Jeremy started to talk. He couldn't say *Gilbert.* Instead, he'd run around the house shouting "Guilt! Guilt!" Ironic and funny, until Gloria heard him one day.

"What's he saying?" she asked, squinting her eyes at Jeremy. "What?"

I couldn't look at Gloria that time. Shortly after that, Gilbert stopped coming over.

"Winning that money around here would be a curse," I say.

"What do you mean?"

"Like stink-bait. Guys like old Gilbert would come sniffing around looking for their meal ticket," I say.

"Oh, Carmel." Gloria sounds disappointed. "So cynical."

"Not cynical," I correct her. *"Practical."*

Gloria gets a dreamy look in her eye. "Well, if I won that money I'd do something that would make us all get along. I'd start by sending Junior on one of them ministries to get him healed."

I laugh. "Gloria. I don't think being gay's a disease."

"Junior is *not* gay," Gloria says forcefully. "I told you that already." Then more softly, "He's confused."

"Does the booze help him get un-confused?"

She ignores me. "Then I'd buy me a big old bedroom set."

"Oh Lord," I roll my eyes.

"And Gilbert would come back to me."

"Hallelujah," I say, waving my hands in the air.

"And we'd spend all day in that king-size bed, like rich people, with fancy feather pillows and duvets and other French-sounding stuff that you can get for beds."

"Well, you know what they say?"

"And we'd eat bonbons from a red satin box shaped like a heart," she goes on.

"A woman without a man..."

"Bonbons are French too."

"Is like a fish without a bicycle."

"Oooh. I can just picture it. Can't you, Carmel?"

"I can, and it's making me nauseous."

"What? I don't know what you're talking about," Gloria says, snapping out of her daydream.

"You know what I'd do? For real?" I ask.

"Hmmm." I can tell Gloria doesn't want to know, doesn't want to hear me say it.

"I'd pack all my stuff into my rusty old Civic and drive as far as that money took me."

"That's what I'll put!" Gloria exclaims, picking up her pencil.

"I wouldn't stop until I was broke."

"Loves to travel," she says as she writes.

"I'd only stop if the wheels fell off my car." I squint my eyes and talk dreamily, looking out the window at my lush green grass, at the Civic sitting in the gravel driveway. But no amount of squinting can make that car look better.

"Although *interested in travel* would cover Jeremy off in Ja – wherever."

"And then I'd buy more wheels," I persist with my story.

"We can't really say *interested in live chickens*," Gloria ponders, chewing on the pencil.

"I'd drive to the edge of the earth and look over."

"That would make you sound like a nut..." she trails off.

"I'd go until my car fell apart and I was so broke that I didn't have a hope of ever getting back."

I feel Gloria staring at me. "I guess I can't really say *sensitive,* can I?" she asks.

"Hopefully I'd be lost too. Just to be sure."

"Not if I'm going to maintain *honest.*"

"That's how damned bad I want to get away from here."

My kitchen is silent. I keep my eyes on the window.

Finally, Gloria says, "You're always so sure." Her voice is soft.

"Hmmm?" I pretend I don't hear.

"Don't you ever have doubts?" she asks, picking at her fingernail.

A large cloud rolls quietly over the sun, casting a dim shadow on my front yard, making my "grass" look a little less lush.

I stand up and toss Gloria my keys.

"Don't smoke in the car."

just pretending

In my family I have a mother, a father and a sister, none of whom are real. Just like me. As if we're all just pretending. About my fake mom, my so-called dad says that the sixties came and went and nobody bothered to inform her. She wears Birkenstock sandals, droopy socks and a horrible patchwork denim skirt that she wears high up over her pot belly, which stubbornly resists valiant efforts to make it budge, efforts that include hours too numerous to count standing on her head in the vain hope that it will force the migration of belly fat into the area of her flat chest. Tiny shoulders and a skinny neck incongruously support a massive head of fuzzy hair, once shot through with clever streaks of white but now gone nearly completely grey. She gives the impression of a dandelion gone to seed. I vow never to be such a hopeless case. I'm secretly pleased we're not really related.

She's a socially conscious vegetarian with armpit hair and skin that smells like hemp. She's no Einstein or genius. So last fall, after I met Joe Jackson on *Geeks and Social Justice* and we just kind of hit it off, she never caught on to what I was up to. She would drop me off at the library on campus, never suspecting that I was doing anything other than "studying." She liked the idea of me being smart, even if she didn't understand it. I had a floor I liked to go to in the main library. It was quiet, in a conspiratorial way. You knew people were all over the place, in the carrels and browsing the stacks, but no one made any noise. Sometimes I fell asleep there, numbed by fat books with old, smelly pages. No one asked me questions, and I could be whoever I wanted there; maybe I was even being myself.

Joe Jackson. I fell in love with his name. Can you admire a person for their name? Probably not. You can admire their parents for thinking up an agreeable name, so I admired Joe Jackson's parents for their baby-naming aptitude. Then again, it was hard to imagine that Joe Jackson was ever a baby. He was at least six feet tall and all angles and points and unusual creases. Even his body structure was clever. I had to admire his parents for their engineering abilities as well.

When we met, Joe Jackson and me were logged on to *Geeks* at the same time, debating (but really sort of agreeing) over the whole English hegemony thing, hogging the group chat when Learningnerd posted *Get a room!* and we agreed to take our conversation private, both of us duly ignoring the sexual suggestion in Learningnerd's post and pretending a purely intellectual interest in each other. Finally, we agreed that since we lived in the same city, we should meet in person to continue our debate. "Discuss the issues."

He brought some papers from his school, something called Students for a Democratic University (turned out he was WAY older than me, but I never did tell him I was only fourteen), and then he proceeded to try to convince me that democracy is a constructed concept that doesn't really exist in any practicable sort of way. I lost him after a while but continued to nod and say *hmm* as though giving thoughtful consideration to his arguments. Soon, I realized he didn't really need me to be listening, so I concentrated instead on watching his pointy bits as he gestured here and there over his remarkable thesis.

"I plan to pursue this more intently in my graduate work," he said.

I could see he took himself way too seriously, but still an inexplicable longing came over me, made me want to watch his every move and listen, uncomprehending, to his voice. It was both delightful and dismaying. There was a time I would have thought myself too smart for that.

Joe Jackson and I continued in this way, week upon week. He

would bring books or papers, editorials and articles, presenting them to me as suitors in the past might have presented flowers or boxes of candy. Between our meetings I would log on to the *Geeks* site to try to catch a glimpse of him, but I found him there less and less.

We walked on campus, where he held my hand awkwardly at first and then with more ardent concentration. I found his attempts funny but didn't dare laugh because of how serious he was. I let him hold my hand, my fingers laced between his long fingers and bony knuckles, as though I'd given my hand up for good. After a while of walking like that it felt a bit like being towed around like sea-drift, but I didn't know how to get my hand back and didn't really think I wanted to, except my finger-tips were getting numb, not to mention sweaty. I imagined pulling my arm inside my shirt and leaving him holding my empty sleeve.

Alternately, he was like a bright spot that I was drawn to and a sore, sinking place in the pit of my stomach. I couldn't make up my mind. I spent a lot of time feeling like I was acting dumb and wanting more of the same.

Someone tied up a baby goat near a patch of grass outside the student residences and the goat's back was spray-painted blue. He gave me an explanation for that, but I forgot. Instead, the image of the blue goat settled like dust in my imagination.

"My dad's a goat farmer," I blurted. "Well, he *was*," I added. "He died." I looked at my sneakers sadly. Joe Jackson didn't know what to say, so I filled in the silence. "We had chickens too," I said. "On the farm." We didn't have a farm, my dad wasn't a goat farmer, and of course he wasn't dead. At least, my *pretend* dad wasn't any of those things. But somewhere, *out there*, I had a *real* family, and anything *could* be true. Even a goat-farming dead father. But my counterfeit mother's sister, my aunt Gabbie, *did* have a farm with goats and chickens, and we spent a lot of time there when I was young, so that was where my story came from. "We used to have to catch the chickens," I said, trying to impress Joe, but my confession-lies weren't getting much of a response out of him. I didn't know where I was going with this, but I decided to try harder. "Once, my mother chopped the rooster's head right off, right in front of us. Just to teach us a lesson."

"What? Really?" Joe said, disbelieving. Finally, he seemed to be listening.

"We had a cousin, Norman, a small little fatty, who we teased."

Joe Jackson's gaze drifted to a group of girls sitting on the grass, talking. My voice got louder as we walked past them, and I stepped up my story.

"There was a rooster who chased us and pecked our legs until they bled. Roosters can be vicious," I said, tugging his hand in emphasis. "So me and my sister, Trish, we climbed a hay bale to get away from the rooster. And Norman comes to try and get up on the bale with us, but Trish wouldn't let him. She pretends she can't pull him up. Then she stands up on the bale and shouts, 'Run, fat boy, run,' while poor Norman runs around the yard trying to get away from the rooster." This part of the story is mostly true. I leave out the part where I joined Trish's chant.

Joe Jackson was listening, but I had the impression he was just waiting for me to finish so he could talk more about his thesis.

"My mom comes along and catches us. She hauls us down from the bale and makes us go with her to the chopping stump. She keeps on saying, 'I'm going to teach you a lesson,' over and over while she shakes Trish by the arm. She makes us wait there." I shook my hand free from Joe's and continued. "And a few seconds later she comes back with the *axe* in one hand and the *rooster* in the other." I held up one hand and then the other, as if to demonstrate how she wielded these two items.

Joe Jackson caught his breath and I escalated my story, making sure to include as many horrible details as possible. I told him, "For some reason, the rooster didn't struggle. I don't know if he felt the authority in her hand, gripped around his neck." I shook my fist. "Or maybe he knew it was futile to fight back." I looked at Joe; his face was pale. At least I had his attention.

"Without saying a thing, my mother held his body on the

chopping stump, her hand on his chest. I *bet* she could feel his heart beating. If you had asked me before, I would have said she didn't have something like that in her. Boy, she sure surprised me." I shook my head and gave a low laugh that very nearly sounded sinister. "Without a second to let us catch our breath, *chop*, she did it." I made a chopping motion with my right hand into my left palm. Joe flinched.

"The little head rolled one way and the body went the other way, blood pumping out of his neck." I laughed out loud, spit flinging from my lips. "Finally, the body fell over and the head stopped rolling."

"It was dead silent," I told Joe, "and then Trish says, '*Cool.*' And she looks at our mom and says, 'Can you do it again?'" I laughed when I delivered the last line, as if it were the punch line to a lengthy joke.

"Wow," Joe Jackson finally said. "Your sister – what a jerk!" I had expected Joe Jackson to laugh when I told him about Trish's response. That's what other people did when I told them that story – they laughed. But just then I remembered that Joe Jackson was a vegetarian. The story must have resonated differently with him, I thought. And yet, I wanted something more from Joe Jackson, at that moment, but I'm not sure what. So I made up an addendum to the story, on the spot, to try to really impress him.

"That night, my mother did a terrible thing," I said. My face was hot with the lie, but I was enjoying the deception. "She served up his tough little carcass for supper, *his whole body* – it still looked like him! He was plucked and roasted to a shiny brown and laid out on the good serving platter." I made myself stop there. I was getting carried away.

"Did you *eat* him?" Joe asked, horrified.

"Well, *they* did." I pointed my finger in the air at my imaginary family. "I said I was sick, and my dad let me leave the table."

"That's an awful story," he said. "Your family sounds crazy." We didn't talk much after that, and we didn't hold hands any more that day. I knew I had crossed a line, some invisible line, but I felt justified, mad that he was so sensitive, offended that he made me feel like I'd done something wrong. *Who does he think he is, anyway?* I kept asking myself. I realized later what upset me most was that he had dared to judge my pretend family.

The next time I met up with Joe Jackson, he was cool to me – still put off, I guess, about the chicken story. I made it up to him by letting him kiss me outside the biology building, with its freaky sponges and sucking, amorphous creatures. He bent down and I stood on my tiptoes so our lips could touch. I'd never kissed a boy before, unless you counted Ricky Gerolamy in grade six, but that was on a dare and neither of us even got off our bikes. Besides, that was gross. Kissing Joe Jackson turned out to be nice. His lips were warm and soft. He pressed his body against mine. My stomach turned somersaults. After, we went inside to check out the aquarium. I think we both felt better.

It was almost the end of the term. I had the vague understanding he was planning to go home when his exams were finished. Home meant back to his small town, with whoever his family was – he refused to talk about them, even when I asked. He expected me to take his leaving as a matter of fact and so I did, hiding my feelings of rejection and impending loneliness.

He invited me to a year-end party in one of the residences. The party involved dressing up in your best clothes and bringing the cheapest bottle of wine you could possibly buy. Joe Jackson brought the wine. I packed my outfit from last Halloween into my backpack – a retro white '70s tuxedo that I thought was funny. My mother dropped me at the library, where I would be "studying," and made sure I had bus fare to get home. I changed in the public bathroom and ran across campus to meet Joe Jackson.

I thought the people at the party were going to be Joe Jackson's friends, but he didn't talk to anyone. I talked for a few minutes with a boy who asked me what my major was. I didn't know what to say, and then "women's studies" lurched out of my mouth.

I must have looked guilty after I said it, because the boy put a hand on my shoulder and, grinning, said, "That's okay. We like you anyway."

Joe Jackson steered me away from that conversation, and he and I sat on the floor and passed the bottle of cheap wine back and forth until I was dizzy and warm and we had to go outside for fresh air.

Campus was quiet. Lots of students had already finished exams, packed up and left. Joe Jackson took me to a still place between the health sciences building and administration. A grassy forgotten spot between the buildings, enclosed by trees, open to the sky.

I lay back on the grass, and he lay stiffly beside me. I could feel the heat from his body all down my right side even though we weren't touching. It was a warm, clear, almost-summer night, and all the stars were visible in the night sky.

"Look, the Big Dipper," I said, tracing my finger in the air down the handle and around the bottom of the scoop. I traced an imaginary line upwards from the lip of the pot. "And the North Star." I rested my finger on the slightly brighter North Star, exactly the same way my dad used to show me. Joe Jackson said nothing. He lay stiffly beside me as though this was something he'd never done, lie in the grass and look at the stars.

I thought about telling him how my dad showed me the Big Dipper and the North Star the first time when I was five and made it seem like magic. Orion's belt. The story of Orion and how he got put in the sky with all his favourite animals. And one lucky night, northern lights. Dancing in the prairie sky. But I didn't get to say any of this because he suddenly sat up and swung himself over top of me, straddling me with his knees. I smiled, thinking this was a game and we were going to kiss again. He took both my wrists and brought them up over my head, held them there with one hand. I tried to look into his eyes, but I couldn't see his face, dark with shadows. I heard him breathing hard. My smile faltered. "What are you doing?" My voice cracked like I didn't want it to. I sounded weak and afraid, and I wished I didn't. Joe Jackson wouldn't answer me. Instead, he lay down on top of me with his whole hot body, as if he was trying to keep me warm. His weight pushed the air from my chest. "Get off me," I

111

said breathlessly into his ear. He was still holding my arms over my head. When I struggled to get my arms free, he pinned them harder to the ground. A sharp pain shot through my wrist and I cried out.

He raised his body some, and I could breathe again. His free hand fumbled at the button on my pants. I tried to lift my knees, twist my hips away, my hands pinned tight to the ground above my head. He used his legs to hold mine down, and his fingers moved so fast over my pants even though I was trying to slow him down with my mind. His hands moved faster than my brain could keep up with. My pants loosened around my waist, were pulled and twisted. I've never felt so unable to stop something in all my life. Joe Jackson was on top of me, I could feel his hand undoing my clothes and I had no way to make it stop. Suddenly, his fleshy thing was poking between my legs, sticking to the soft skin of my inner thighs.

"Don't." I managed that one breathless word, tried to make it a command. He didn't listen. He shoved his chin into my neck, his weight taking my breath away, and still I felt his thing poking between my legs. I squeezed my knees, still wrapped in their pants, as tight as I could. The skin on my thighs pinched and tore. Then he heaved himself up, shifted his weight to one side, took his foot, his hard shoe, and scraped it down between my legs. The polyester pants of my once-hilarious tuxedo burned my skin as they ripped down my legs to my ankles. He kept kicking, forcing my shoe off my left foot, pushing my pants off my leg. He contorted his body so he could look down at the job he was doing, get it right. At that angle I could see his face in the moonlight, shiny with sweat, his pale lips drawn down with effort. His eyes, like nickels in the shadows of a wishing pond, wouldn't look at me. I'm not sure he knew I was there at all.

I'd been saying no, like a chant, over and over, but I stopped. He put his weight on top of me again, and I struggled to keep this thing from happening. He held my wrists so tight I was afraid he'd break them, squeezing, pressing, sharp and painful. I stopped thinking, focussed on looking past the burning heap on top of me, looked up at the night sky, traced the Big Dipper with my eyes, found the North Star. I imagined I saw Orion's belt, even though I knew it was the wrong time of year for it. But it was the right time for Aquila the eagle, so I searched for him. *The flamingo called Grus might be around now too,* I thought. I imagined they were all out. Again and again I traced those familiar sky-scapes like lifelines, critical work that had to be accomplished or the world would fall apart. I counted them. I counted on them.

When he rolled off of me, the cool relief of night air hit my skin, my wrists were released, my hands were numb. I rolled on my side away from him, curled into a ball but only for a moment. I heard him behind me, doing up his pants. I sat up, fumbled at my feet, somehow found the pant leg, tugged myself back together, did up zippers and buttons, pulled on a shoe. He stood beside me and we walked, as if this was any other time, any other evening. We didn't hold hands; we didn't talk. We walked out to the paved pathway that cut through the heart of the university campus and out to the ordinary street that signalled the end of university grounds. We stopped on the sidewalk at the bus stop, and he put his hands in his pockets. I couldn't bring myself to look up, all the way up, into his face. Instead, I stared stonily ahead.

"Do you want me to wait with you? For your bus?"

I shook my head.

"Okay then. See you later," he said, and I managed a small wave with my hand. I was just barely aware that he walked away. The bus came; I got on. I didn't think about my clothes, about the grass in my hair, about the thumbprints on the inside of my wrist, about the friction burns on my legs or ripped skin on my thighs. I didn't think of any of this. Instead, the inexplicable blue goat came to mind, producing a deep blue haze that descended to follow me home on the bus, where I sat with damp legs and scorched thighs. I avoided looking out the window because I knew my reflection was there.

After that night, I didn't see Joe Jackson again. I guessed he went home to whatever pretend family he came from. I didn't ever go and look for him on the *Geeks* site – I couldn't bring myself to log in there. But I thought about that place, on campus, where it happened. I didn't want to be afraid of it, so I revisited it. Off the bus, brisk walk to the health sciences building, duck in behind the bushes. Whoosh. Silence. I was not really surprised that it was cool and silent, soothing. I sat on the grass, my back against the stone of the health sciences building, and picked thick, waxy leaves from a bush. I folded one of the leaves between my fingers, and it resisted, then snapped as though I'd broken its bones. Sickened, guilty, I dropped the leaf. After that, I was more careful. I touched the leaves and put a branch between my finger-tips. I tenderly examined the veins on one of the leaves. I pulled blades of grass one by one from their roots, carefully sliding each blade from its sheath before chewing on the ripe white end. In my throat, the smell of green. Ordinarily a good smell. After a while, I figured out that it wasn't a bad place.

It wasn't until the start of June that I realized I was pregnant.

To hear my mother talk, getting pregnant made me the equivalent of a crack-addicted prostitute. "Oh my God," she cried when I told her. "I can't believe it." She threw her hands up in the air and shrieked, "Just like your real mother." Those were her words. I slapped her in the face. We were standing by the sink in the kitchen, and when I looked out the window I saw the apple tree had come into bloom, as though it had happened just in that moment. I was sorry as soon as I did it, but she picked the wrong moment to say that thing about my "real mother," who she thought I was protecting, which in turn hurt my pretend mother's feeling. That's right, I said *feeling*. She only had one, and it involved tears and was cleverly designed to inspire guilt in all others. Maybe someday I would tell her she was wrong about the protecting thing. It's hard to explain, but I didn't slap her because she said "just like your real mother," I slapped her because she said those words, "your real mother," to remind me *again* that I was different, didn't really belong, adopted and therefore not real. Every time I let my guard down and sort of forgot and just got on with things, she had to bring it up.

She decided I'd have an abortion. My dad, more unreal than ever, avoided talking to me altogether. Trish, who was real trouble by that time, was too busy climbing out her bedroom window and into cars with boys to notice anything was wrong.

My pretend mother took me to talk to a social worker. I went into his office alone, without her, and instead of what my mother thought we'd talk about, which was me being pregnant, we talked about my real mother. I wanted the social worker to look in his big files and give me answers more substantial than the basic background he was allowed to share. Instead, he had me write a letter to her so he could put it in the file. That way, he said, if she ever called to ask about me, it would be there. I didn't believe him when he said this was all he could offer.

I wrote, *I'd love to see you again sometime. We'll meet by the fountain in the mall. I'm the one with the red scarf and dark hair, narrow eyes like my father, whom you may or may not recall. If I see you again, will I know you by your smell? Touch? Voice? Aura? The social worker tells me you took care of me for the first two weeks. I know I never took my eyes off you. I looked and looked, but still I forgot.*

The image of me with my mother was so strong: I could see myself, swaddled in baby blankets, staring, glued to her every move. Yet, for some reason, I just couldn't bring myself to remember. My brain refused my deepest desire. I knew the memory was in there; I just couldn't get to it.

In bed that night, I talked to my stomach. "I won't do that to you," I whispered under my sheets. "I won't double-cross you. I promise," I murmured solemnly, "not to leave you."

I fell asleep and later woke up wet, having soaked the sheets. When I turned on the lights, I was covered in blood. I woke the woman who calls herself my mother, and she drove me to the hospital in silence. My legs were shaking when we arrived. I said I wanted to go in alone.

In the emergency room cubicle, a gentle doctor touched her

fingertips to my leg, just above the knee. "Scary, huh?" she said, and I wished for her to stay. I distracted myself by pretending she was my real mother, there to offer me comfort. *She must be some- body's real mother,* I told myself. I imagined us strolling down a sunny street, like in a movie, her hand raised to make a light touch on my back. We laughed about something and looked breezily at one another; no one thought about the idea that the other could just disappear. She linked her arm in mine, and we licked our ice cream cones and smiled. I moaned as my stomach cramped and I rolled on my side, tucking my knees tighter to my chest. I won- dered if I was being taught a lesson for something I'd done.

I miscarried by myself on a narrow cot behind a thin blue curtain. I felt my pretend mother's shadow hovering in the waiting room, where I hoped she was suitably worried – I sin- cerely expected I wouldn't live. She came and stood outside the curtain once. I could see her feet waiting there, unsure.

"Go away," I wailed, clutching myself tighter. "Leave me alone." I swear I could hear her wringing her hands. Her stupid sandals went away.

The doctor/mother came in only a couple of times to explain things to me and to order some medicine. In slow motion, my insides churned themselves into a purple pulp while I curled into a fiery ball.

Finally, in the bathroom, my body expelled the fetus in one shocking movement, a pale waxy shape, a suggestion of some- thing else.

the times in between

"Vince is in la-la land again."

I ignore Joy and resume my struggle with the passage I'm working on. An hour ago I woke with a hangover and an epiphany and headed straight to the writing table, an island in the middle of chaos. The kids have gotten up, and Joy's got a visitor. They all know enough not to cross the imaginary border between their space – strewn with toys, bits of clothing, beer bottles and stuffed ashtrays – and my space, cleared for writing in the middle of it all, a certain sanctity within it.

Last night one of the poets from down the street came to the house for the first time. He's being hailed by the writers' union as "recently emerged" to indicate he's at the beginning of his publishing career, even though he's nearly forty. The whole "emerging" thing makes it sound as though he's coming out of the closet or something. Joy invited him to do a reading; of course he was brilliant, the fucker. I remember starting out, when the words came like gifts and everyone thought I was exceptional. Some writers talk about it getting easier, but it's been the opposite for me.

It wasn't until he was here that I recognized him. At first I had difficulty placing him, but the niggling feeling that I should know the man wouldn't dissipate. I must have been staring because he caught my eye and took it as an invitation to lope over to where I huddled on the couch, already drunk.

"It's Vince, isn't it?" He stuck out his hand, which I ignored. "Marcus Quinn," he persisted. "I know you from Sheppard. You were a couple years ahead of me."

Christ, I thought. I didn't immediately make room for him on the sofa, as perhaps he might have expected. I left him standing there with that stupid grin on his face, waiting for me to congratulate him on his work, as I was sure he had come to expect. Instead, I downed my drink in one swallow and stood for the refill, tottering on my heels. I tried to push my way past him.

The determined little bastard grabbed my shoulder; his grip was surprisingly firm. When I felt his hand on my shoulder that way, I hoped this wouldn't lead to a drunken brawl in the living room but was prepared to deck him if circumstances warranted. I tried to shrug his hand off, but he was insistent. I turned my face to his, only inches from my own, and breathed my sour breath purposely toward his nostrils. He pretended not to notice, but I saw his demeanour shift. He hung on tighter just then, and I saw him change his mind about what he would say to me.

"How's your father?" he asked, squinting his eyes.

"Dead," I said, refusing to be drawn into a let's-reminisce-about-the-old-times conversation. What the fuck was he up to? I wondered.

"Oh, I'm sorry," he said.

"No you're not," I said. My tone implied he was an idiot. "Why would you be?" I asked. "Who the fuck's 'sorry' when the town drunk dies?"

His smile faded completely, and he readjusted his body slightly like someone faltering from a slap but trying to conceal the effects. Still, he kept his hand on my shoulder. "Vince," he finally said, low and conspiratorially, leaning toward my ear. "I just wanted to tell you, I mean, I thought you should know. Everyone could see what was going on and, well, it was terrible – what happened to you." He paused to be sure he had my attention, then said, "We all felt *so sorry* for you." Then his hand dropped.

I lurched past him and into the kitchen, where I had to steady myself at the sink, my head bowed, as though praying to the holy mountain of dirty dishes. I must have looked to be contemplating sickness; someone asked me if I was okay. I shakily poured another drink and stumbled out the back door into the changed atmosphere of the evening.

How could a single sentence uttered by a stranger so shatter a person? *We all felt so sorry for you.* I was quite certain, just then, that my glass insides were rattling around in pieces by my ankles.

The beatings weren't the worst of what my old man doled out, yet that's surely what Quinn the outed poet was referring to. Did they really all feel sorry for me? Is that what it looked like from the outside?

"Tell me about your mother," Joy said, shortly after we started going out. All she knew was that I had lost my mother when I was young.

"She died of a brain aneurysm," I said. "I didn't even know what that was. The principal had to explain it to me." I didn't tell Joy that I was convinced I'd witnessed the beginning of that injury. My mother and father were fighting when he pushed her and she fell, hitting her head on the corner of the stove. I thought she was dead that time, the way her head bobbed on her neck as she went down. My father left her where she fell and staggered out the door, leaving me to try to rouse her. Remarkably, there was no blood, just unconsciousness, and then the quiet complaint of a headache for days afterward.

But my father wasn't always a mean drunk. Sometimes he was funny. One time he laughed as he picked my mother up in his arms like a groom taking his bride over the threshold. I thought it was good sport too until I saw her face, her eyes wide, her voice scared as she begged him to put her down. He took her to the large freezer chest where we kept the meat he brought home from hunting, after it was butchered and wrapped in its brown paper. I followed them, the smile quickly fading from my lips. He staggered as he carried her, even though she must have been light as a bird. From behind them, I watched her slender fingers as she clung to his neck and said his name, over and over.

"Richard, put me down. Richard, please."

He flipped open the freezer chest lid with one hand and held her over the void, as though he would place her inside.

"Richard! Richard!" she cried, louder, on the edge of hysteria. She struggled, her slight body twisting to escape his grasp. My father laughed his gravelly laugh from the back of his throat. He held on tighter to her and continued to pretend he would put her into the freezer. Finally, he took a step back and let her legs drop to the floor. She stood for a minute, breathing hard, on the verge of crying, her one arm still around his shoulders.

"Chicken," my dad said. He still seemed in a good mood.

My mother put a trembling hand to her mouth and caught my eye. Then she pushed past him, took me by the arm, and we fled to the bedroom.

The beatings weren't the worst of it, though, as Quinn's comment would imply. The worst were the times in between – the times when you didn't know what would happen next – when maybe you could feel the trouble building inside the dusty house, ricocheting like an undercurrent off the crowded furniture. Instinct told you to run, and you did, but in the cold prairie winter in a musty little town where you had made no friends but everybody knew you as the son of the town drunk, how long could you stay away? People's pity was just that, and you learned early not to mistake it for kindness. There may have been many who felt sorry for me but none who were willing to get involved.

I notice Kit and Casey, crouched on their haunches with their tiny, bare toes pressed to the edge of the invisible line that keeps them out. They wait for the spell to be broken, for me to be released from my self-imposed exile and notice them. I've found that when I pay attention to their antics, they get overexcited and lose control. I try, for Joy's sake, to be a good father. Or at least a good enough father. But I see it in their eyes, they're guarded with me, already, at their young age; they seem to have learnt not to trust me.

"Daddy! Daddy!" Casey used to shriek whenever I came in the door, running to show me some creation or to offer me a taste of whatever she was eating. After so many times of me pushing past her, saying, "Not now, Casey," and, "Later, Casey," she finally seems to have given up.

I don't want to dislike my own children, and for the most part I don't. I'm just not certain I like them all that much. And I'm probably overstating that. After all, what parent doesn't wonder at the innocent softness of their child's sleeping face, the perfection of ten tiny digits? I'm not immune to all of it. It's other times I can't bear – their sorry hopefulness, their persistence. I have an unnatural dread of being left alone with them. Joy rarely asks it of me.

In my drunken anger last night, I returned to the kitchen from the cool evening air of the backyard. I pushed through the people crowding my tiny house – writers and poets and their partners – making my way to the writing table where everyone knew not to touch the workspace or set their empty beer bottles. *Sanctum sanctorum* in the middle of chaos.

It was then that I saw them, Joy and Quinn, standing in the small hallway. He leaned against the wall with his shoulder, and she did the same, facing him. She held a drink with both hands, twirling the glass in her fingers. There was something playful in the casual turn of the glass, the cock of her head. It looked *off*, somehow. Too much like flirting, it seemed to me. Even though she was turned away from me, I could tell she was smiling.

I pushed my way to the writing table and grabbed the journals with my most recent notes, poems, sketches and outlines. The notebooks are where it all starts for me – where poems are born. Of course there is no copy of any of them. I stalked back through the kitchen and out to the yard, slamming the screen door carelessly. Into the fire pit I dumped the entire burden. Fumbling in my pockets for matches, I pictured Joy with Quinn. The congested papers wouldn't light, and I was forced to handle them once again. As I tore and crumpled individual sheets, I averted my eyes from the inked words, the individual letters on the page – the little blue-black inflections, like stutters, t-t-tripping across the pages. I was afraid the sight of those letters, forming into words, might bring me to my senses.

Joy sets a glass of water cautiously on the table near my papers. I grunt acknowledgement, and she shoos the kids away. I can see by her demeanour that she's waiting for me to be finished. I have the intense urge, just then, to explain myself to her. The words *I love you* hover on my tongue, urgent, and yet I'm not able to say them out loud. I'm sorry. That's what I want to convey. None of those silly girls, most of whose names I can't recall, ever meant a thing to me. All drunken distractions. She knows that. I always thought she knew that.

I would have liked for her and my mother to have known one another. It was after my mother died, and my father was drunk with an impossible regularity, that I made my way to the city. In my own drunken moment, at the party of an acquaintance from the Friday open mike, I spotted Joy across the room. I promptly walked up to her, mustered all the charm of a toad and blurted out Who the fuck are you? which, roughly deciphered, meant I've never seen you around here before. To my surprise, she was able to translate Drunken Asshole to English, and I went home with her that night.

She found me last night, smoking my unfiltered cigarettes one after another, my last drink long gone, the papers in the fire pit reduced to smouldering brown ashes. I refused to acknowledge her touch on my back or to hold her hand when she slipped it into mine, irrationally blaming her for bringing the outed poet to our house. For making me burn my papers.

Rather than go pick a fight with the poet, as I imagined would bring me satisfaction, I allowed myself instead to be led inside and put to bed like a child. The sensation of letting another man get the better of me in my own house dogged my dreams all night.

I've been thinking about it all day, trying to make sense of what really happened last night. Before I know it, the shadows get long and the stereo begins playing the cool sounds of Chet Baker. She's purposely chosen my favourite. A glass of wine appears on my table, and I emerge from my cocoon to see the kids leaping around the couch in their underwear. Joy enters with a cup in her hand and perches on the ottoman, ignoring them. She notices me watching her and lifts her arm, bearing a toast. In the twilight window frame I see the ill-formed beginnings of my own reflection, watered down as it is by the light of a near full moon.

The look on Joy's face is wry, as if she doesn't quite believe in the toast herself. "To us," the toast implies, but that look tells me it can't deliver. Her look seems to question what the "us" is, any more. Or maybe these are just my own insecurities, projected onto her.

I don't know why, but I drop my pen and get out of my chair. I kneel on the floor in front of her and place my arms alongside her legs. My head falls into her lap. I can sense a moment where she hesitates even to touch me, there on my knees in front of her. I don't cry, but I just stay there, head down, feeling her warm legs against my cheek and my ear.

"What is it?" she asks, concerned. There's a bit of an awkward laugh behind her words. The laugh tells me she's afraid, afraid of what I'm going to say. Finally, she lays her free hand across my back, the other still holding her wine. "Vince?" she says, and then she repeats my name more insistently. "Vince!" She shakes my shoulder. "Vince, what have you done?"

drinking wine spo dee o dee

ash, you tell a good story. You should write some of them down, you. People like that kind of thing.

That's what Sadie was always saying to me. Fucking Sadie. After she got on that bus, Roy and me each drank a whole bottle of Two-Buck Chuck in the bus station parking lot. That usually makes me sing the Spo Dee O Dee song, but I just wasn't in the mood that time.

I tried to act like I was happy she was going. She didn't even look back. I called out *Bitch!* as the bus drove away. Then I almost had to pound some guy staring at me. Asshole. That got me and Roy kicked out of the station altogether. Roy passed out beside me, little Scruffy tucked in his shirt. It was another damn cold night.

Fucking Sadie. Who goes from Winnipeg to Toronto anyway? I told her she'd find out. Being on the streets is a lot different in a big city like that. I told her when she came back, saying she's sorry, that she was wrong, I wouldn't be here waiting. But I guess we both knew that wasn't true.

Sadie only went to Toronto because she thought her kid was out there. She was thinking it was her last chance to find her, I guess. What the hell did she think she was going to do? Have some kind of happy reunion or something? What did she have to offer that kid, I asked her? I wish I'd never said that to Sadie now.

She was only out of the hospital two days before she left for Toronto. While she was in there, I waited for her every day, outside, for almost a whole week. Hospital staff wouldn't let me in to see her. Not since the first day and the incident in her bathroom. How was I supposed to know the bathroom is only for patients? And what did I do all that waiting for, anyway? So she could take off on me? But I suppose she had a good reason.

The day she got out, I was waiting for her, camped out near the doors, panhandling for change. Sadie always wore a black tube-style neck warmer on her head and I'd gotten used to the look of it, the way it stood straight up on her head, to make her look like a Russian Cossack dancer. But the day she came out of the hospital, I noticed she'd gotten hold of a large yellow metal binder paperclip and clipped the top of the neck warmer shut in the middle, at the top of her head, making it look, more than ever, like just a toque. I was disappointed that she no longer looked like a Russian dancer, but I did like the yellow paperclip against the black fabric of the neck warmer. It was the first thing I noticed when she came out the hospital doors.

"Sadie," I yelled at the yellow paperclip, bobbing away on top of her head. She didn't see me there when she came out, sitting next to the door with my back against the building. I jumped up, scooping up my cup with its bits of change and the piece of cardboard that I'd been sitting on, and trotted along to catch up with her. She looked back when I called her name, but she was determined not to slow down.

"Well?" I asked, finally catching up to her.

Sadie ignored me and kept walking.

"Where's the fucking fire?" I asked, looking around to see if she was being chased. Maybe she was AWOL from the hospital, I thought. But no one was following us. I knew she'd come around and talk to me, sooner or later, so I just walked with her. "Roy and Scruff are over at the library," I told her.

"So?" she asked.

So this is how it's going to go, I thought to myself.

"We got enough for a bottle. We'll celebrate you getting out of the hospital, hey?"

Sadie's steps slowed a bit. We walked some more. I could tell Sadie was warm to the idea of a bottle.

I heard the footsteps, running behind us, more than one person. I should've realized what was coming, but I didn't think anything of those running steps until it was too late. They were right on us, and then Sadie started fucking screaming at the same time as one of the little punks grabbed the yellow paperclip and pulled her hat off her head. The pricks kept running down the sidewalk, whooping and hollering, swinging Sadie's hat in the air. When they threw it and it landed on the sidewalk, they kicked it along like a soccer ball.

Sadie ran a bit down the street, screaming at the boys. "You! You! You!" she kept repeating, not able to spit out the rest of what she wanted to say.

I ran after the boys for a block, which made them laugh louder, but they kept running, throwing catcalls over their shoulders.

"Come and get it, Grandpa," they taunted.

"Yeah?" I shouted back. "Fuck you." Grandpa. What the fuck?

Finally, they left the hat on the sidewalk and took off. I walked the last block to get it, snatching it up and turning around to go back to where I'd left Sadie. By the time I got there, she was leaning against one of the buildings, having a coughing fit. She tried to hide the bloody napkin she was coughing into, but I saw it plain as anything.

Sadie never talked too much about her life, except when she was drinking and she got into that funky mood. Her eyes would go glassy and the tears would leak like someone was fiddling around with a tap. Those times, she would tell me how much she loved me, how she couldn't live without me. Those were good times, those.

One of those times, she told me about the baby.

"I feel it, sometimes," she said to me. And when I didn't say anything, she said, "My uncle, he had a leg amputated, from diabetes. After it was gone, he swore he could still feel that leg. Sometimes it was itchy. Sometimes it hurt. And he'd go to scratch it or rub it, and it wasn't there. There was nothing for him to scratch or rub. Phantom pain, that's what he called it." She paused and then said, "That's what I got. Phantom pain. That baby grew here." She thumped her ribs. "And sometimes I still feel it there. I swear, I feel it kicking me, nudging me from the inside. Like it wants to remind me – so I won't forget about it." She paused. "I never looked, you know?" she said to me, her eyes searching my face to see if I understood. Then she added, "I never looked at my baby to see if it was a boy or a girl. And nobody told me."

"I went home after that. Home free. Empty handed. I was supposed to act like it didn't happen. I always had a feeling it was a girl, so that's how I think of her now. A little orphan girl."

"After I got home, I stayed in my room a long time. The first time I dared to go out, with my friends, I went out to a party. A house party. I got a bottle of vodka that night. I tipped my head back with that bottle and I drank and drank. I didn't know how to drink hard liquor; I never had it before. I let it burn my throat and my sinuses, it felt good to hurt myself that way. I kept wondering how come no one noticed I was bleeding. Course I wasn't, really. I just felt like it."

Another time she told me, "I could have done it. I could have. We'd have been poor, but so what? There's worse things for a kid than growing up poor."

After the coughing fit, I fixed Sadie's hat on her head. While we walked to meet up with Roy, Sadie explained to me why she had to go to Toronto. "I imagine her wearing her life like a lie," she said. "Slipping in and out of crowds of people and going completely unnoticed. No one knows who she is because she don't know herself. How will she know who she is?" Sadie pleaded. "I dream she has one memory again and again – the memory of my heart beating out a message to her. I want her to know she's not alone."

And so Sadie went on the bus and left me here with Roy. My good friend Roy.

"I hate Winnipeg," Roy says, rubbing his hands together, stomping his feet. "The coldest fucking city in the world, or some shit like that."

We're outside the Louis Riel, hoping to get some change. I put little Scruffy under my arm and hold the cup out at a woman passing through the doors into the hotel. As if on cue, Scruff gives a small whine.

"Sparesomechange?" I ask. She pauses – a good sign. A couple of coins hit the bottom of the cup and I say, "God bless." She grimaces and goes into the hotel, avoiding eye contact.

"Fuck, it's cold," Roy says.

"Dat reminds me of a joke," I say. "A drunk sits in a bar and watches a guy walk in. The guy sits beside the prettiest girl there. Pretty soon, they get up and leave together. Next night, same thing happens. The drunk watches as the guy scores, night after night."

Roy's still dancing around in his work boots, rubbing his hands together, but he's watching me with a smile.

"Finally, the drunk can't stand it," I continue. "He goes up to that guy and asks him for his secret. 'How do you get all those women to go with you?' he asks. The guy says, 'Okay, first thing you do is go up to a woman and say, *Tickle your ass with a feather.* If she acts good to that, then you go from there. If she says, *What!?* you say, *Typical nasty weather.* You got it?' The drunk nods his head and stumbles away to find himself a lady to try this on."

Roy's smiling now. He takes Scruff from me and puts the pup under his coat to keep him warm. "Keep talkin'," he says.

"So the drunk, he sits down beside a woman at the bar and he says, 'Scratch your cunt with a twig.' She says, 'What!?' and he says, 'FUCK it's cold.'"

Sadie liked me telling stories. "It's how we know who we are," she was always saying, whatever that meant. But my stories are different than Sadie's. Sadie's stories are older than mine – they're about where she comes from, her whole family, like. Ancestors and shit like that. Mine are just life stories. Jokes and life stories.

Hey, I got a story from my life. Most of the people around here don't know about it, but me and Roy, we used to be part of something big, something historic, us. Did you ever hear of AIM? Red Power and all that. American Indian Movement. Yeah, well we were there. We were there on the front lines at Wounded Knee, down in South Dakota, getting our asses kicked along with all those other Indians.

It was really something, all those Indians in one place, standing up for our rights. That's how it went back then. We done a lot of scrapping, a lot of fighting, 'cause we knew what we wanted and we knew what was right.

We watched the seasons turn there at Wounded Knee. Something like seventy-two days. A baby was born there, a spring baby. I wonder sometimes where that baby is today. He must be at least thirty years old now, him. Older, even. God, was it that long ago? I wonder if he's a warrior, like his mom must have been.

We were all warriors then, us, to be at Wounded Knee, taking on the fucking US army. Women, children, babies. No one was afraid. You're talking about a bunch of people with nothing to lose. That's how revolution works – when people got nothing to lose.

On our way into the camp, we had to try not to get fucking shot by those *moonias* people who were pissed off about the roads being closed and all those army guys being around. They were taking pot shots at the Indians from the hills along the highway.

In the end there, I was one of the ones who got arrested. Me and Roy. When those soldiers took me down, I was running with my guts in my throat, I never ran so scared. I honestly thought if they got me I'd be dead. I'd already seen two other Indians die over those seventy days. One of them, he was shot by a fucking machine gun.

I saw other things too. Like when twelve people left from the camp to go for supplies. Gonna pack them in on foot, through what they call there the "badlands." Not one of those guys came back. I never heard of anyone finding out what happened to those guys. People talked about a mass grave and stuff, out in the desert, but I never heard if that was true, me.

So I'm running from the soldiers, the taste of iron in my mouth, pumping my arms and my boots slippery on the hard ground. I didn't look back because I knew looking would slow me down. That and I didn't want to see the fucker that was going to shoot me. Any minute I knew I'd hear a gun crack.

And then I did hear it. I stumbled and fell, sucking that dusty grey-shit dirt through my front teeth. They gave me a licking with the boots and rifle butts until I went unconscious. I woke up in the back of a truck, handcuffed, bleeding; Roy was sitting near me and we were headed for jail.

That time with AIM, that wasn't my first time in jail. First time I went to jail was when I met Roy. I was fresh as dew, me. I can imagine how I must have looked – bony shoulders sticking out, little tough guy, scrappy, big-eyed, fresh and tender baby meat. Six-fucking-teen.

If it wasn't for Crow I'd have been torn apart inside a week.
Who's the punk, Crow?
Fuck you, he's my nephew.
Didn't anyone ever tell you that's fuckin' incest?
Laughter.
But nobody fucked with my uncle Crow.

"Don't you let no one in here call you that, nephew," Crow told me later. "Punk," he said, when I looked confused. "You don't wanna wear that jacket. You hear?" To be somebody's punk was to be his girlfriend. Jail's the only fucked up place I know where forcing another guy to suck your dick proves you're a man.

I seen it happen to another guy. Little *moonias* kid, same age as me. I can still remember his name was Adrian. We met in the buckets, were on the same bus ride out, and we hit the block

131

together. First-time offenders.

The cop at the holding cells looked real hard at him and me. Then he said, "You going to the Pen?" When we said yes, he shook his head, mocking us with his *tsk, tsking,* and walked away, grinning. The bastard. He saw how fresh we were.

It didn't take long – that kid Adrian was turned out by his cellmate inside of two days. You could hear him pleading with the guy. I asked Crow why nobody done anything to stop it, and he said they don't even patrol the blocks after lockdown.

We were on the same work crew for a while, me and Adrian.

"Heya, Adrian," I said to him one day. Just being friendly was all.

His rake stopped moving. His head stayed down, and he stood like he was frozen. It took a couple of minutes for me to see he was fucking crying.

"What the fuck's the matter?"

He didn't answer.

"Fucking quit it, before someone sees you," I said, looking around.

Then he said, without looking up, "You're the first person to say my name since I got here. My name is Adrian. I'm not a fucking punk." Then he started raking again and moved away from me.

Like I said, Sadie's stories were different. Bigger, somehow. Larger than just one person's life. Sadie, she told me about her uncle telling her a story once about a giant that lived on the reserve. A giant and a weasel. That weasel, he ate the giant's heart out there, at the end of that story. They're fast and sneaky there, them weasels. That's how that story went. I know how the old people's stories work, how they're told over and over because kids don't really listen. It takes lots of times to hear the story before you remember it.

Sadie said that time with her uncle was different. It was special to have him tell the story in his slow way that made a person hang on to the end of each word, waiting to see if there would be more. I knew just what she meant when she said that. She didn't dare breathe because it might make him stop.

When Sadie's uncle finished his story, she said there was no way to get him to tell another one. Instead, he went outside for a smoke. Seven months after that, he was dead from the cancer.

"He didn't tell any more stories after that time," Sadie said. "Think about it. All the stories he didn't tell. Just gone."

The more I think about it, the more I see that Sadie was right, it's all about the stories.

Beside me, Roy cracks his knuckles, a habit that gives me the willies. I first heard him do it in jail that first time. After I hit the block, it didn't take long before this guy, a big halfbreed with a rep, started to fuck with me. Just a little at first, he'd bump me in the food line and whisper *Cousin* in my ear, or stare me down in the chow hall.

Crow's advice was important. *Someone gets in your face, you fight back. Don't let nobody fuck with you.*

One night, four weeks into my sentence, I go to get a coffee and the big halfbreed takes my spot. He takes my spot and then turns away from me and starts joking around with those guys at the table. Only he's not just joking around, he's cracking his knuckles, loud and aggressive-like.

I'm not your fucking babysitter, my uncle Crow's voice echoed.

So while I'm at the coffee counter I put my hand in my front pocket, feeling for the smooth metal, warm next to my leg, which is shaking. I palm the combination lock, looping the string that's tied to it around my hand. Then I turn around, ready to come back to my seat, my arm stiff at my side. The big halfbreed's still turned away from me, on purpose, pretending it's not a challenge, him taking my seat.

You want to make it in here? Draw blood, hurt somebody, get a rep for being crazy – that's what you gotta do.

I could let it go, could find myself another seat. But I know the price of not sticking up for myself. So I wait until I'm close before I break with two strong steps, drop my coffee and bring my straight right arm around, my whole hundred and thirty pounds behind the blow with the lock that catches him on the temple.

His head, it goes all the way down, and on the bounce back up I clock him with the lock to the back of the scalp. I hit him so many times I lose count. The string finally breaks, and the lock falls. I look at my unconscious halfbreed friend, blood pouring from his scalp, soaking his hair, dripping from the ends like water.

"Cousin," I say out loud.

A week later, when I see the big halfbreed for the first time since the attack, I'm ready for trouble. The bruises on his face have faded, yellowed around the edges. The whites of both eyes are still blood red, but even they've started to turn yellow. His eyes, with the broken blood vessels like that, make him look fierce. But it's not like I thought, with him. Instead of pulling a knife on me, he pulls a deck of cards.

"Play," he says menacingly, holding up the well-worn deck and nodding to an empty table.

Okay, I think, as he deals out a hand of whist, me wondering all the time what his game is. Any time a guy tries to sit down at the table and join the game, the halfbreed says, "We're fucking busy here," and stares the guy down until he backs off.

"Someone's gonna think we're on a date," I say, and he looks at me sharply. Then he laughs out loud, shuffling the cards.

I win the game in four hands, and he puts the cards in his pocket and stands up. He's still got one hand in his pocket and I watch that hand, bracing myself for what's going to come next. My calf muscles are tense under my seat as I lean my weight onto my toes, ready to spring up and defend myself.

But instead of attacking me, the halfbreed just says, "We'll play again tomorrow."

Twice more we play cards before I figure out he's maybe not as menacing as I thought. Then he starts sitting with me at mealtime. At first, I think he's trying to power me out. But he don't do anything, just sits. And that's how it goes, for my whole sentence. When we got out of the Pen, we just kept on hanging around together, me and my halfbreed friend.

I poke Roy and pass him the bottle. "Cousin," I say.

Roy shifts on his cardboard and sleeping bag. "Fuck, it's cold," he says.

"Scratch your cunt with a twig," I say, and we both laugh.

Roy rubs his hand over his face, and his thumb grazes the spot near his temple where that scar is. He tips his head back to drink out of the bottle. You can still read most of the word *MASTER* imprinted there, backwards and lopsided, if you look at it in the light. We've had a laugh or two about that over the years, me and my fucking halfbreed friend.

We should go to the shelter tonight, but they have rules about us drinking. Good old Two-Buck Chuck. *Drinkin' wine spo dee o dee.* Wish I knew a sad song, me.

"Hey, Cousin," I say, "wanna go to the Fort Garry there and watch those rich *moonias* people pretending to be broke?"

"Ehhh," Roy says, putting the tip of his tongue on his bottom front teeth, like Indians do, as if to say, *Good joke.* And then we laugh, which helps to warm us up. At the Fort Garry, we panhandle enough for another bottle and then, like a gift, the weather breaks.

A few days later, me and Roy are outside the bus station after a pretty good afternoon at the hotel there. We're feeling all right about things just then. A car full of Indians pulls up to the curb, and two people get out. I'm thinking about whether or not to ask them for money before I see that it's Sadie's family, her brother and a cousin. They've come to find me, something I know right away ain't good.

Her brother shakes my hand. "Hash." He says my name like

I'm an old friend. He offers me a smoke. Roy goes inside with Sadie's cousin. We stand around near the wall of the bus station, me and Sadie's brother, dragging on our smokes, not sure what to say to each other. We both look up and down the street as if this will help. Neither of us wants to look too hard at the other. I have the feeling I don't want to know what he's come here to say.

"How you been?" I ask.

"Okay," he answers. He nods his head a bit, his thumbs hooked in the front pockets of his jeans. "Yep. I been okay."

We're both silent for a while.

"Got a call," he says finally.

I nod.

"It's Sadie," he says. "She died."

"Oh," I say. "I didn't know that." Even while my voice stays the same, talking to Sadie's brother there, everything inside me changes.

"Oh," he says. Then he adds, "You didn't, hey." He nods his head some more, drags on his smoke before saying, "She's in Toronto – her body. We're gonna have a funeral there. It's where we're from, you know."

I nod again, just as though we're talking about something ordinary. My ears buzz and it's sort of crazy, but there's nothing I can do about it.

I let him tell me some more stuff, about how she died on the bus before she even got to Toronto and nobody noticed until they got to the Toronto station and everyone got off and the driver checked the seats. She was already long gone by the time he found her. "Natural causes," Sadie's brother says. The discussion ends with him giving me money for a bus ticket, so I can go.

Later, I say to Roy, "That was nice. Him making a point of finding me. Yup."

I took the money and all. Roy and me even went in to buy that ticket there. Then I thought, *How can I get on that bus?* I'd have to wonder which seat she was in. Did she look out the window here? Did she see that same shack out there in the field;

did she watch those same shadows sliding around over the snatches of snow? Where was it that old Wesakechak played his last big trick on her? Was it just outside TO where she quietly stopped breathing as the bus churned up the dust on the road? How could I get on that bus and have all them thoughts, me?

Instead, me and Roy drink up the money. You probably guessed that. But after, I start to have second thoughts. I start to wonder what's the right thing to do and I think maybe, maybe I'll still have to get on that bus. Maybe after it warms up. When the seasons change again. Find that kid, tell her Sadie's story.

Sadie would like that kind of shit.

hungry

When Lucy Wingfeather was small, she lived with her real mother, where she was kept, for a time, in the basement, on account of being bad. A puppy came to the basement one day, and Lucy reasoned that he must have been bad too. He came to her, to the place where she stayed in the corner with the blankets and old clothes. He was soft all over and warm and wiggly. His black fur was like velvet. Lucy wanted to hold him but he squirmed away, scratching her with his small sharp nails.

"Jesus!" she said. She clutched his rump but he squealed and scared her, so she let him go. He ran to the bottom of the stairs and started to cry. Too small to climb the stairs, he just stood at the bottom and whined. Lucy wondered why he didn't like her.

"Shhhh," Lucy hissed, but he didn't pay any attention to her. She called to him in whispers. Lucy could tell the puppy didn't know how bad it was to cry at the stairs like that. Lucy stayed in the corner. There was only one small window in the basement and it was by the stairs. The puppy could be seen in the light that came in through the window; he whined and looked up the stairs. Lucy, still mad at him for not staying with her, threw things at him to try to get him to quit.

After a while, the puppy figured out how to get up onto the first step. Once up, he couldn't get down. He cried even more. Lucy wanted to go and help him but she was too afraid. A little while later, he made it up one more step, where he curled up and fell asleep.

Later, Lucy consoled herself with the thought that she tried to tell the puppy. Lucy knew bad things happened if you cried by the steps. *Stupid puppy,* she thought.

The puppy was still asleep on the second step when Lucy's mother, with her heavy steps and hard-landing heels, was heard on the floor overhead, moving to the door at the top of the stairs. Lucy held her breath when her mother came thumping down the stairs. It only took one of those heavy heel strikes in the centre of the puppy's back to break it. Puppy made a terrible noise.

"Jesus," Lucy's mother cried, surprised, crashing down the remaining two steps before she caught her balance. Still holding Lucy's plate of supper in one hand, Lucy's mother leaned over to examine the crushed puppy. "Stupid little bastard," she said.

She set Lucy's plate in the usual spot on the counter beside the stairs before turning to clomp back up, avoiding the puppy, which was making small, awful noises. Lucy was so afraid of the noises that she didn't dare go near her supper plate. In the morning, when the sun came in through the little window, the noises had stopped and Lucy could see the still curve of soft black fur on the step.

After the strangers came to get Lucy out of the basement, Lucy was sent to a series of foster homes. The longest foster home stay was Lucy's last one – she made it almost to the end of grade eight. On her first day at her last foster home, Billy, the real kid of the foster parents, took her into his parents' bedroom and showed her a cupboard with piles and piles of porno magazines. "Look," he said, flipping a magazine open and showing her pictures of two girls kissing. "What do you think of *that?*"

Lucy didn't know what she thought about it but could tell Billy thought something about it, and he wanted some kind of reaction from her. By then, she'd learned a thing or two about when to give boys what they wanted and when not to.

"So?" she said, in the face of the dirty magazine. "Who cares about that?"

When his mother came in and caught them looking in the cupboard, the first words out of Billy's mouth were, "She made me."

By the time she was in grade eight, Lucy knew too well what

Billy thought about the pictures in his dad's magazines and how he expected her to respond.

The day she saw the group of boys from her grade eight class at the school playground, Lucy didn't turn to go a different way. She wasn't afraid of them. The opposite, in fact. Lucy had wanted to have a boyfriend since she was in grade seven. She sometimes dreamed so vividly that Davis Anderson, the most popular boy in grade eight, had asked her to "go out" with him that she had to remind herself that it wasn't real when she woke up. She imagined how her life would be different if she got herself a boyfriend. A real boyfriend that is. Billy didn't count.

The boys waited until she walked right into the playground and stood by the fort before they paid any attention to her. It was the school's new playground and it was supposed to be some kind of a boat, although Lucy could never see the resemblance. It was officially named the "Friend Ship." The boys were all in Lucy's class except for the black-haired boy, who Lucy knew went to a different school. He laughed like an excited girl when he saw her standing there. One by one, the boys jumped off the fort and stood around her. There was Tremaine Sheppard, a yellow-skinned Métis boy with a long face and a lumpy nose, the black-haired boy with thick, dark-rimmed glasses whose name she didn't know, and a French boy called Gilles with long hair that fell in his eyes, who got picked on because of his girl's name. Normally, they all ignored her.

"Lucy Wingfeather," said Tremaine in a mocking tone.

Even though they were in the same class at school, Lucy was surprised he knew her name. She tried to smile.

"Lucy Weirdfucker," said Gilles, and the other boys laughed. Lucy noticed the black-haired boy's nose was runny and he snuffled a lot trying to keep the snot inside.

When Tremaine stepped forward to take Lucy by the shoulders, she thought he was going to kiss her right there in front of the other boys and she began to close her eyes in anticipation of her first real kiss. Instead, Tremaine turned Lucy around so that her back was to him and he pulled her close and hugged her to his body. He held her tight to him and bent over at the waist, forcing her to bend too. His elbows dug into her sides while his hands slid up the front of her top to cup her loose breasts both at once. Lucy didn't try to stop him. The hug felt good and she didn't even so much mind his hands. The other boys laughed and encouraged him, and Lucy felt like she was a part of something. Tremaine held her like that for a moment before removing his hands from her shirt.

"Come on," he said, and took her hand. He jumped onto the hanging bridge that led up to the fort, or "ship," as it was supposed to be known, and Lucy followed. He lay down in a corner of the fort on the hard wooden boards and pulled Lucy down on top of him. They were partially hidden behind the short walls of the fort. Tremaine rolled over on top of Lucy and put his hand up her shirt again. This time he kissed her too, sending warmth spreading through her belly and tingling inside her chest. Lucy had never felt this before and she thought it might be what it felt like when you fell in love. He took her hand and pulled it down to make her feel his hardness through his jeans. She knew he wanted her to touch it, and so she undid his pants. He exhaled deeply when she reached inside his underwear. Right away, Lucy could see that being with Tremaine was different from Billy. For one thing, she liked that Tremaine kissed her and acted like they were doing something together. With Billy, it always seemed like he was making her do something that was just his idea. Billy never tried to kiss her. She wondered if kissing might be the thing that made people fall in love.

After he was finished, Lucy tried to hug him. She thought that Tremaine Sheppard, despite his lumpy nose, wasn't entirely unattractive. Lucy just wouldn't have picked him first, is all. Lucy consoled herself about her second-string boyfriend with the fact that he did have a silver front tooth and it made him look tough. She firmly told herself she was pleased that he was going to be her boyfriend now. Tremaine didn't spend long before he did up his pants and whispered, "I'll be right back." He jumped off the fort from the top and she could hear the excited voices of the other boys as Tremaine joined them.

She waited and imagined that the other boys must think she was daring for what she did with Tremaine. They'd know Tremaine was now her boyfriend.

She heard him coming back up the hanging bridge and smiled expectantly. Instead of Tremaine, though, it was Gilles, the small French boy, who entered the fort. He came over and sat beside her on the wooden floor of the fort, slinging his arm around her neck. She let him do this, and soon he had his tongue deep in her mouth, his lips pressed so hard on hers that tears sprang to her eyes. This kissing wasn't nice, she thought to herself. She wondered about Tremaine and then thought that this must be what he wanted her to do. She was determined to think of Tremaine as her boyfriend, and if he had sent Gilles up to the fort to do this, then she would go along with it. Maybe it was a test, she thought. She had heard stories about other girls, popular girls, doing things like this. This might be what it would take to get to be popular, she thought. So she let Gilles grind away on top of her while she daydreamed about how her newly enhanced status at school would feel the next day.

After Gilles, Lucy waited again for Tremaine. Instead, the black-haired boy came up to the fort. She didn't want to kiss him, so she asked him his name.

"Greg," he said, and she knew he was lying. She didn't know why, but she knew it was something boys did.

He tried to kiss her again, and so she said, "Can I try on your glasses?"

He looked at her strangely, like he didn't trust her. Lucy didn't like that look. But then he took off his glasses and put them on her face, jabbing her ears with the arms. She couldn't see through them and they made her dizzy. She reached up to take them off but he grabbed her hand and held it, took them off her with his other hand.

"My mom will kill me if they get broke," he said, and giggled his high-pitched laugh.

Lucy put her hand on the fly of his jeans, but he didn't want her to do that either. Instead, he took his own thing out of his pants and then rolled on top of her and jabbed it between her legs. Lucy looked at the sky, clouding over, and waited for him to finish. She quelled a feeling of disappointment by thinking about how she would hug Tremaine when this was over.

After "Greg," she waited for Tremaine to come back to the fort. It took a while before she realized that the boys had left the playground. It was getting dark. Lucy left the fort and walked home with the scent of the boys on her fingers and her clothes.

Seven months later, Lucy arrived at school after the bell but before the teacher. All the kids in the class were in their seats, talking loudly. Randy Rhode, who sat at the back, saw Lucy come in and he said, at full volume, "Look, I think Lucy's pregnant." This caused the other kids to laugh because Lucy's belly was so big she could hardly manoeuvre into her desk anymore – of course she was pregnant. Lucy went to her seat, which was also at the back. "Everyone says it's your brother did that to you," Randy said. "Is it true?"

Lucy turned and looked into Randy's face for a long time. Finally, he looked away. But Lucy wasn't trying to shame Randy into looking away. She was trying to imagine what his words meant. *Is that what people thought all along?* she wondered. *Do people really think that?* Randy was talking about Billy, her foster parents' "real" kid. Billy didn't go to Lucy's school. He went on the bus to some special school for smart kids. There was a word for those kids, but Lucy could never remember it – she just knew it wasn't the same word as they used in Lucy's school – "special ed." Billy's word was a better word than that.

Finally, she crossed her arms and put her head down on her desk and mumbled, "He ain't my brother," which was just stupid, she realized too late, because it was like she was saying it was true that Billy got her pregnant. If they didn't say it before, they said it then, that Lucy was pregnant by her brother.

"She lets her *brother* fuck her." After that, things only got worse. Eventually, Lucy was expelled for fighting even though it wasn't on school grounds. Lucy told herself it was okay, she was used to people making excuses to get rid of her, and so, *Fuck them,* she thought.

Lucy Wingfeather had her baby. Less than a day old, he lay in his Plexiglas bassinet beside Lucy's bed in the hospital. A dimpled beige curtain provided the only privacy in the hot room with eight full beds. A woman who wore her paper hat like a disposable lid couldn't bring the breakfast tray fast enough, as far as Lucy was concerned. Lucy scooped dry corn flakes to her lips at first with the spoon but then with her fingers. She chewed the flakes into clods and swallowed them in chunks. She guzzled the milk from the carton, a sweet white line running to her chin. She tore the two paper sugar packs open and poured them, one at a time, in small white cascades onto her tongue. She looked at the Plexiglas cot and thought, *He sleeps a lot.*

That afternoon, a nurse snuck in and caught Lucy lying back on her pillow with her eyes closed. The nurse plucked up Lucy Wingfeather's baby just like that from his plastic space-alien bed. And Lucy, who wasn't really asleep anyway, and who had never had anything of her own before in her life, sat up straight away and followed the nurse. "Where are you taking him?" she asked.

The nurse turned and blinked through thick lenses, unsmiling. "He needs a bath."

"Not yet," Lucy pleaded.

The nurse blinked again and said, "But you were asleep," as if this was some kind of logic.

"No." Lucy shook her head like a child. Lucy hadn't been asleep. "Uh-uh." Lucy stood with her arms out, waiting for her baby to be returned.

The slight tightening of the nurse's lips told Lucy the power game was on. The nurse turned and walked away, the baby tucked firmly in the crook of one arm. "This baby needs a bath."

Lucy, with leaky breasts and torn perineum, shuffled after

the nurse. Lucy watched the nurse clip along the silent corridor, getting farther and farther ahead.

Finally, Lucy caught up to them in a small room, where she looked on helplessly as the nurse stripped the baby. With a dish of soapy water on hand, the nurse rubbed each fold of his newly hatched skin with a soapy cloth. The creases at the backs of his knees, his underarms, his groin. Nowhere was safe. The nurse worked silently and, it seemed to Lucy, angrily. The baby's head and fine black hair were sudsed and scrubbed before she held him like a football under one arm and rinsed his head under the tap over a large industrial sink, where the falling water made a hollow metal echo. His face was scarlet from the screaming.

The nurse squeezed cream on his bum, diapered him, wrapped him like a tight twist of grease bannock and handed over a small alien that smelled like antiseptic and soap.

Back in her room, wide awake, a knot in her throat, Lucy Wingfeather examined her baby. She sniffed his head, his ears, the folds in his neck. All of it was gone: the smell of her body, the hot, peppery scent of birth, the metallic ping of blood. None of it lingered.

Finally, she found a small streak of dried blood behind one ear. But it wasn't enough. She put the baby in his bucket and let him cry.

Lucy Wingfeather was sent home.

The social worker, whose name was Joni, had helped her find an apartment. It was one of the few close to the rent allowance rate. She only had to take a bit from her food money to make up the difference. Lucy found little brown bugs in the cupboards. The bugs seemed to like the dry cheese in the noodles and found ways to burrow into the packages. Lucy couldn't really blame them.

Joni came to do a home visit and asked the same question she'd asked before. "Who is the baby's father?"

Lucy knew what the social worker wanted. She wanted the welfare to pay less for the baby because Lucy was supposed to file for child support from the father. Lucy did what she normally did with this social worker – she started to cry. It usually worked. The social worker seemed to think that the memory of the baby's father was so painful that the mere mention of it made her cry.

"Oh, Lucy," Joni said and slid over on the couch to put a consoling arm around Lucy's shoulders. Joni fished a tissue out of her purse and handed it over. "Lucy," she said in a sympathetic voice, "honey, you've got to put your burden down. Aren't you tired of carrying it all by yourself yet?"

When it became apparent that Lucy didn't have an answer about the baby's father, Joni prepared to leave.

"You're leaking," Joni said. Lucy looked down to see her thin white t-shirt soaked with warm milk. Lucy didn't like the way the nurse had insisted on binding her chest in the hospital when she chose not to breastfeed, so she'd taken the binding off almost immediately after coming home. As a result, she spent most of the day soaked with her own milk.

"That's okay," Lucy said, "it makes me smell sweet."

Joni was gone and the baby was crying again. To Lucy, it seemed a lonely sound in the empty apartment. Lucy turned the volume on the television louder and tried to think what to do. The basement came to mind, but Lucy was in an apartment and there was no basement. Well, there was, she thought, but it had other apartments in it and a laundry room with coin-operated machines that never worked.

She had learnt a brandy trick from a foster mom who took in all the babies – brandy in the baby's milk made it sleep. She had no brandy or anything like it – she wasn't old enough to buy alcohol, even if she had the money. Besides, she was out of baby milk anyway.

Instead, she left the baby lying on the couch and took his soother to the kitchen where she dipped its wet end into the sugar bag. The white granules coated it like a thin crust of jewels. Returning to the living room, she plopped on the couch beside the baby and put the soother to his lips. Instantly his cries stopped. His eyes went wide and he sucked hungrily at the rubber end. Lucy ran a finger over his head, feeling the dark hair, as soft as fur. He watched her with intensity. Pop. The soother burst from his lips as if he'd purposely pushed it out. They both waited, each scrutinizing the other for a dumb moment, and then the baby twisted up his face and released a loud wail. Lucy went to the kitchen to retrieve the sugar bag, brought it back to the couch. She dipped the wet end in again and watched as the baby greedily took it. Over and over again, Lucy and the baby repeated the ritual until finally his eyes glazed over and he fell asleep.

Lucy snapped off the TV. In the silence, the image of one rural foster home came to mind – a farm, and the dry, lazy heat she associated with her summer there. Lucy lay down beside her baby and fell asleep. She dreamed of fresh butter, sliding down her throat. She woke to the afternoon sunshine filtering through the thin curtains.

The baby's small black-capped head squirmed beside her, but he wasn't crying. He turned his head and smacked his lips, rooting. His fist found its way to his mouth for a moment before jerking out of reach again. Then Lucy Wingfeather's baby found Lucy's breast with his tiny bow mouth and he sucked on the damp fabric of her t-shirt. Lucy lifted her shirt and the baby latched on. Both their eyes widened with surprise. Lucy felt the baby's sharp tug on her breast. He stared into her eyes like a hypnotist, refusing to release her. She watched him, eyes dark and serious as he rhythmically suckled, taking what he needed. Gradually, he dared to close his eyes. She longed to tell someone, but there was no one to tell.

Afterward, Lucy held the baby to her face, where she inhaled the scent of her own milky whisper on his breath.

fine stuff

That's a beauty of a tent you got there. Looks like it's brand new. Need any help?" The father of the red-haired kids from the next site was hunched down at Bob's side, admiring the tent and smiling good-naturedly. Looking at the man, Bob could see where the children had gotten their doughy looks. Bob told himself this soft look likely belied the fact that the man was as strong as an ox. At least, thought Bob, he was the size of one.

Before Bob could answer, the neighbour had picked up one of the poles and started inserting it into the tent.

"Um, I'm not really sure that goes..." Bob trailed off as the pole slid perfectly into place and the neighbour picked up the next one.

"Oh yeah, this is a real beauty. Here, hold this," he said, handing Bob the end of an inserted pole and moving around the tent with the last one. "Me and my wife camped for the last fifteen years with the same tent. That's ours over there," he said, pointing with his chin. "We got a new one for the kids but it's nothing special. Maybe it's time to get something good. I wouldn't mind one of these babies." With this, the neighbour gave a little grunt and the pole Bob was holding snapped out of his hand and into its proper position on the ground. "There," the neighbour said, slapping his hands together, removing imaginary dust. "Now you just have to stake it."

Bob's blank stare prompted the neighbour to pick up the bag of stakes and the shiny new hatchet and begin hammering.

"I have a mallet for that," Bob protested weakly, seeing that the neighbour was nearly finished already.

"Oh, I'll bet you do. You've got some real fine stuff here. All new. Let me guess, first time camping?" The man straightened up and looked at Bob inquisitively.

Indeed, Bob thought wryly, his mind wandering to his job, where, thankfully, he didn't need to know anything about camping gear. The near-empty campsite looked bleakly back at him.

"You got me," Bob said to the man, smiling. He stopped himself from adding, *I'm here to relax. Doctor's orders.* Instead he said, "My wife's joining me tomorrow." Roxanne. This had been all her idea. She would deny it, but he understood it was her attempt to bring him out of the funk he'd been in since his heart attack three months ago. Before he left, she'd forced him to surrender his Blackberry, iPad and laptop. He'd had some fleeting thoughts of being able to tap into an unsecured wireless network at the town-site, but Roxanne would hear none of it.

"Hey, thanks a lot for your help," Bob said, extending his hand. "I'm Bob, by the way."

"Laverne," the neighbour said, offering a chunky, freckled hand. "Good to meet you."

A gust of wind blew through the coin-like leaves of the tall, slender birch trees that surrounded the campsite. Bob looked up to see the thin trees swaying, their leaves flipping in the wind.

Laverne followed Bob's cue.

"I think we're in for some rain pretty quick here," he said. "I was going to get some wood under a tarp. C'mon, I'll show you where the woodpile is."

They had just gotten their wood under the tarps when Bob was motivated by a rare spontaneity. He pulled a beer from his cooler without thinking and offered it to Laverne. "Join me?" he asked.

He was surprised how easy it was to sit in the dull light of the campsite in his new folding chair with this virtual stranger, and how much he enjoyed the cold beers and small talk. Completely out of his element, Bob felt decidedly relaxed already. As the empties piled beside their chairs, Bob and Laverne talked about cars, soccer, football and music. Mostly music.

"I don't care what you say, Dylan was a great influence," Laverne insisted. "Just look at Neil Young," he exclaimed, as if this solidified his argument.

"Man, what about the English bands like the Clash and the Sex Pistols?" countered Bob.

"Don't you dare start talking to me about Duran Duran or I'll lose all respect for you," Laverne warned.

"I'm talking about punk. It had its moments. It defined things. Not that I ever went in for that stuff. I'm just against thinking it's all about the Americans." He paused. *"I'm afraid of Americans!"* he sang loudly. "Bowie. Now there's an influence."

"Fucking rights," Laverne agreed, leaning back in his folding chair.

They enjoyed a moment of contemplative silence before Bob said, "Okay, best concert, what's yours?"

"Live?" asked Laverne.

"What other kind of concert have you gone to? Dead?" Bob teased.

"The Guess Who. Toronto. When I was seventeen. We drove down from the Peg. There were so many of us in one car the girls had to sit on our laps." Laverne laughed. "That music's classic."

"Mine's Bowie," offered Bob. "Played in Winnipeg in about '83. I've never seen anything like it."

"Was that when he was dressing like a chick and stuff?" asked Laverne.

"The androgynous phase," said Bob. "No, he was long past that."

"I don't know what you call it, but it was weird," said Laverne. "But that would have been a great concert."

They sat nodding their heads and drinking their beers, each lost in his thoughts. Every so often, one of Laverne's kids came running down the gravel road and into Bob's campsite to tell on a brother or ask for money to go to the store. Laverne's pat answer was "Go see your mother," and the kids would run off again. Laverne showed no signs of leaving and Bob had no desire to get rid of him. Bob had a nice buzz going from the beer and was enjoying his freedom. The threat of rain had passed and every now and then a sunny patch would open up in the sky and warmth would land on his back like a gift.

The cooler nearly empty, Laverne leaned in close to Bob, elbows on his knees, conspiratorial. "So you're here to relax. Is that it? You're in a stressful job and you never get away and you need a vacation. So you come camping, with the bugs and the dirt, and the shared toilets and icy showers? I'm sure you won't mind my saying so, but you just don't seem like the camping kind." He paused, then added, "What gives?" Laverne didn't say any of this meanly and Bob was unfazed.

"Okay, I'll tell you the truth." Bob paused as though thinking of how to answer. Instead, he said, "But first, I have to take a leak." He stood, lost his balance, and stumbled backwards.

"Whoa, man," said Laverne. "Maybe we should go for a beer run, too. There's a liquor store at the town-site. All the conveniences of home, hey? I'd better drive though – you're in no shape."

Once he'd manoeuvred the car out of the campground, Laverne turned to Bob and asked again, "Tell me, then. Why camping? Why not some fancy vacation in a luxury hotel?"

"Simple," said Bob, even though it really wasn't simple at all. How to sum up the stress of the last months, the doctors, the critical care unit, his rampant emotions since the heart attack, crying at the drop of a hat, grappling with his own mortality? "My wife talked me into it. She says we leave the cell phones at home, no computers or email, no checking messages, no contact. Those are her rules. We make ourselves completely unavailable, and maybe I'll unwind and live longer. That's it." Bob paused. Something about Laverne and the beers and the setting had made Bob unusually candid. Bob could feel his eyes welling up.

They drove in silence for a few minutes.

"Are you serious about relaxing?" Laverne reached across Bob's knees and pulled a small plastic bag from the glove box. He tossed it onto Bob's lap. "Spark 'er up," Laverne said, handing Bob a Bic lighter.

Bob held the bag to his nose and caught a whiff of the pungent odour. He hadn't smoked pot since, well, since a long time, that's when, Bob thought to himself. He vaguely recalled that it had made him feel paranoid in his high school days but that was such a long time ago. He wasn't the same self-conscious kid trying to fit in that he had been then. Maybe this was the thing, he thought, the thing that would help him relax. And wasn't that what he was here for? The words *medical marijuana* popped into Bob's head and that clinched it for him.

He put the joint in his mouth and lit it like a cigarette. At once, Bob began to cough, his virgin lungs in full revolt. Laverne slapped him on the back and waited for the spasm to pass. Bob looked at Laverne through watery eyes.

"This isn't going well."

Laverne gave him some pointers and Bob nodded, putting the joint to his lips again. This time, on Laverne's advice, he managed to suppress his cough until after he had exhaled. Laverne made a motion for the joint and they drove the next few kilometres passing it back and forth. Bob put the soggy-ended joint to his lips and wondered languidly if he could get an STD this way, not really caring much about the answer. He thought about talking to Laverne, but opening his mouth and forming words was too much effort. Instead, he sat back in his seat and let the pot do its work. Laverne searched the floor of the car, one hand on the wheel, and finally settled for *The Who* to put in the CD player. After that, they drove for what seemed like a long time, touring the marina and blasting the music before heading to the town-site.

When Laverne parked in front of the liquor store, he quickly hopped out of the car and made for the steps. Attempting to follow suit, Bob felt the blood rush to his head as he stood. He put a hand on the car to steady himself. By this time, Laverne had already passed through the doors, unaware or unconcerned that Bob was left behind.

Watching Laverne's back, Bob was struck by an amusing thought. He had the sudden, unbidden urge to play a joke on Laverne. He imagined himself sneaking up behind Laverne and startling him – perhaps poking him in the ribs or maybe slapping his hands over Laverne's eyes and saying, *Guess who?* The element of surprise was the key to what made this joke funny, in Bob's mind. In fact, the longer Bob considered the idea, the more irresistible it became. Bob could barely suppress his laughter as he envisioned playing out this joke.

With the image of playing the trick on Laverne as his only guide, Bob ran from the car and up the steps of the liquor store two at a time. He quickly took in the store layout and saw Laverne peering into a cooler at the back of the store. Bob had his mark.

He darted around the end of the first aisle, marked RUM, keeping a wary eye on Laverne. Then he ran, hunkered down, along the end of the aisles toward the back of the store, closing the distance between himself and Laverne. Bob poked his head over the top of the VODKA aisle to get his bearings. He let an accidental giggle escape from his lips and slapped his hand over his mouth more forcefully than he had intended. This only made him laugh harder and he had to fight for self-control.

He was close enough to make a run for Laverne across the open space that separated them. At once, Bob jumped up, a mad grin on his face, a wheeze-like laugh escaping through his teeth. He ran on his tiptoes across the floor, intending to come up on Laverne and take him by surprise, though he still hadn't decided whether to poke him playfully in the ribs or try and cover his eyes with his hands and say, *Guess who?* Small noises escaped through his teeth as Bob fought to suppress his laughter.

He got within three feet of Laverne when Laverne sensed the attack, heard the strange noises and saw a fleeting reflected image in the cooler. On reflex, Laverne pivoted on his left foot, turned his body a full 180 degrees and followed through with a crushing right to the middle of his attacker's face.

Bob flew, landing with a crash on a display of sparkling wine. Bottles smashed and sticky pink wine poured out around him.

Blood spurted from Bob's face like a geyser. In those first seconds, it might have seemed to any onlooker that Bob was unconscious, maybe even dead. But, in fact, as Bob had landed, or perhaps even as he had been flying through the air, he was taking mental stock of his injuries. The whole incident, over in a matter of seconds, seemed to occur in slow motion for Bob.

He knew that, besides his hemorrhaging nose, which was beginning to throb and make his eyes water, he was intact. More pressing than his injuries was his mental image of himself, tip-toe-running across the store, ready to slap his hands over Laverne's eyes in a grown-man's game of "guess who." The image made Bob start to shake with silent laughter. His body quivered with the effort.

"Jesus Christ, are you okay? What the hell are you doing, sneaking up on a guy like that —" Laverne cut his sentence short when he saw Bob shaking. He had been in enough fights to associate the shaking with convulsions. Thinking that Bob was going into dangerous seizures, Laverne threw himself down on his knees beside Bob, grasping his head in his thick hands. He looked frantically around at the store employees, who had gathered at the sound of the smashing bottles. "What're you supposed to do?" he yelled, frantic. Blood pooled on Bob's lips and spattered Laverne's hands. Bob sputtered in Laverne's grip, laughing uncontrollably and unable to catch his breath and speak.

"His tongue!" one of them yelled. "Grab his tongue so he doesn't swallow it!" Laverne pinned Bob's forehead to the floor with one hand and began trying to pry his mouth open with the other. Bob thrashed in Laverne's grasp, whipping his head from side to side in an attempt to keep Laverne's fingers out of his mouth. Bob put up so much resistance that Laverne was forced to straddle Bob's chest and clamp his head between his knees to try to keep him still. Just as Laverne was about to succeed in prying his jaws apart, Bob let out a huge gasp in an attempt to try to control his laughter. Laverne stopped, looking intently at Bob's wild eyes and shaking head. He loosened his grip.

"Stop," Bob gasped through hysterics. "Stop."

Realization crept up on Laverne and he looked at the store employees crowded around. Then he let out a snicker, sending Bob into renewed hysteria. He let go of Bob's head and watched as Bob rolled around in the mess, unable to breathe. The two of them were like school kids caught up in the giggles, each unsuccessfully suppressing a snort that would set them both off again.

Laverne helped Bob to his feet, still trying to get control of himself. One of the store employees handed Bob a fistful of paper towels for his still gushing nose.

"You guys are together?" an older man asked. Likely the manager thought Bob. The man's lips were tight; he was clearly unimpressed.

Laverne nodded.

"You should probably get him checked out at the medical place. It's over in administration," the manager said, eyeing all the blood and clearly thinking *lawsuit*.

Bob, holding the crimson paper towels to his nose, kept erupting with snorts and giggles.

The manager was even less impressed. "Maybe just leave your names with me, and how to get ahold of you, and we'll contact you about any damages. Just make sure he's okay."

Laverne took the pen and paper from the manager and scribbled something.

The manager retrieved the pen from Laverne, holding it as though contaminated. He looked at what Laverne had written and, apparently satisfied, turned to escort Bob and Laverne from the store, but not before Laverne picked up a case and tucked some bills into the manager's hand. The manager looked at his hand as though it held a steamy turd, but didn't refuse.

Peering sideways at the manager, recognition lit on Bob. He saw how familiar the contemptuous glare and tight white lips of the manager were – familiar because they could be his own, had been his own. The manager's demeanour was one Bob had replicated many times in his own job and life. The realization caused Bob's chest to contract. Despite the laughter playing on his lips, Bob felt slightly chastised. Then the moment passed as quickly as it had come.

In the car, Laverne and Bob took one look at each other and started to laugh again. "Jesus man, you turned out to be one crazy son of a bitch," said Laverne, shaking his head in admiration.

Bob smiled through his bloody, throbbing face and felt a sense of something like inner peace cascade over him.

"Okay, let's skip the medical so they don't get our names," said Laverne, already planning ahead. "I think you're okay but we'll clean you up before we go back. My wife'll freak if we turn up like this."

"I thought you gave the manager our names?" asked Bob.

"Yeah, right," Laverne snorted. "You're Ben and I'm Mike. Mr. Dover, it's nice to meet you. It's Mike...Mike Oxbigg." Laverne stuck out his beefy hand for Bob to shake for the second time that day. Bob laughed at the joke and Laverne said, "I thought he might catch on, but he was a little rattled. Don't worry. They just write off the broken shit as damaged stock. I used to work in a bar – happens all the time."

Laverne pulled in near the bathrooms and they went in to clean up. Bob was shocked by his appearance, seeing another man in the mirror. He was wet and covered in blood from his nose to his trousers. Fortunately, the bleeding had subsided. Laverne, who seemed to be something of an expert in broken noses, concluded that it wasn't broken and once Bob was cleaned up he looked a lot better, even though that wasn't saying much. His nose was purple and blue, his nostrils were caked with blood and his eyes were turning black underneath. Bob was talking as though he had a bad cold and he could feel his nose getting tighter and tighter the more it swelled.

"Okay, here's what we'll do," said Laverne. "I'll drop you at your site and then you can go and change. I'll check in with the wife and make up some kind of story. Then I'll come over and we can have another beer and maybe put some ice on your face to stop the swelling. Sound okay to you?"

Bob was enjoying his newfound camaraderie and every time his old self interjected with doubtful sentiments, Bob would remind himself that he was trying a new approach now. When was the last time he had laughed like this? In spite of, no, *because of,* the bloody swollen nose. What would he tell Roxanne? he wondered fleetingly. "Let's go," he said to Laverne as he took one last look in the mirror at his disfigured face. He smiled a tight smile at himself. He was feeling a bit rugged now after all.

Back at the campsite, Bob retrieved his duffel bag from the trunk and hauled it into his tent. Sitting cross-legged on the floor, he opened it, expecting to see his new clothes from the outdoor store. Instead, he found himself gazing upon an assortment of filmy negligees, satin camisoles, see-through panties, sexy bras, fur-and-feather adorned bed jackets, night-time eye masks and a number of other items intended for Roxanne's lingerie party. He groaned, realizing he had picked up Roxanne's work bag and left his bag behind. All the bags they owned looked the same because Roxanne had won the entire set one piece at a time for having high sales. In fact, she had won so many pieces that they had double and triple of many of the bags. They must have each used the same bag to pack their things in.

He was sitting in his only set of clothes, wet with blood and covered in sugary wine. He stripped down, shivering; the wet had given him a chill. Roxanne would be here in the morning with his bag. She'd be pissed off when she found out she took his clothes to the lingerie party. He cringed at the thought but could do nothing about it now. He carefully selected the most conservative items from the bag. He was momentarily thankful that Vanity Secret made a few more practical items for their shoppers to choose from. He struggled into a pair of hot pink satin lounge pants that were several sizes too small for him – tight enough to show quite clearly the outline of his genitals. He topped it off with a blue stretchy cotton tank top with spaghetti straps. Finally, he tried to cover it all up with a silky white housecoat with faux fur at the wrists and neck. The housecoat came down to his knees and had large, open wrists. Once dressed, Bob sat down in the tent to wait for Laverne, not knowing what else to do.

Tenderly fingering his swollen nose, mostly out of boredom, somewhat out of fascination (for Bob had never had a "fighting" injury in his life), he was suddenly hungry. Of course he'd heard of the munchies before, but this was ridiculous. He wasn't just hungry, he was ravenous. He began to salivate over the thought of the snacks he'd seen Roxanne pack into the food box. Unfortunately, the food box was in his trunk. He considered for a moment the chances of making a dash for the car without being seen. The camping loop was packed for the weekend, every site taken. Small children threw baseballs in the roadway and tore around the loop on bicycles. But he couldn't hear much activity at the moment, which meant that perhaps it was suppertime. Bob decided to take his chances.

Unzipping the tent, he stuck his head out to see what was happening. No one was walking past his site. No children were playing catch on the road. Bob knew he had only a moment to make a dash for the food. He hastily unzipped the flap and lurched over the lip of the tent, only to be yanked back by a faux-fur sleeve caught in the zipper. Bob looked around furtively but could still see no one in the loop. He worked the zipper and sleeve frantically and finally decided to slip out of the housecoat and leave it behind. He made a dash for the car, only to realize the keys were in his soggy jeans inside the tent. As he ducked back inside the tent to retrieve the keys, Bob felt the hot pink pants, made of shiny satin with no give, split neatly along the seam at the back. He reached around and felt a gaping hole. Undaunted, key in hand, Bob made it to the trunk and the waiting Doritos. He grabbed the chips and a box of granola bars before changing his mind and shoving it all back in the box. He grasped the entire box and hauled it out of the trunk. Balancing the box on his forearm, he reached with his free hand to slam the trunk and the box slipped off his arm and spilled sideways into the dirt. Bob crouched on his knees and chucked the spilled contents back into the box.

Reaching for a can of corn that had rolled underneath the car, he heard the familiar crunch of car tires on the road of the loop. He peered out from behind his car bumper to see the plastic dome lights of a conservation officer's car. Bob remained behind the car, determined to wait for them to pass. To his horror, the car stopped in front of his campsite. Two uniformed conservation officers emerged from the car and a couple of curious campers craned their necks to catch a glimpse. Bob realized his chances for escape were slim. In a crouched position, he began to trot like a soldier under fire toward his tent.

"Excuse me, sir!" one of the officers barked, bringing Bob up short. Bob wheeled around, his hand clutching the back of his pants while he slowly continued backing toward his tent.

"Yes," he squeaked, his vocal cords pinched with effort. Bob was suddenly paranoid about the pot he and Laverne had smoked, sure the officers could smell it.

"Could we have a word with you?" The officer put his hand out in front of him as though approaching a frightened animal. His other hand rested lightly on the butt of his holstered gun.

Bob's mind did a double take – since when did conservation officers carry guns? he wondered. The second officer had quietly made his way around the back of the tent, and Bob imagined he could feel the man breathing down his neck. Bob clutched the ripped edges of his pants tighter, trying to turn his back away from the officer to hide his naked butt.

"Are you all right?" The officer motioned to Bob's beaten face. "Looks like you had a bit of an accident there? Do you want to tell me who did that to you?" While the first officer talked gently to him, Bob was acutely aware of the second officer peering in the tent, catching a whiff, Bob was sure, of the wine and taking stock of the floor littered with women's lingerie.

Bob saw knowing glances pass between the two officers.

"Laverne," Bob croaked. What the hell was wrong with his voice? He thought of the marijuana smoke tearing at his throat. "It was an accident..."

Bob was cut short by his friend's voice as Laverne rounded the edge of the campsite, ice pack in hand, case of beer swinging easily in his other meaty fist. "Okay, I got the ice! Let's get this party started!" Laverne stopped short upon seeing the officers and Bob. "Whoa, what the hell?" Laverne said, waiving his hands at Bob's clothes.

"Thang God," Bob chirped. "Laverne, tell them id was an accident."

"*This* is Laverne?" The second officer's voice took on a hard edge. Laverne held up his hand with the ice pack.

"Hey man, I didn't do anything. Bob, what did you tell them?" Laverne looked hurt, as though Bob had betrayed him.

Bob started to protest when the first officer interrupted. "It's okay now, Bob. Everything's going to be fine." Bob could see the second officer had retreated to the car and was using the radio. He clearly heard the words "domestic situation." The first officer continued to speak in soothing tones that suggested Bob might be a hysterical victim who needed calming down.

"Doe," Bob shook his head. "Doe fugging way." Bob shook his head even more emphatically. "You guys hab got this all ronck. This is ab-h-soludely not..." Bob's voice cracked, and he imagined it would sound, to the officer and anyone else within earshot, as if it was from emotion.

The second officer had left the car and the radio and was approaching Laverne, hand on gun, serious expression on his face. "Sir!" he barked out, as though it were an order rather than a salutation. "I'm afraid I'm going to have to ask you to come with me. Have a seat in the car until we can get this all sorted out."

Another car came crunching down the loop and Bob felt his swollen face, already engorged with blood, become a deep shade of purple as his blood pressure spiked and his heart made a rattly *farump* in his chest. "Rogs-anne!" he exclaimed when he saw the nose of the mauve Camry sniffing its way down the loop toward them. The officers, Laverne, and the spectators from the loop, who seemed to have gathered in hordes to watch his humiliation, all turned with curiosity to see who Roxanne was and how she would add to the situation at hand.

The Camry came to a sudden stop and Roxanne, who was ordinarily high strung, looked practically crazed as she ran to Bob's car.

"What's going on here?" Roxanne demanded and then caught sight of Bob. "Bob, is that you?"

"Ma'am," the officer tried to interject.

"What the hell is going on with your face?" Roxanne was staring at Bob in disbelief.

The officer tried again. "Ma'am?"

But Roxanne was having none of it. "Are those my *clothes* you're wearing?" She was practically shrieking now.

"Ma'am!" The officer's tone was insistent.

This time, Roxanne turned to him and lowered her voice. "Yes?" she asked in an over-controlled way that signalled to Bob she was barely keeping her cool.

For a moment Bob felt as though his head separated from his body and twirled in the air as he fell dizzily to the ground. For the second time that day Bob looked up through the slender trees at the dappled sky above him, hints of sunshine and vertigo balanced precariously on leaves that looked like fluttering discs.

For a moment, he thought he knew exactly what it was all about.

delicate on her tongue

When my mother's marriage disintegrated, she stepped over that pile of rubble no bigger than a doorstep and made moving on look simple. The morning she left, she did not have the nerve to say goodbye. Instead, she slipped away at five a.m. and disappeared in a cloud of exhaust from an idling taxi at the front of the house. Her "things" would follow her, but not before sitting like unwelcome guests in the front hallway for days that seemed like weeks. And when they were finally picked up, the empty spaces they created echoed through the house.

The night before she left, however, she did visit each of us, one by one. I can only imagine what her visits to my brothers must have been like. All three of the boys in one room like that – the room they shared for their whole growing-up lives. What intimate affection could she have shown those boys each, individually? And yet I have no doubt that she did. She was accomplished that way.

When she came to my room, which I was obliged to share with no one, being the only girl and getting to "that age," whatever that meant, she sat with a sigh on the edge of my bed. My mother wasn't one for tears, and so there were none. I refused to disappoint her by crying. Instead, I mimicked her composure. She held my hand for several moments and looked all around my room before finally meeting my eyes with her own dry and unremorseful ones. Then she put her fine and perfect hand to my cheek and stroked it once, slowly, and did the one thing that was guaranteed to lodge itself within the minute crevasses of my heart forever. She said my name, *Moss*, with such a tender affection that her voice has echoed inside me for all these years. *Moss*. And there it hung between us, my name like a pungent odour, suspended, until it finally fell to earth when she let go of my hand and rose to leave my room. I suspected she had more to say, but when she stood, the moment was shattered and there was nothing else.

And now, all these years later, she has returned.

When my mother and father announced their divorce, I wasn't angry or sad, as I believe the boys were, but secretly elated. No one in my class at school had parents who were divorced except for my best friend Holly, who had only just recently made her dramatic announcement, attempting to look stricken but unable to keep the shadow of a smile from creeping onto her lips. Our impression of children of divorce was that they were exotic and worldly. Children of divorced parents stood to be spoiled. Parental guilt and neglect translated into money and presents. Trips to a new household, Disneyland, who knew how far it could go? A whole new world opened up with divorce, and with it, the promise of a whole new self. With divorce, it was entirely possible to imagine yourself living a parallel, but *different* (and this was the key), life. But we knew we were supposed to be upset, so we tried.

Of course, my family was different. In 1969, how many *mothers* up and left their families – and to go to such a far away, mysterious and yet mundane-sounding place as *Philadelphia?* Who even knew where that was, except to say in America?

And being the children of divorce, although not as glamorous as we once imagined, did turn out to have its rewards. At the end of each summer, we would return to our ordinary working-class neighbourhood from summer holidays, brown and happy with stories of a splendid house and a notorious, rakish new stepfather – one so different from our own father that it was difficult to imagine the two of them inhabited the same world – were even the same species.

"Miss Moss," my new stepfather called me affectionately and I blushed every single time he spoke to me. Parties at their house were the norm; no one seemed to work, or get cross or be busy.

Those summers seemed endless and full of promise.

Those were stories for my friends, though, not for my father. My older brothers likely didn't see things the same way. I recall my genuine surprise as they, one by one, stopped going on the summer visits, opting instead to stay at home and keep my father company – to build their transistor radios and spend the summer reading and eating small sour apples from the tree in our back yard. Those apples were a favourite of my father's and he never missed commenting with wonder each summer when the first apple turned from green to red on the branch. He made it special to be the one offered that first apple of the season. After that, they were more abundant than we could eat, and the fruit would eventually drop and be raked up with the fall leaves into piles to be burnt in the back garden. It had never occurred to me that my father might be lonely while we were away, or that he missed us at all. I never thought to wonder what he did all summer. I assumed he worked, but I can't say for certain if he did.

Eventually, we all married and started families, with the exception of my oldest brother, who, looking back, had been the one most genuinely devastated by the divorce. He remains to this day a confirmed bachelor – something that the rest of us are, by turns, both sad and envious about. My visits to Philadelphia ceased for a time when my children were small and I was busier than I could have imagined; when the visits resumed, I was surprised to find the scale of everything diminished. Perhaps in my brother's mind, the scale of it all had always been clear.

I have not been to visit my mother since my father died a little over ten years ago, when she didn't have the decency to get on an airplane and come to the funeral. In fact, in retrospect, I realized that she'd never had the consideration to inquire about my father over all those summers we visited as children. Yet when we returned home my father would always ask, *How's your mother?* His interest was genuine, his heart on his sleeve. Somewhere in these last ten years, I found I stopped caring about what she thought of me, about whether or not I was worthy of her approval. I stopped calling to tell her in an affected, offhand manner about the degree I had earned or the award I had received. I can't pinpoint when exactly that happened but I can recall the relief of waking up one day to realize it was gone. It was like a miraculous recovery from a chronic illness that one doesn't notice until the last phlegmy cough completely clears the lungs.

And now my mother has returned.

I can't help but think it merciful that my father is dead, for my mother has changed so much. Frail hardly begins to describe her. And if she understands what has happened to her, the ways she's been betrayed, she doesn't let on. She maintains her digni- fied, upright posture despite her condition and circumstance.

Do I find it ironic that the life she left us for has abandoned her, pushed her aside, stepped over *her* like a small, crumbled pile of dust? Perhaps, but I haven't any cruel intentions. I like to imagine myself to be resigned and indifferent, a state that has taken a great deal of effort and time to achieve. And yet I have found in the days that she has been here, after being dropped off by taxi at my front door while I watched from a window – an uncanny reminder of the day she left – I have found myself supple, bendable, pliable to her touch. Though not a physical touch, I feel it all the same. But I have come to understand this one thing about my mother – that one word she spoke between us on the eve before she left, *Moss,* my name, delicate on her tongue, that word and the way it left her lips was no accident. She meant for it to stick.

I reach for the tea from the top cupboard and flick the switch of the kettle, my watery actions reflected in the dim evening twi- light of the kitchen window. My mother waits in the back yard, the *garden,* she calls it, even though it's just grass. She's acquired certain affectations from her life in high society. What is there to do but make the tea and carry on? It's what we've always done.

But if I were to tell the truth, I might say that I'm waiting to see if perhaps she came back to tell me what she meant to say next, that last night in our house, after she said my name.

ayekis

as we walk up the road, scanning the ditches for treasures, I tell Kyle, "We saw a whole herd of elk here last year. They were on the sides of the road and just in the trees there." I point, but he's not looking.

"So?"

"So you have to be pretty careful around them. If you make eye contact, they could charge you. Just telling you, in case we see any."

"Yeah, well, I know a guy who killed a moose with a slingshot before," he says. I consider this for a few moments.

"That's impossible," I tell him. "Moose are huge. You couldn't kill one with a slingshot."

"Well he did, smart ass." Kyle pauses.

"How?"

"How he did it was he waited until the moose was having a drink. Then he shot it in the nuts with the slingshot. It was so surprised it sucked up a bunch of water and drowned." Kyle makes the motion of firing a slingshot, closing one eye, pulling his arm back and releasing his imaginary projectile.

"Sick," I say. We plod the rest of the way to the store in silence.

Weekends, when I go to my Kokum's with my dad and camp on the couch, there are cousins who stay too. They call me *moonias* and laugh when I can't understand the Cree my Kokum talks. I've long since stopped telling them I'm not *moonias* – it just makes them laugh harder.

"C'mon, little shit face," Kyle calls to me. Kyle is what you might call a dink. At least that's what I call him. He's got a gland problem (says my Nana) that makes him have a fat problem (says me). His dad takes him to the barber and gets his hair cut down to stubble so you can see the pink, fleshy rolls at the back of his neck.

I think Kyle's jealous that I get to live with our grandparents. My Nana tells people they're "co-parenting" me with my dad, who works up north in the mines. I know Kyle wishes his dad would go away and work, too. My dad says Kyle's headed for the reformatory. I don't know what that is. It sounds like the word he told me for the place where they burn dead bodies, but I don't think that's right. That gave me nightmares after he told me about that: the place where bodies get burnt. Kyle's pretty bad, but I don't think he deserves that.

Because I get to stay with Nana and Grampa, Kyle thinks I have it easy. Maybe he's right. But then maybe there are things Kyle doesn't know about being the only brown kid in a white neighbourhood, about being the "little Indian" and getting called "chief," even by some of the teachers. What Kyle does know about, though, is how to be a first-class ass.

But once in a while he can be okay. Like the time he made me a walkie-talkie out of a block of wood. It was just pretend, but it was really cool the way it fit in my hand just right and I could hold it there at my side and then bring it up to my mouth like I was talking to someone. It would have been better if there were two of them, even though it was just pretend.

On the narrow beach behind the store, Kyle picks up stones and throws them at the water, at first half heartedly, and then with more effort to skip them. He has a shitty throw and the little rocks fall, *ploop,* into the water. I wonder if I should try skipping stones too, but I would probably be better at it, in which case he'd be likely to pound me.

This is the place I found the rock last year that looks almost exactly like a candy corn. It's even the right colours – orange where it should be orange and white near the tip. It's even better when it's wet and you can see the different layers of orange getting lighter and lighter as the rock comes to its point.

I have that rock at home in my cigar box, the one that Grampa gave to me, with the parrot on the lid. Sometimes I take the rock out and rub it with my thumb, just to feel its polished surface. I put it in my mouth and slide it over my tongue, feeling its cone shape, slightly flattened on one side, clicking it between my teeth, tasting its mild nothing flavour.

I imagine this little candy corn rock making its journey with the waves, getting polished by the rhythm of the water, the rubbing of the sand and the nibbling fishes. Maybe it even came all the way from the ocean, all the way to this particular shore to be found by me. Sometimes I look, wishing I could find more, thinking I could make a little dish of candy corn rocks if I found enough. But then I think that would kind of spoil it, so I don't look too hard.

I hear voices, and then two kids, a boy and a girl, burst through the trees. They're fat, pale and red haired. They stop and squint suspiciously at me and Kyle. Their doughy noses, uneven ears and little pink eyes remind me of the grunting pigs my Mooshum keeps. Kyle looks over his shoulder and then goes back to pretending to ignore all of us.

"Hey," I say.

"Hey," the boy echoes.

We watch Kyle twisting his body and flinging his arm out from his side. The stones all land with a single plop several yards from the shore.

"You guys staying in these cabins?" I ask.

The girl shakes her head and the boy points in toward the campground. "We're in the campground over there. How about you?"

"Yeah, we are too."

Kyle has given up on the rock skipping and comes slouching over to where we stand. He knows we're watching him as he pulls out a pack of cigarettes, takes one out and puts it between his lips. Looking up, trying hard to be cool, he says, "Gotta match?"

Your face and my ass, I think to myself. I don't say it, even though it's a good burn, because I don't feel like being pummelled. Not only is Kyle two years older than me, he outweighs me by a ton, the porker.

When none of us answer him, Kyle digs a box of matches from

his pocket and slickly lights one with a flick of his thumbnail.

"You *smoke?*" the girl asks. Kyle smiles, glad to have impressed someone.

"Yeah, but I'm trying to cut down." I have to give him credit, that was pretty good. Then he spoils it by sneering at me. "Hey, little shit face, you'd better keep *this,*" he jerks his smoke at me, "to yourself, if you know what's good for you."

As we walk back to the campsite with the red-haired kids, Kyle talks all loud and pisses me off by pulling my hair and putting me in a headlock every two frickin' minutes. Jesus Christ, I wish I were bigger and could give him a licking.

When we enter the campground and turn up the main road leading to the camping loops, Kyle starts walking ahead of us and then calls over his shoulder, "I'm going ahead. Meet me at the campsite, ass face."

"I have a name," I say quietly under my breath as we slow our pace and watch Kyle walk quickly away.

"How do you know *him?*" the red-haired boy asks me.

"He's my stupid cousin."

"What a jerk."

I guess this kid doesn't really look so much like my Mooshum's pigs.

"Hey," I say, as we turn down the road to our campsite. "Do you want to see something cool?"

Instead of turning toward the campsites, I lead them the opposite way down the loop. We cut to the cooking shelter and I take my new friends around to the back of the building, to the place I found earlier, alone. It's mine, I found it, and I plan never to show it to Kyle. We step into the unnaturally cool shade and I hunch down at the edge of the stream that runs through the dirt at the bottom of a small incline. The stream is a good secret, lying in the dim, cool place where the sparse sun can't reach. The towering trees and shade from the cook shack make this place dark and damp. A very good secret. Brown rotting leaves line the edges of the bank. On either side, small, scrubby brush inches hopefully toward flecks of sunlight dancing at the tops of the trees. The stream seems to come from nowhere and disappears quickly into the bush. We listen to the sound of the trickling water and breathe in the musty smell.

A tiny brown frog jumps across the stream. It would ordinarily be perfectly camouflaged by the rotting leaves, but now its little hind legs have missed the bank and splashed into the water. I reach across and scoop it into my hand, where I feel its frantic struggle. Cupping my other hand over it, I slowly open my palms. The frog jumps, and I clamp my hand down again. Soon it tires and lies quiet. I open my hands to see its moist brown sides heaving; its delicate feet tickle my hand. Then it jumps unexpectedly into the bushes and is gone.

"*Ayekis,*" I say to my friends.

"What?" asks the boy.

"That's *Ayekis* the frog. My kok...gramma told me a story about him. Lots of times."

"What's the story?" asks the girl eagerly.

"She told me you're not supposed to tell the stories in the summer. Stories are for the winter. I can't remember why."

"Please tell us," she begs. Her freckles, dashed across her nose, are dotted with sunlight, reminding me of how some piebald horses look.

"Well, I'll just tell you a bit," I say, feeling guilty. No one has to know, I think. I dip my hand into the running water of the stream and feel its coolness. I try to remember the *Ayekis* story my Kokum has told me forever, wishing I had listened more carefully.

"Once, *Ayekis* the frog lived on the banks of a river," I start. "He had short, stubby legs at that time. And he had a beautiful voice. He sang songs every night and *Wesakechak* would hear him singing. *Wesakechak* would send tasty flies to *Ayekis* as a way to thank him for his singing."

"Who?" the girl interrupts.

"Shhh!" the boy says, smacking her in the arm.

"*Wesakechak* is someone who lives across the river," I say. "He's kind of – magic." That's lame, but I don't really know how to describe *Wesakechak* to someone who's never heard of him.

"Then what?"

"Then one day, *Ayekis* decides he wants to meet *Wesakechak*. But he can't get across the river because he can't swim. Did I tell you he had short legs back then?" Two red heads nod.

"Anyway, so *Ayekis* asks a bird, I can't remember what kind, to help him. He tells the bird he wants to send a present to *Wesakechak*. He makes a package and he fills it full of *kinikenik*." Before they can ask, I say, *"Kinikenik* is a kind of Indian tobacco."

As I'm talking, we all watch the trickling stream. Down here in the shade, it's like a different world. Suddenly, another little frog hops on the bank close to us. The boy reaches out and places his hand over it. He scoops it up and holds it cupped in his two hands. Once the little frog calms down and we've all had a look, the girl asks, "Can I hold it?"

Reluctantly, the boy holds out his hands, offering the frog, "You better not let it go."

The girl sits perfectly still with the frog and whispers, *"Ayekis"* They both look at me.

"Okay, so *Ayekis* makes up this package of *kinikenik,* but he leaves a little extra space in the package. Just before the bird comes to pick it up, *Ayekis* crawls inside and pulls the flap shut. The bird comes and picks up the package and is surprised how heavy it is. As the bird flies over the water, *Ayekis* starts to slip. Just before they reach the other side of the river *Ayekis* falls out of the package. He's falling and falling toward the water. No, wait. He's falling toward the rocks at the edge of the water. That's it." I have the feeling I'm not telling this completely right.

"Wesakechak sees that his friend's going to be killed if he hits the rocks, so he sends some magic out, and at the last minute *Ayekis* gets snagged in a tree branch at the edge of the river, which saves him from hitting the rocks. He's hanging there upside down by his feet. He squirms and wiggles but he can't get his feet free. He hangs there for such a long time that his legs start to stretch. They get longer and longer until he's almost touching the water. Finally, the branch lets go and *Ayekis* slips into the water without getting hurt.

"After that day, *Ayekis's* legs were stretched really long, which made him feel embarrassed and shy. So he hid from everyone and hardly ever came out of the water. That's why frogs are the way they are today."

I look at their intent faces and am just about to say, *The end*, when I hear, "That's a real sweet story, chief brown streak. Tell us another," and Kyle jumps over the side of the shelter, landing hard in the dirt. The girl tries to hide behind her brother. "What're you doing here, telling your little gay stories with your new *girl* friends?" Kyle turns to look at the red-haired kids. "Lemme see the frog," he demands. The girl simply holds out her cupped hands. Roughly, Kyle takes the animal.

The frog hops in Kyle's hands as he tries to get a look at it. When he cracks them open, the little frog tries to jump through the narrow opening. Kyle clamps his hands together and barely catches the animal by its hind feet. He closes one fist around the frog's legs and lets it dangle upside down from his hand.

"Quit it," I say.

"What's the matter, little baby? Are you scared I'll hurt your stupid frog?"

"If it's stupid, then you must be a retard." I don't care if he beats me to a pulp. I yell, "Put it down, you're scaring it with your ugly face."

Kyle, still dangling the frog in one hand, fumbles in his jacket pocket with the other. "Oh? You wanna see me scare it?" He pulls out a wooden match.

"Quit it," I say.

Kyle flicks his thumbnail over the match head and it flares to life. He holds it up in front of the frog. The frog squirms.

The girl starts to cry and I can't help but stare. She makes snivelly noises and cries in a way that doesn't make you feel sorry for her at all, like crying should. Instead, it sort of makes you want to do something really mean like give her a lighter-burn pinch. I can tell Kyle's thinking the same thing by the way he looks at her and smiles, shark-like.

The frog is frantic as Kyle pokes the flame at its writhing body. I lunge at Kyle and shove him hard. Kyle's solid, but he's taken by surprise, and while he's distracted, the flame from the match touches his fingertips.

"Shit!" He drops the match, shaking his hand. He yells something at me, but I don't understand it. Then Kyle turns to the red-haired girl. She starts to back away but he reaches out and grabs her by the arm.

She doesn't even try to snatch her arm away like most people would. She just starts to twist and squirm, rotating her arm around in his hand, leaving red marks on her flesh where his hand is rubbing her skin. She makes feeble attempts to pry his fingers off her arm as if she doesn't really expect to get away, as if she is just going through the motions – as if she believes she should take her punishment, whatever it is.

Kyle holds on to her arm because he wants her to stay, to see what he'll do next, because it's for her that he does it. Because she has it coming. He drops her arm and with the frog still clutched in his hand, he jumps awkwardly onto the ledge that forms the partial wall of the cooking shelter. He looks down at us and then, all at once, he raises his hand with the frog high above his head.

He brings his arm down with all his force, his body bending at the waist, as he flings the little brown frog onto the cement floor of the cooking shelter.

The girl's face collapses and turns a dangerous shade of red, shiny with mucous and wet. The boy stands frozen, his lips hanging open. Then he grabs his sister's hand and runs. I listen to the sound of their sneakers on the gravel and the girl's fading wail until all we are left with is the soft sound of the shuddering trees.

Kyle, still standing on the ledge, seems stunned, as if the sudden quiet has broken a spell.

"Why?" I ask. "Why'd you have to do that?"

Kyle, quick to resume being Kyle, shrugs his shoulders with mock carelessness. "Why not?" he says, as he jumps down beside the mangled frog and walks away. I watch his retreating back long after he's gone. Over my shoulder, the cool rolling stream mutters its secrets to no one in particular. The light through the trees begins to fade.

delivery

Ruth Ann looks out the bedroom window and registers the shifting light through the grey drizzle. She wonders if Ray will come home soon. She imagines him sitting in his car on the shoulder of the highway, just before the turn off to the rez, chain-smoking and watching their house. She knows it's a test. He wants to see if she'll try to escape.

Her belly tightens and she rocks her hips in an effort to keep the contraction at bay. Ever since Ray pushed her down this morning, she's felt the cramping with more and more urgency. When he pushed her, she had the feeling of witnessing the event from outside her body, from a distance, as if she were a spectator. She remembers flying across the bathroom in a backward spin, her arms spiralling to try to catch her balance. She was brought up short as her legs caught the edge of the bathtub and she fell in. Her lower back smashed against the back of the tub and her head struck hard against the wall. The impact moved through her body like a wave, through her belly, through the baby, and into the thin air of the room.

The shock of the impact sharpened her senses and she searched her mind for the best move she could make. Her ears rang as she lay in the bathtub, perfectly still, except for placing her hands protectively over her belly. Experience told her not to show her pain, to put up the front that she wasn't vulnerable. She looked up and met his eyes as he stood over her. He was breathing hard, waiting.

"*What* are you doing?" she said, trying her best to keep her voice steady. She achieved a tone that seemed to imply this was a startling, singular event.

His pupils were so dilated his irises were like black saucers, the surrounding whites tinged a sickly yellow. In the back of her mind, she registered the yellow, associated it with a character flaw rather than the ill health it likely represented.

"You're not going," he said, then turned and walked out of the bathroom.

She struggled to get out of the tub, to regain her feet, and followed him into the bedroom in time to see him take the car keys from her purse.

"There." He tucked the keys into the front pocket of his jeans. His voice was flat, his eyes daring. "You're not going anywhere."

Another contraction, stronger and sooner than the last one, jars her from her memory of the morning's events. *This is it,* she thinks, *active labour.* She's seen enough babies born to know the second baby comes a lot faster than the first. Her mother's admonition to the women she midwifed: "You can't wait with the second baby. As soon as those contractions are coming regularly, or your water breaks, you call for me." She has no idea if Ray will be home in time to take her to the hospital.

Ruth Ann decides to call Old Man, beg him to come and get her. To hell with Ray and his stupid games watching the house. Old Man isn't afraid of Ray. In Ruth Ann's mind, he isn't afraid of anyone. She fumbles her cell phone out of her purse and picks out Old Man's number. "Come," she says just as a contraction builds to its crest. She clenches her jaw against it and says, through gritted teeth, "I need you." She's surprised by these words. She thought she was going to say "help" – *I need help.*

Old Man doesn't ask any questions. "Hang on," he says, his voice taking on an edge, a you-can-count-on-me edge, purposely reassuring. The sort of macho thing she might ordinarily find irritating. "I'm coming to get you."

She breathes deeply in and out, focussed on riding the contraction to its end. She whimpers into the phone and hates herself for it.

"Don't panic," he says before he hangs up.

She drops the phone into her purse and thinks about Old Man, whom she's known all her life – her oldest friend. Maybe her only friend. Old Man is only a nickname – he's not old at all, same age as her. They went to boarding school together.

Three months ago, Old Man returned to the community. He'd been away, in the city, trying to work. "Got tired of it," he said when she asked why he came back. That was all, just tired of it. He didn't elaborate.

"What about you?" he asked then. "You doing okay?" And the tone of his voice combined with the look on his face told her he knew she wasn't. But she couldn't tell him how bad it was. Instead, she found ways – made excuses to see him, to be the same places he was. First, she volunteered to work the Tuesday bingo because his uncle ran the hall and she thought he might be there. When he didn't show up the first two times, she decided to look in town.

She parked to go to the grocery store further east on Main Street than was necessary. This was so she could walk past the café she knew he frequented. As she approached the café door, her chest tightened. She told herself she was going in just to use the washroom and grab a quick cup of coffee. She would pretend she wasn't looking for him. The door jangled as she walked in and her face flushed. She was sure everyone was looking at her. She saw him at the counter and he smiled. "Howdy, stranger," he said, and she sank into the seat beside him, faint with relief. That was how it started. He was someone to talk to like they were familiar friends and they quickly found their old connection, eventually getting bold enough to talk on the telephone in stolen moments. She knew it was risky. They both did. Old Man was the only person she trusted enough to tell about her plans to leave, her intention to go to her mother's and have the baby without Ray.

She leans on the bed to get through the next contraction. As it builds, she thinks about Ray, watching her, watching the house, and again has a thought she's had often – a semi ramming his parked car from behind, leaving him in a twisted metal wreck on the highway. The police at the door to tell her the bad news.

Fatal. He's gone. She imagines their words. Or maybe a bar fight gone too far. He's such a prick when he drinks, this isn't hard to imagine – him picking a fight with the wrong person and getting beaten, maybe by a group of men, beaten to the ground and kicked again and again in the stomach, the ribs, the head. Maybe a call from the hospital to tell her he's in a coma. On life support. Dead. These sorts of things happen. Would solve everything, in some ways. But each time she has wished something like this, she regrets it when he shows her another side – a shift that suggests he might come around – the times when he gets better for a while. Full of a hundred promises, bargains – earnest in his resolve, he seems, to her, sincere. And so, once again, she allows herself to be tugged forward by hope until it all comes crashing down anew, as it did this morning.

When the pain subsides, she caresses her belly as she walks across the bedroom, opens the closet and takes out an old gym bag. She sets it on the bed and begins to pack, opening and closing her dresser drawers. She fills the bag with socks and underwear, leaving little room for the rest of her clothes. Then she returns most of the socks and underwear to the drawers and starts again.

She leans her forearms on the dresser as another contraction builds to its peak, a pair of socks gripped in both hands like a prayer. At the end of the contraction, she hastily puts a few more items into the bag and closes it, stroking her belly, wishing for her labour to slow down – for a clear-headed moment.

As the next strong contraction spikes and then passes, she feels an urgent need to pee. She closes the bathroom door, willing herself to stay alert to sounds of Ray entering the house. The door might as well be wide open for all the privacy or protection it gives, the useless lock long ago smashed by one strong kick with a heavy workboot. It's remained broken – a reminder that he won't be denied.

As she stands from the toilet, a thump deep inside her body is the only warning before her water bursts in a cascade down her legs. Her legs begin to shake as she grabs the towels from the towel bar and sinks to her knees on the floor. She tries to soak up the clear fluid pouring from her body.

Her chest tightens with renewed fear. After the last pregnancy, she read books about prolapsed cords and breaking water. She consulted endlessly with her mother, read as much as she could, paid special attention to those things that might go wrong. The last time, the first time, her baby had made it to full term. When he was born, he had a smooth, round face accented by a tiny mouth that looked as though it was waiting for a kiss. Silky black hair cupped a round skull that fit in her palm like a baseball, and he had long-lashed eyes that never opened. It was Ray's fault the baby was born still and lifeless. Her overdue placenta had been knocked from the wall of her uterus. Her baby had drowned.

She stays on her hands and knees on the bathroom floor, afraid that any downward pressure of the baby's head on the cord might cut off its oxygen. She's convinced that, again, her baby is dying, right this moment, inside of her. She can't think of what to do next. She leans her head against the edge of the tub while waves of contractions pound her body.

When she feels the baby shift downward in the birth canal, she fights a surge of panic, certain the baby is dying. She rolls onto her back, half of her on the towels, the other half on the cold tile floor. Immediately, another contraction rocks her body and she closes her eyes and wills herself through it. She's afraid to move because each time she does, the movement triggers another contraction. She gingerly stuffs another towel underneath her hips and takes quick, shallow breaths in an effort to stay focussed.

She panics as another contraction rises. "Nooo," she begs, out loud. She rides the crest of pain to its peak and eases down the other side. More contractions follow quickly and tears spring to her eyes as she finally gives in, bearing down to let sound escape from her throat like hot steam. Her work is purposeful and she listens intently to her body as it guides her.

When the head is born, she cries out, relief washing her in a chill. She guides the baby from her body and quickly wipes mucus from its face, looking for signs of life. She lifts the floppy infant to her stomach, pulling at the corner of a towel to work it free, wiping at the baby's nose and mouth, desperate to clear its airway. She scoops mucus from its mouth with her finger while images of her lifeless first infant threaten to choke her. She lifts the baby to her face as though she's going to kiss it and bends her head forward to place her mouth over its innocent nose. She sucks out the mucus, spits it to the side and sucks again. She's rewarded by a sputter; the baby's face contorts with the effort. Then its chest moves, heaves, and it takes its first real live breath. It gives a small cry, at first only sputtering, but as she rubs its body with the towel, the faltering sounds finally give way to a tiny bawl.

All at once, Ray is there. When she looks up into his eyes they aren't hard and suspicious, as she's come to expect. Instead, she reads concern.

"It's okay," Ruth Ann says. "Listen to her," she laughs, cupping the baby close. "She's alive. Look. She's a girl."

Ray reaches out to run a finger lightly over the baby's hair, ruffling it back. He looks intently at the infant, who lies wide-eyed and alert on Ruth Ann's chest. For an instant Ruth Ann is hopeful. Together they look into the mystery of those deep, fluid eyes.

"That's great, babe," he says.

Ruth Ann wants him to say more. She wants him to show some emotion, maybe cry; she wants him to be moved by this miracle. She watches him for a sign that he has empathy, for a sign that maybe she can trust him. She wants it to be different – a new start for all of them. And for just one moment, while she and Ray look at their new baby together and he tenderly touches her soft head, Ruth Ann believes that this new beginning might just be possible.

Ruth Ann's legs begin to shake. Ray leaves the room and is back within seconds with towels from the hall closet. He wraps her legs with them and places towels over the baby to keep her warm.

A sharp knock at the back door causes Ray's eyes to narrow and the line of his jaw tightens.

Ruth Ann's scalp prickles as Ray strides from the bathroom. She shuffles her hips, blood gushing as she moves, so she can see through the bathroom door – across the hallway into the kitchen, where she can just get a glimpse of Ray at the back door. He has it open, and she hears Old Man talking but can't see him. Ray steps forward and pushes Old Man with one hand, likely on Old Man's chest, from the angle of Ray's arm. Pushes him back firmly, but not violently, out the door. She hears Ray say, "No, she's not," as he closes the door on Old Man.

Ray returns to the bathroom and as Ruth Ann meets Ray's gaze, her face turns hot. She gives an involuntary shudder. She knows by his look that he'll make her pay for Old Man's presence. She knows Ray well enough to understand that he's calculating, now, just how to do this.

Finally, he curls his lips back and says, "Clean this mess." His gaze takes in the bloody and fluid-soaked towels; his look implies that this detritus from having the baby is something foul and obscene. He makes sure to look only at her and the surrounding scene in the bathroom – he purposely ignores the baby. He leaves the bathroom doorway and goes to the bedroom, where Ruth Ann can feel his presence, his keyed-up anger, radiating through the thin walls.

Her breath comes in panicky waves. *What now, what now?* she asks herself. She shifts, the baby still in her arms, trying to get up to her knees. As she rises, a strong contraction delivers the placenta. She feels the cramping pain in her stomach as hot blood rushes between her legs. She realizes that her bleeding is more than what's normal and lies back again, hopeful that reclining will help staunch the flow. Her muscles go weak and every bit of strength leaves her body.

"Ray," she calls out faintly. He should be able to hear her, even though her voice is small. "Ray, please. I need an ambulance," she tries again.

Another crisp knock at the back door brings Ray striding out of the bedroom and across the hallway. "That mother-fucking – I'll kill him," Ray barks at her as he stomps to the door. He grabs the doorknob and jerks the door open, ready to strike. But then his tense and sure body recoils.

Ruth Ann can only imagine what he sees on the other side of the door. Does Old Man have a weapon? Is he threatening Ray just outside of her sightline?

"What?" Ray demands, defiance in his voice.

Ruth Ann thinks about Ray's baseball bat, behind the speaker in the living room. She wants to warn Old Man. "Don't," she tries to call out, but there's no power in her voice.

There are loud male voices, more than one. She can't make out their words. Has Old Man brought friends? Her neck muscles are painfully tense as she strains to see and hear what is happening. Her trembling arms fall to her sides and she's too weak to raise them again, to protect the baby, still lying on her chest. The blood is thick, congealing on her legs but still moving in a steady stream from her uterus.

"...Some sort of problem," a male voice, closer now, cuts into the house.

Ray takes a step back as the back door is pushed open. Ruth Ann expects to see Old Man enter. Instead she sees a volley of blue and grey; a yellow stripe down a dark pant leg makes her think of the track uniforms the older kids wore in school. For a second, she wonders why Old Man would wear his old school tracksuit to her house. She closes her eyes for a moment.

"I have rights. I can say no," Ray says.

"No, sir. You can't." The male voice is firm.

She opens her eyes as the yellow stripe comes through the kitchen and across the hallway, toward her. The black boots look familiar but she can't quite place them. They're speckled with small, perfect raindrops. Ruth Ann desperately tries to raise her arm, to tell the person to take the baby to a safe place, but she's too weak.

She hears static and a beep, followed by a woman's radioed voice: "Unit twelve, we have confirmation." The radio crackles and clicks. A hand is raised to turn the volume low.

"Are you all right? Can you hear me?" the officer asks, standing over her, his hand still on the radio at his hip.

"I want to go home," Ruth Ann whispers. She closes her eyes

and tries to listen. Through the ringing in her ears and the voices that make no sense to her now, Ruth Ann hears sirens, far away. Her mind drifts to a time when she was young, at home with her parents: warm amber light, a quilt made by her Kokum, and her father's strong, wide hands around a chipped mug of hot tea with honey. The baby's movements, its heartbeat next to her own, force Ruth Ann back to the present. The sirens seem closer now.

Almost there, she thinks, willing her spirit to stay strong.

She opens her eyes to see Old Man bending down by her side. He places one warm hand on her shoulder and the other on the baby's back. Almost there.

billy bird

You can stay if you like."
But Billy doesn't like the curtain zipping shut, the drawers being yanked open, and Billy's grandfather throwing his head from side to side on the pillow – bloated eyes, neck craning, *my things my things* – just before the nurse whips the sheets off to expose his stick limbs. She tugs the gown away and Billy's Mooshum lies stiff in silent protest, as if to say he won't do a thing to make this easier on any of them. Turned on his side, a patch of white gauze just above the buttocks is peeled back to show where the pressure of lying all day has broken open the old man's skin to a crater the size of a grapefruit. Billy can see the hole goes right to the bone, edges raw and inflamed. Billy wonders when things got this bad, as if it might be possible to pinpoint a moment over the past twenty years when the decline started in earnest.

The nurse gone, the woman in the next bed begins her scream again. Thigh-high stumps thrash beneath a thin white sheet and Billy doesn't need to see it to know it's happening just the way it's happened every day for the last how many months or years. And the woman is ignored, her flaccid grey hair pushed away from an afflicted full-moon face; her eyes search and of course no one comes. Billy's grandfather groans low and deep and Billy wipes the old man's crusty tears with a damp cloth. No less than eight beds, this is a mixed ward where modesty has been presumed irrelevant. Women and men are stripped and sponged, and when no family is present there seems little reason for privacy curtains. His grandfather's silent weeping isn't new. He's been doing it for years – around the same time he stopped wanting to eat. Sometimes he used to laugh – slyly, like someone had told him a dirty joke.

Billy Bird heard his Auntie call his grandfather an ugly word. A vegetable.

Convince me, Billy thinks, *that this is the man, the same man who, as a boy, saw his own beloved grampa attacked by a demented muskwa.* The story Billy knows so well.

"Tell me again Mooshum," Billy whispers, his lips close to Mooshum's ear.

Billy's been mad at his Mooshum for twenty years for not being able to tell him the stories.

Tell me who I am Mooshum. Billy thinks.

A Mooshum should tell a grandson the stories.

Billy sees himself as part of a circle, part of a never-ending circle he shares with the grampas and grannies of his past. Each of them holds a fine red thread that reminds him of a fresh-spun spider silk, but a red one, and one that can't be broken. His whole family is there sharing the circle with him, people he looks like, people he's connected to, people whose traits he shares, people whose history is his own, grannies and grampas, *Nêhiyaw* and Métis, all connected by that silky red thread. Because of the circle, Billy grew up thinking of the *muskwa* story as being about himself and his own Mooshum – a whole two generations removed from the facts but not so removed from the truth in the mind of Billy.

When his Mooshum was a boy, he saw his own grampa killed by a bear. In the season *miyoskamiki,* when the frogs will start their singing right before dusk, a great sickly bear burst into the small cabin the boy-Mooshum shared with his grampa. An enormous noise, followed by a great stink, entered with *muskwa* – the noise of wood splitting and hinges tearing, along with an angry bawl from the maddened bear. The stink was musky fur and something else that Mooshum didn't know yet but later would identify as desperation. Boy-Mooshum crouched behind the wood box, and sent spiders scurrying. The scent of sap and fresh-cut wood enfolded him as the murderous look in *muskwa's* eyes chilled his scalp like a sudden winter wind. The bear rose up ten feet in the air, towering over his grampa, the big man who boy-Mooshum had known all his life, now *kiseyinisis,* old and small in *muskwa's* shadow.

Grampa lashed out at the bear with a first pre-emptive strike. It seemed to boy-Mooshum that his grampa had himself turned into a *muskwa,* rising to slash the bear with the razor-sharp claws of a fire poker that tore half of *muskwa's* face away with a single blow, sending him reeling. The animal shook his snout with such furious wonder that little Mooshum was splattered with a warm red cascade. *Muskwa* swiped one massive paw, belting out his fury in time with Grampa's bodily thump as he was flung across the room easy, like an old muskrat pelt. The bear pounced and set to work, throttling Grampa until it seemed the bear would tear Grampa's head off. Finally the bear stopped after seconds that seemed like forever, great steaming breaths escaping from his massive snout. Boy-Mooshum watched as *muskwa* turned to look directly into his eyes. It was then that Mooshum felt the fiery surge spread as he wet himself and *muskwa* lumbered his way before hurtling through the open cabin door and into the woods. The *onipahtakew,* murderer, was gone.

Mooshum remained behind the wood box until well into the night, unable to loosen his grip on the rough-hewn boards, tiny red spiders zigzagging across his fingers. The door of the cabin was torn clean off, and it was the angry buzzing of flies around Grampa's body that brought Mooshum to his senses enough to be afraid of other animals who might come for the smell of fresh blood. He found the courage to move from his hiding place and fix the battered door over its frame and build a large fire. He spent the first lonely night sitting beside the body, vainly trying to prevent ugly blue-black flies from laying eggs in Grampa's flesh. In the morning, boy-Mooshum prayed to the east and the eagle, as his grampa had taught him, before dressing the body in a shroud made from some of Grampa's clothing. Finally, he left to follow the road that led to his parents and siblings. They returned together and held a three-day wake before burying his grampa behind the cabin.

It was this story of his Mooshum's grampa that made Billy so mad to watch the bit-by-bit, year-after-year stripping down of Billy's Mooshum. *Tell me the stories Mooshum. A Mooshum should tell the stories.* For twenty years, this plundering had been occurring, sometimes while Billy had been away in jail where he couldn't see it, and other times right under his nose.

At night, after one of his visits, Billy would consider the turns in his own life – his name well known by local cops and JPs, an unhappy drunk to be counted on to smash a few skulls after last call at the Prairie Inn or the Embassy. But then a thing had happened between him and Shelby. First, Shelby made it known she was special, different from the girls he usually went with. There was no question about that and just because she knew about his past in jail didn't mean he ever wanted her to have to visit him there. Second, Billy heard one night he was going to be a father, and it was what he needed, not as an excuse to slop away another twenty-six, but to find himself tired of bar rooms and split-knuckle hangovers. He got a punishing job on a construction site that offered all the overtime he was willing to take and he worked his body into submission until he no longer craved a drink, was too exhausted to lust after any fight. He resolved that he would be a good father and when that unborn baby died one night in an oily hemorrhage, he still denied it as an excuse to pick up a bottle. All that time, his Mooshum was there in the Watershed Rehab Centre, mashing his head into the pillow and laughing slyly.

In the public bathroom down the hall from Mooshum's room, Billy Bird looks through the slits of his fingers and sees his knees wrapped in the denim of his jeans, the toes of his runners, ordinary, as if they're patiently waiting for him to be finished. Billy's run himself down, run it all out in throaty sobs that caught and choked like barbs tearing up his insides, and he thinks he might be finished now.

Looking through his fingers, he thinks about putting his hand to a light, like a flashlight, and how a person can see through it to blood and dark and creases, crimson fingers laced with veins and nerves and what else Billy can't remember. But he knows as he sits on the toilet with his pants on and looks at his fingers from this close-up view, mashed against his face, that he hasn't done that flashlight trick since he was a little boy and he should, because he couldn't feel more like a child than he does right now, helpless in this public toilet, looking through his fingers, no idea what he'll do next.

The usual thing is to go home, to his woman, to the home he's made, at last, with one woman. Where he can finally finally convince himself that she'll be there when he gets back, patient and calm. He wonders what he ever did in his life to deserve Shelby, besides nothing. Seven years they've been together and he hopes he won't go fucking it up.

But these times with Billy's Mooshum, they make him low, and Shelby is just intuitive. She knows how to wait him out like a bad cold or bitter weather while he hides his head under the hood of the Chev. He tinkers and slams and mutters and bangs at the altar of the Chev and pretty soon her lack of intervention soothes the sore, hard lump in his chest, below his throat that's raw, and the little boy inside Billy slowly loosens his grip like he's had him by the balls all this time and Billy didn't notice until the moment when he got let go. And then Billy can go inside and take a sip of Shelby that eases the knot down to a softer spot, where it doesn't pinch and bind so bad.

A little earlier, he watched his Mooshum watch him as he touched Mooshum's stuff. Mooshum growled at Billy but that was okay because by now Billy's used to it. And Mooshum pitched his head about on the pillow. Billy knows his Mooshum likes to keep a close eye on his things, the dozen or so things that belong to the old man in this whole world. Pyjama tops and bottoms, folded neatly into the drawers, plastic framed eyeglasses, twenty years out of date, and a framed photo of Billy's family lined up in his Auntie's back-yard, smiling into the sun, the brown fence behind them like a backdrop. Billy touches and messes with all of Mooshum's worldly possessions to agitate the old man, to see if Mooshum is still in there, somewhere. And then Billy comes in here to the public toilet to do his secret weeping thing that's probably not so secret. Those nurses must have seen it all before.

In the early days at the Rehab Centre, Billy's Mooshum would masturbate earnestly, making deliberate eye contact with the nurses, his one good hand working furiously.

convince me convince me convince me

(Convince me I'm still alive convince me I've something to live for, even this.) Hopeful good eye casting about.

convince me convince me

"That's enough now, Mister Bird," the nurse's singsong pleasant voice suggesting *you're not shocking me, little-boy-old-man* as she took his hand from under the covers, his one good hand, while he giggled and grinned so she had to wipe the drool. Tucking him in, straightening him out, keeping him tight, smoothing wrinkled sheets and applying comfort like a salve with cool, competent hands to hover over and offer blessing to a big full-grown-man-child.

That's what's become of his Mooshum, Billy's grandfather, one arm frozen for all time in a rigid bend, hand a down-turned claw, skin so fine his bones can be seen right there by anyone who cares to look. None of it made any better by the nurses who try to feed Mooshum as he clamps his lips shut to the mush. Billy tries to get him to eat too, but hasn't had much luck, though he's willing to stick with it longer. Some days the old man will take the water, but Billy can't deny the dry smell of tepid breath, and now they say he's lost another twelve pounds.

Billy returns to Mooshum's room just as another nurse is finishing. She leaves Billy with his cheek on Mooshum's pillow, lips whispering into the old man's ear a chant something like this – *convince me convince me*. Billy moves the pillow, damp with tears, from beneath Mooshum's head and places it so gently and quietly over the old man's face that none of the other patients are even aware.

When the nurse returns, Billy's gone and Mooshum lies quiet on the pillow, his bent arm at ease. The woman in the next bed halts her screams for once, and they all hear a sound like a mighty *muskwa* bawl just outside the window. The lids of Mooshum's eyes are still, no longer mapping the fine red stream of veins, the ruby tendril threads.

grapes

ast time I saw Cowboy, I told him he looked like a chief, and
then I patted his belly and laughed. Later I was sorry because
that wasn't very nice to call him fat like that. Around here, you
gotta be careful with your jokes – someone takes what you say the
wrong way, then they start some rumour about you. *Jeez.*

Like my poor cousin Shirley. Her, she's just walking down the
highway one morning hoping somebody will give her a lift into
town 'cause she's gotta be at work at nine and already it's at least
nine-fifteen. So she keeps looking over her shoulder to see who's
coming. The only place this road goes is between the rez and
town, so you know right away if somebody doesn't stop to give
you a ride, well, it must be one of them stuck-up Indians. There's
a few like that around here.

Anyway, Shirley sees this big green car – well, hears it really –
cruising down the highway behind her, and she knows right away
it's gonna be Reuben. So she puts her head down and keeps
walking and concentrates real hard on chanting *don't stop don't stop
don't stop.* Even so, Reuben pulls up beside her in his big old
Monte Carlo – the car that makes him look like a pimp and got
that rumour started around here. And Reuben, he leans across
the seat and opens the door for her, not because he's a gentleman
but because his handle's broke. And at least three cars drive past
while this is happening. Round here, those are called *corroborating
witnesses.*

So Shirley, who's real nice and doesn't want to be stuck up,
gets into Reuben's car quick before anyone else sees her standing
there, and lets him give her a ride. Before she even gets home
from work that day, everybody's heard Shirley is Reuben's new

girlfriend, on account of those *witnesses*. And even though nobody necessarily saw them together after that one morning, when Shirley shows up later in the fall for the bannock and stew fundraiser and everyone can see that little bump under her sweatshirt, they all *know* it has to be Reuben's baby.

Around here, when a person gossips, someone might call them out for being part of the grapevine, but usually only because that person's already heard the story and isn't too interested in hearing it again. But it's not too nice to be called out like that.

So when I hear Sally Cooke telling Kimmy Frank about Shirley's baby, I decide to try and teach her a lesson.

"I'm sorry to hear about yer old man," I say.

"What?" Sally says, sharply.

"You know. With Glenda what's-her-face," I say, pointing with my chin toward the other side of the hall.

That makes Sally take straight off to look for her old man.

While we watch Sally scuttle away, Kimmy says, "What a grape," and then we both have a real good laugh.

lost

When I Was Fifteen

I was supposed to take care of Marty, but then we got ourselves lost. Who leaves a fifteen-year-old city kid alone to look after her baby brother in the woods, anyway?

Two irresponsible morons who want to fuck like teenagers in a tent, that's who.

Me and Marty heard the water before we came upon it. It was a narrow river, maybe fifty yards across. Silver fish suspended in the current curved this way and that to keep themselves in place. It seemed a lot of effort to go nowhere. Several feet away, a group of ducks sat in the riffles, greedily sucking insects from the bubbles.

The water looked clean and clear and I knelt to drink from its flow where it rushed over the stones as if from a tap. Instead of being cold, as I had expected, the water had absorbed heat from dark rocks warmed by the sun. I held my cupped hands to Marty Junior's lips. *Open your mouth a little.* He did, and I let the water trickle in. We repeated this several times until he was satisfied. After another long drink, I rested on my haunches while Marty poked the soft bank with a stick. Somehow, the ducks' frantic nibbling helped me feel hopeful.

When I Was Twelve

In Italy, with Monique and Dee, and of course Martin – when they were still into pretending we were one big happy family, just after Martin moved in with us and spoiled everything – the tour guide, Daniella, had kept us all in check with her bright pink umbrella, which she held high above her head, arm extended, elbow straight. We followed that tattered beacon dutifully, like moths to a flame, all over Vatican City.

I remember she spoke to us in English but had a lovely Italian accent that I tried to imitate for weeks afterward. "And now we are entering de Vatican Pinacoteca, de art-eh gal-lery, built most recently in-eh 1932-eh." Her hair was dyed a stunning shade of blonde, but I could see just the beginning of black roots. As we went from one attraction to the next, I observed her switching from English, when she herded us around, to Italian when she spoke to the security guards or admissions people. As we waited our turn to enter St. Peter's Basilica, she stood with a young man who was managing admissions. They talked quickly and closely, then she threw her head back and laughed when he said something to her in Italian. He smiled as his eyes danced along her lovely long neck. The switch from one language and persona to the other was seamless and intriguing, something I also tried to imitate. I desperately wanted to be able to speak Italian, and so for the rest of the trip and even after we returned to Canada and our boring lives, I would insert small words here and there, practicing my Italian accent. *Buonasera,* I joyously greeted shop owners. *Grazie,* I told the waiters in the hotel, rolling the *r* in a circle on my tongue in an effort to banish my flat Canadian accent.

I thought Daniella must be rich and famous until later, when we were in the midst of the tour and I sat close to her as we waited in one of the churches. I saw the crow's feet around her eyes and then noticed her shoes were badly scuffed. There was a hole worn through near the knuckle of her big toe. She smiled warmly when she saw me staring at her, and I blushed.

Fifteen

So that morning, in the woods, I held my stick above my head in imitation of Daniella the Italian tour guide. Of course, Junior didn't remember Italy, because he hadn't been born yet, but he followed along anyway.

"Tour guide of de forEST-eh!" I hollered and marched ahead with the stick in the air, yelling commands over my shoulder in an

Italian accent. "Hurry! Keep-eh up or you will be left behind-eh! Just ahead you will see the amazing evergreen-eh, indigenous to dis part of de world-eh." And then I would stop and turn abruptly to face my audience – tour group of one. Junior giggled as I used my stick to point out features of the forest in my overdone Italian accent, which began to sound like I was from Transylvania after a while. "And here ve have-eh an aMAZing example of u-MONG-gous fungus! U-MONG-gous fungus is a giant-eh mushroom of de forEST-eh," I said, pointing to gigantic white and red mushrooms growing from the cracks in a tree stump.

Twelve

In Italy, even though we were all under strict orders to stay together and follow the tour guide's ridiculous umbrella, it was inevitably Dee who wound up lost, left behind with a group of Germans at the tapestries gallery in the Vatican museum. Afterwards, she complained bitterly to me about Martin's unreasonable response and how nobody understood her.

"I couldn't tear myself away," she said. "They were so beautiful. Exquisite," she said, with their depictions of women and saints, martyrs and icons, the Virgin Mary, the baby Jesus. The semi-sarcastic smile that played at the corners of her mouth told me something different.

"Do you expect us to believe that you didn't notice the group you stayed behind with were all speaking *German?*" Martin asked, looking from Dee to Monique and back again. He seemed to be imploring Monique to help him make his point. "I find that hard to believe," he said drily.

"Oh, so now you're calling me a liar," Dee fumed, throwing up her hands in a way that implied this was the most unforgivable insult.

"You have no idea," Martin said in small, measured tones, "how difficult it is to spend any amount of time with those paintings. Access to the interior of the Sistine Chapel is limited. The noise deteriorates the paintings. I have no idea if we'll ever get this chance again." We all stopped listening because this was, like, the fifth time we'd heard Martin say this.

Then Dee said, "Well, maybe if you're so worried about the noise, you should just shut up then."

Martin's lips clamped shut and his face turned really red, like almost purple it was so red. He took three long strides to reach the hotel room door, which he slammed on the way out.

"Dee," Monique said quietly. But that was all.

A Twelve List

Mom made me go to bed early that night in Rome, as if I had done something wrong. I spent my time making up a list of things I wanted to change about myself:

My name. *Sunny* was a tall order. Sunshine, rainbows, happiness, lollipops. Perpetual summer. Give me an ugly name any day. Make me a *Eugenia,* with its associated low expectations. I really wasn't up to *Sunny.*

Bad things. Stop doing them. Stupid things too.

Body hair. Grow some. Its absence was giving me a complex. Normal was overrated but necessary.

Mom, I mean *Monique,* tried to pretend she wasn't crying, but later I woke up and heard her rush to the door when Martin came back. It was long after I had fallen asleep. I knew then she was pathetic.

Fifteen

How long me and Junior played the tour guide game before I realized we had strayed from the rough path I couldn't say. The mosquitos were getting thicker, biting our faces and through the thin fabric of my hoodie. Junior began losing interest in the game and I started to look for the path to get back. Only by that time everything looked off – both familiar and unfamiliar at the same time. I couldn't see any of the landmarks I had just been pointing out to Junior, or else I saw too many of them. Each time I thought I recognized a mossy rock or a diseased tree, by the time we arrived at it, it looked all wrong. I thought that if only I could see the path, I'd know what to do, so I scoured the ground for a sign. I no longer held my stick in the air. Junior started to whimper and when he had to pee I tried to help him, but he peed all over his pants anyway because he was only three and still incompetent. At least that's what Dee would say. Peeing on his pants made him cry, so I had to help him feel better before we could go again, giving him hugs and telling him jokes so he wouldn't think about his pants.

"What did one toilet say to the other toilet?" I asked. Anything about toilets or farts was usually a hit.

"I dunno," Marty said, brightening.

"You look a little flushed!" I paused. "Get it? You *flush* a toilet."

Junior laughed.

I made a farting noise with my mouth and held his hand.

He laughed and we started walking, making farting noises back and forth.

"What did one clown say to the other clown?" I asked.

"What?"

"You look funny."

Junior smiled.

As we walked, I showed him how to put his bare forearm to his lips and blow on it to make farting sounds, and we did this until we found the river.

Sitting on the bank, I admitted to myself that we were lost. I tried not to let Marty see me crying, but after a while he came up to me and took my face between his hands, one flat open baby palm pressed against each of my cheeks. It reminded me of a joke where you squish your own face between your palms and say, *Buth Driver, open the door, I'm not in yet!* But Marty Junior didn't know that joke. He held my face firmly in his hands and looked into my eyes. His face was close to mine.

Finally he said, "Sunny, will you marry me?" and he was so serious and his words were so unexpected that I just had to laugh.

I hugged Marty and told him *sure*.

I convinced myself to follow the river upstream. I was sure we'd seen this river before, earlier in the camping trip with

Monique and Martin. We drove by the river twice on our way out to look at the marina (boring), and I kept expecting to see the overpass of the road any minute. If we followed the river long enough, we had to come to a road or someplace where there were other people. Didn't we? Once we were out of sight of the ducks, I began to feel less certain.

Twelve

A little while after Mom met Martin, we stopped calling her *Mom* and started calling her *Monique,* which was weird at first but seemed okay later. She said she needed to get her own identity back, whatever that meant. Dee said it was stupid and refused to call her anything but *Excuse me* and *Hey.* She tried *Moan*-ique because of the whole thing about the disgusting noises coming from their bedroom in the middle of the day and everything, which Dee said was just gross. Martin went into her room and threatened her about that one, which was what I learnt from Dee before she left. They all said Dee didn't leave because of Martin but I couldn't see any other reason. Martin moved in. Shit changed. Dee moved out. It might have taken a whole year to unfold but it looked straightforward to me. When I tried to ask Monique about it, she only said, "It's complicated," which made me want to scream. All's I knew was that every time Dee came in and let the back door bang behind her like an announcement, I could see Martin's shoulders square up and his knobbly spine stiffen a notch like someone had adjusted the pole Dee said he kept up his backside. Only Dee didn't say "backside" either. Then Dee started not coming home, and the door banged less, and Monique looked anxious and relieved all at the same time.

I was also not supposed to call Martin Junior *Marty* – so said Martin Senior. It was *Mar-tin.* In two crisp syllables. So I called him *Marty* when Martin wasn't listening. I was also not supposed to let Marty dress up in my flower girl dress from the wedding and put on my shiny white patent leather shoes so he could click around my room on the hardwood floor that Martin put in for me. Sometimes Marty wanted me to put makeup on him and pull his hair back with a headband. When Martin caught us, he got very angry. The next day, he took Marty to the barber's for a haircut. Dee said that pretty soon the poor kid would have no hair left.

Fifteen

How had more than three years gone past and Martin was still here? I had to reconsider my approach. Hadn't I tried with the pictures of my father all over the house? Didn't I show my disdain for the idea of being an *art historian* with his clean fingernails, crisp button-down shirts and stiff laugh? Wasn't it clear how pale he was in comparison to my *real* dad, who was a logger and a miner, who worked and laughed hard and who told stories and played the guitar? Wasn't it obvious that Martin didn't hold a candle to my dad? And yet, there he was, three years later, still hanging around with his stiff white shirts, still trying too hard to make us see his way of thinking. Like on family movie nights.

"Jim Carey's funny," I said, defending my choice when it was my turn to pick.

"Slapstick funny is different than being cleverly funny," Martin said. We all knew his bias for being "witty."

"Well I like him," I replied, staring at the TV, refusing to look at Martin.

Halfway through the movie, Martin went to his study and quietly closed the door, which I thought was rude, since we'd all sat through *Annie Hall* when it was his night to pick.

Twelve

One night, early on, I came to the dinner table in my Groucho glasses and nose. I was planning to conduct a social distancing experiment. Instead of sparking a discussion, which was what I had hoped for, and which is what would have happened before Martin moved in, grumpy Martin bit my head off. "Take those off," he demanded. Monique didn't even say anything because they were already having a fight. I considered going to my room and sulking but then decided that would be too easy for Martin. Instead, I took the glasses off and then pretended to be made of granite. I sat there still as stone at the kitchen table, quietly seething, willing my mind cold instead of boiling. My eyes burned everything they touched but refused to look at Martin. I glared at Monique, but she wouldn't play that game. My jaw was so tense I thought it would snap.

While I sat there, I promised myself *again* that I was always going to remember what it felt like to be a kid so that when I had kids I wouldn't treat them that way. I wouldn't go around being a jerk, hurting the kid's feelings over nothing and making the kid feel irrelevant and small and useless and a nuisance. I would definitely make an effort to make my kid feel *not* stupid. Martin had this way of making you feel so stupid that you started to feel like you might actually be a retard. I spent a good deal of time being concerned that I might be mentally retarded and then trying to keep people from finding out. I sometimes did these crazy things where I got angry and completely freaked out. I'd throw things and yell and it was like I couldn't help myself. At those times, grown-up people would say things like *There's something wrong with her,* which didn't help. Once, a woman told me, *You have a chip on your shoulder,* and she was staring at me so hard I thought she meant for real, so I looked at my shoulder to see what was there. But there was nothing. Then I really did feel like a retard.

I made up a new list of the ways Martin was different from my real dad.

My dad was Métis like me. Martin was not.

My dad loved me because he did; Martin said he loved me because he had to.

Martin was alive.

Twelve

At first, before Marty was born, Dee said Martin had no idea what it was like to have kids. I thought she must be right, judging by the way he tried too hard to make us like him at first, grinning and exclaiming all over himself in a way that you knew was all about Monique and had nothing to do with us. After a while, that changed. It's like when you go somewhere and you're on your best behaviour and then after a while you can't help it and you start to act like your true self. That's what happened to Martin after they got married and he moved in – his true self came out. I personally thought he should have tried out his true self from the start, although I don't know if it would have made Dee like him any better. But it might have made her despise him less. Martin did things to try to hide his true self from Monique. They had this sickening thing they did together where they talked in fake voices and teased each other about their age difference. Martin was only thirty-one, whereas Monique was forty, so they said stupid things like "robbing the cradle," which Dee said meant our mother had married a child. It was at those times I could see that Martin was not being his true self with Monique.

Thirteen

Martin was only one vowel away from being Martian. I wouldn't have been at all surprised if Martin were an alien disguised as a human, brainwashing us so that the other aliens could take over earth. Or maybe they were here already – all the step-dads on earth were really part of a sinister alien plot. Could happen. Maybe that's why step-dads were so different from real dads. But that made me feel bad for Marty because Martin *was* his real dad, and if his real dad was an alien, then that made poor little Marty part alien too. Unless maybe it worked like you either got to be one or the other, like blue eyes and brown eyes. In that case, Marty was definitely human.

Thirteen

Peppery sweat, men's cologne, and leather. These were my dad's smells – they were all I had left. My Métis dad, black hair, black eyes, smooth and young. Before Dee went away, her and me, we used to talk about stuff when she was in the mood and not so grouchy and wanting to be left alone – sometimes after she'd been out late she'd come and sit on the end of my bed to see if I was awake, and I could always tell if she was there even if

I was asleep. I'd feel the bed shift and I'd wake up right away because I knew it was her. She'd tell me how she missed our dad and she remembered him so much more than I did. I was jealous for her to tell me how he gave her horse rides on his knee, played his Johnny Cash records and sang along and how the songs were fun but sometimes depressing too. Our dad loved Johnny Cash – he dressed like him, the boots, the black shirts. I knew what she meant; I'd seen the pictures with his Brylcreemed hair, narrow eyes, holding his guitar with one leg up on a chair or a stump at the lake at our campsite. Dee didn't remember this, but I did: camping with my dad and Monique when she was still our mom, snuggling in the big quilt at my mom's feet on the long cot, lines from the webbing marking my cheek, eyes on the fire, my dad crooning bits of Johnny Cash tunes while his fingers strummed the guitar strings. When I fell asleep, he'd pick me up and carry me to my sleeping bag, tuck me in, make sure I was safe. Even if I woke up when he lifted me, I'd still pretend to be asleep, just to have him put me in bed like that.

Fifteen

By the time me and Marty got lost, I'd been making lists for more than three years. I was fifteen and Marty was three and Monique and Martin were too busy screwing to realize we were gone until it was nearly dark. It had gotten cold. The wind picked up and the sun got lower, and being next to the river made everything damp and chilly. I'd been making lists since Martin. Sometimes I kept them in a notebook. Sometimes I kept them in my head. Me and Marty sat by the river again to take a rest, and I told him my list of things I wouldn't change about myself even if I could:

Being Métis. Even if Martin acted like it was irrelevant.

Being smart. Even if it made me weird.

Being a tomboy.

Hating Ramona Peck and her so-called popularity. Wait. To say I hated Ramona Peck was overstating it. It implied an emotional investment that was inaccurate. Revise: Irritation inspired by Ramona Peck and her so-called popularity.

Disdain of popularity in general.

Independence. Ability to be a non-conformist. Which Monique called loneliness and alienation only because she lacked imagination.

It didn't matter that Marty didn't know what I was talking about, he was a good listener. I asked him for his list of favourite things, which was a mistake because all he came up with was stuff like ice cream and hot dogs and macaroni and cheese because he was hungry. And doing that just reminded us both that we were lost and wanted to go home.

I was worried about the dark. I didn't know what I was supposed to do. I thought about the fish, swimming upstream, caught up in the riffles and trying to get food. We had only seen them that morning but it seemed like days ago already. I thought of all the effort they expended to go nowhere and I realized maybe I was doing the same. Maybe we were going the wrong way.

The air was getting cold and the sun was setting fast. I broke a branch off a small soft tree and pulled the string out of my hoodie. I tied the string to the branch and used another branch to dig a hole in the bare ground beside the river. I put the stick in the hole and tried to get it to stand up. I got Marty to gather a few rocks to help prop the stick up. If anyone was looking for us I wanted to leave a signal so they'd know we were there.

I got Marty to help me as I tore branches from pine trees and threw them in a pile on the ground near the base of a big tree. My hands were covered in sap and scratches. Once we had a pile of branches, I sat on them and let Marty crawl into my lap. His skin was cold.

"I want Mom," he said.

"Me too," I told him. I was surprised I said that. I had spent three years thinking I wanted my dad.

For once, there was no one around to remind us to call her *Monique.*

"Will she be mad at us?" Marty asked me.

I hugged him tight. "No way," I said. "She's probably looking for us right now."

Marty's little body relaxed into my arms.

"I'm scared of the dark," he said.

"Let's memorize what we see now so when it's dark we can still see everything, 'kay?"

As we counted the trees, darkness fell. Huddled together for warmth, Marty and I fell asleep.

I dreamed of being at the lake with my mom and my dad. I was small. I was on the lounge chair and my blanket had fallen off. I was cold. I wished, in my sleep, that someone would cover me up. Then I felt my dad put his arms around me, one arm under my knees, one across my back and under my armpits. His arms were warm. As he picked me up, I kept my eyes closed on purpose, not wanting to break the spell of the delicious dream.

I'm not sure exactly when I became aware that it wasn't a dream, but as I awoke, I saw I really was being carried. It was pitch dark and I could hear the snapping branches underfoot of the person carrying me. I had no idea how long I'd been asleep. For a moment, I was still able to imagine it was my dad carrying me through our campsite to my waiting bed. I could feel the warmth from his chest against my cold body. Then I really did wake up.

"Marty," I called, realizing we'd been separated.

"Shhh. It's okay. He's here." It was Martin who had a firm, steady grip on me.

There were beams from flashlights and calling voices – a search party. My eyes adjusted, and in the sporadic flashes of light I saw that close by was a uniformed officer carrying Marty. I closed my eyes then and let it all happen.

From the trees, an owl asked us its relentless question again and again.

in simpler times

In simpler times, no woman called mother would ever have given her thirteen-year-old daughter Luanne her whole pack of cigarettes and all the coins and crumpled bills dug from her jeans pocket and said, *I won't be needing these any more*, before walking away somewhere forever.

And later, much later, when Luanne's own boy was seven, she wouldn't strike the metaphorical match that burned the house of his childhood clean to the ground, walking out on her marriage, dragging the boy with her as she went. And the whole time she stood back, detached from the emotion of losing everything, willfully unaware of the slow ripping sound underscoring it all.

In simpler times, Luanne would not have heard his pleading *no no no* out of sync with his shaking head, as if he could stop her from saying what she was determined to say in the car outside McDonald's while the food turned rancid in his stomach and caused him to throw up – a smell that would never leave the car – the word *divorce* ringing in the air. Later, at the park, he wouldn't have refused to play with her and they wouldn't have had nowhere to go.

When the boy was nine, she would not have had to pray not to be killed by her boyfriend while her son sat in the next room eating sugared cereal he had made for himself and watching Saturday morning cartoons turned up too loud.

And later, she would not have taken him to yet another city only to watch in dumb wonder as he got expelled from school for smoking pot with that damned older kid and then cried in the car on the way home as she wondered out loud what to do with him.

In a simpler time, Luanne would not find him outside the King George on the concrete steps and herself with no one to shake her fist at, wanting to kick the asses of the mysterious bastards who had sold him the drugs. She would not know about his wasted frame hidden beneath the cumbersome coat, black with dirt, or the hollows of his cheeks and the tense outline of his still-beautiful jaw. She wouldn't understand his inability to eat, that he had no appetite for anything but junk. She wouldn't have to hold his uncomprehending body in her arms or lie down clumsily on the steps to cry into the bulky coat shoulder, with him not knowing she had been there except for the sixty bucks in his pocket.

Luanne wouldn't have to lay the photos out, examining each one, seeing them become fewer and fewer the older he gets until there is nothing left. She wouldn't still be able to smell the stink off his coat and know without thinking that she would do it again tomorrow if she could find him.

In simpler times, Luanne would have laughed when he jumped impulsively onto the back of the decrepit, slow-moving snow plough to ride home after Winter Carnival, Old Eddy Kirk, not really old at all, turning to smile at him just as she snapped the picture. She'd tread lightly behind, watching as he moved away from her, knowing she could always catch up.

how to tell if you are poor

Now listen, I'm going to tell you a story. One day, we were out walking by the river, the bunch of us. This was at a time when we weren't so young any more, any of us. Old enough, maybe, to know better, but not too old yet either. Things were pretty much settled just as they are now. Animals were animals and people were people. Spring had turned the corner into summer and we were enjoying a warm, slow day. We were waiting, as usual, for something to happen.

Angel was the first to see it. She skipped over to pick the dark bottle out of the long, sandy grass near the water's edge.

"There's something in it," she said in a singsong voice, dancing on her tip-toes. She swung the wine bottle by its neck with the tips of her slim fingers. Angel had a way of looking graceful even just doing things like that. Personally, I found her beautiful no matter what anyone else said.

Angel barely had a chance to jiggle the bottle to demonstrate its heft before Cydric yanked it out of her light-fingered grasp.

"It's mine," she cried. "I found it." That was Angel – full of split-second emotions.

"What happened to sharing?" asked Cydric, holding the bottle by its slender neck, just out of Angel's reach. We all stopped to watch. "Relax," he said to her, more command than request. Angel usually knew how far to push it with Cydric, so she snapped her mouth shut and backed off. Her eyes narrowed to slits.

Cydric polished the label with the sleeve of his forearm, but it was too faded and revealed nothing. He wiped all the glass until it was free of dust and shone in the sun, which was peeking from between skiffs of clouds.

"Open it," Réal said. He was always so decisive, that one. We all crowded in close to get a look.

Cydric jostled the cork only a couple of times before it popped. A slow wisp of smoke rose from the rounded rim.

"Hey," said Gabe, cocking his head, "smells like sweetgrass."

Out of the bottle's neck the smoke continued to rise, getting thicker and more voluminous until it was practically pouring from the opening. Cydric dropped the bottle onto the grass at our feet and took a step back, flicking his fingertips as if maybe they'd been burned.

The smoke quickly became so thick we all started to wave our hands in front of our noses. I took a step back. Mika coughed a bit. The smoke began to twist and turn until it took a human shape. We watched as the smoky form solidified and became more defined. The thickest smoke cleared and within the remaining wisps there stood an honest to goodness flesh and blood man, as if he had been there all along.

"What is it?" Mika breathed.

"Black magic," whispered Gabe speculatively.

"Witchcraft," added Réal.

"There's a policy against that, you know," Christian said. He turned his back and pretended to ignore the man. Every few seconds I saw Christian peek over his shoulder until eventually he joined us again.

The air cleared. The man's dark hair was greasy and hung in tangled ropes. His flannel shirt, unbuttoned to mid-chest, fell loosely from his skinny shoulders and hugged a narrow potbelly. He removed his backpack and set it by his feet.

Cydric took several steps back. Then one step forward. We all did. I felt like part of a messy marching band. No one spoke.

The man from the bottle stood in the grass in front of us, his back to the river. He let out a loud belch.

"S'cuse me," he said and then hiccupped into the back of his hand. The smell of hangover breath pushed past my nose. I saw Réal take a small step forward.

Of course, I thought, *Réal will make this right.*

Réal paused before the stranger and regarded him with a shrewd eye. Réal was always smart, him. I believe it's what made him irresistible to women. That and his poetry. After all, what woman can resist a man who writes poetry?

We held our breath, waiting for Réal to speak, and when he did it was a great surprise, as it often was.

"*Wesakechak.*" Réal breathed the name. How he knew I couldn't tell.

"All my friends call me Wes," the man said. "So you guys can call me *Mister* Wesakechak," he said, and then he laughed at our serious faces. "Aw, c'mon, just jokes, hey? You guys can call me Wes, too." He laughed, but no one else joined him.

"What are you doing in my wine bottle?" Cydric demanded angrily. But then, Cydric always sounded cranky.

"Oh, was it *you* who put the cork in when I passed out?" Wes asked, turning to Cydric, matching his tone. Cydric's puffed-out chest deflated just a bit, and he scowled.

Angel said, "Am I tripping here? Ho-lee. My teachers were right; I shouldn't have done all that acid in high school. Flashback!"

"Want me to pinch you, see if you wake up?" Mika offered generously.

"Ahem." Réal cleared his throat, preparing to address the newcomer. "Mister Wesakechak, brother to the animals," he began solemnly. But Wesakechak wasn't listening.

Wesakechak yawned and stretched his arms high, clasping his hands overhead, his shirt lifting to reveal his small, brown belly. I noted grey fuzz stuck in his belly button like dryer lint and I saw Mika looking at it too. Beside me, she giggled. It was funny to think of Wesakechak having dryer lint in his belly button. Mika's giggling got his attention and he immediately pulled himself straight.

He walked over to her and slung his arm lightly around her shoulders. "If you like what you see, sweetheart, there's more where that came from," he said. Mika just kept giggling. He added, "I'd invite you over for a drink, but my place is a little small right now," and he pointed to the discarded wine bottle. Mika giggled some more.

"Careful, Mika," Angel said and then turned to Wesakechak to say, "She gets pregnant just looking at a guy. Better not get her started!"

"That's okay, there's plenty of Wes to go around," said Wesakechak, smiling broadly but letting his arm drop just the same. Anything he was about to say was interrupted by his growling stomach. He frowned and looked down at his belly as if it were alive.

"Where can a guy get some grub around here, anyway? I'm hungry. The three *H*s after a night of drinking," he said to Angel, putting his arm around her shoulders.

Angel looked quizzically at him and he said, "Hungover."

Angel nodded.

"Hungry."

Angel nodded again.

Wesakechak paused for effect and then added, "And Horny!" throwing his head back and laughing.

Angel smiled but ducked away from his arm. Wesakechak didn't seem to notice.

"Okay, I get it," said Cydric. "Don't you all see what this is?"

We turned to look at Cydric, who was antsy and keyed up.

"The bottle, the smoke, this guy here.... He's, like, you know, the genie. The genie in the bottle. You know what that means?" He looked at us inquisitively, and when we remained mute, he yelled out, "Three fucking wishes, that's what! This guy owes us three wishes!"

Wesakechak looked down at his moccasins sheepishly. A tiny fart escaped with a beep.

"Is that true?" asked Gabe.

"Well, technically..." Wesakechak began.

"No fucking *technically,*" Cydric mimicked. "Fucking really. Three wishes. And they're mine 'cause I found him."

"I found the bottle first," Angel challenged, her eyes flashing.

"That's true," said Réal thoughtfully. Gabe nodded his head

to back Réal up.

"Well, I uncorked him," said Cydric defiantly.

"Only after you stole it right out of my hands," Angel said. She was the only one who would stand up to Cydric. Angel was all about the jokes and the laughs, but the others knew it was only a cover. She'd been known to say, as if it were a joke, "I got a lot of pain – I'm laughing through it!"

"Let's ask *him* then," said Cydric.

"Well," Wesakechak looked around at the group, feeling his power. He made us wait for his answer, and then, like the parent of bickering children, he proclaimed, "You'll have to share."

After that, a squabble ensued about how we would choose what to wish for. Angel and Cydric kept insisting they had special rights to the wishes since they had both touched the bottle.

Then Wes had a great idea. "We'll do a talking circle," he said. He cited tradition, and none of us could argue, although Christian looked as if he might burst into tears. It was all too much for him. Then Wes pulled a giant bong from his bag and set it on the grass. After watching him fish through every pocket for a lighter, Gabe finally handed him his. We sat on the grass in a circle and watched Wes light up. Smoke rose from the tube and wound itself around his head.

"Okay," Wes said, holding the smoke in his lungs, "whoever has the bong gets to talk." He passed it to Gabe, who was sitting on his left.

Gabe took a toke and then sat back, looking thoughtful. We all waited. "Pass," he finally said and handed the bong over to Mika.

Mika copied Gabe, saying, "Pass," as well. She tried to hand the bong to Christian but he shook his head and put both his hands up like an innocent at the inquisition. Cydric made a mocking sound with his teeth – Cydric hated everyone, but especially Christian. I wanted to tell Christian he'd be the first to be shot at an inquisition but it wasn't my turn to talk. Mika reached around Christian and gave the bong to Réal. One by one, each of us, Réal, Angel, Cydric and me, did exactly the same thing as

Gabe and Mika, all saying, "Pass," until the bong once again rested in Wes's hands.

"Nobody's talking," Wes observed.

"I'm looking for some inspiration," Gabe said, rubbing the scar on his forehead. "God, aren't we all," Angel muttered.

"I can tell you a story," offered Wes.

"I like stories," Mika said, settling into her spot on the grass. She reminded me of a little kid, even though we were far past that.

"Once, after the people had all been made from the clay of the earth, and the animals were in their proper places, and the spirits were honoured, and all was right and balanced in the Indigenous world, the Creator decided to go on a holiday," Wes began.

"Wait a minute," said Cydric. "Why are we doing this?"

"Shhh," Angel hissed.

Wesakechak continued. "And when She went on Her holiday, She left Old Wesakechak in charge." Wes was talking about himself in the third person, as if he was a storied legend. "That was back when She still thought She could trust him. He meant well. Really he did.

"He fell asleep by the fire after a fine feast. Oh, that was a good feast that time. And the fire was warm. And Wesakechak's belly was full." As if on cue, Wes's belly grumbled. He looked down sadly at it, remembering the time of the good feast. "After Old Wesakechak had that fine feast, he fell asleep. And a terrible thing happened."

We were listening carefully.

"Wesakechak, he fell asleep, but not before he gave instructions to his rear end to wake him up if anything went wrong."

Mika giggled.

"Well, he was so full from his meal, and so warm from the fire, that he fell into a deep, deep sleep. He never even heard if his rear end warned him or not." Wes looked miserable at this part of the story. "What happened while Creator was on holidays and Wesakechak slept, you ask? The Europeans came in and colonized the place! When Creator returned, She exclaimed, 'Wesakechak! What have you done!?!'

"Ever since that time, we've been trying to find a solution to the European problem." Wes shook his head unhappily.

"Each time Creator and Wesakechak came up with a plan, it backfired. Creator tried to distract the Europeans with their own bureaucracy. She sent them an idea but it got muddled in the translation and eventually turned into the Department of Indian Affairs and the Indian Act. Creator help us all," Wes said, rolling his eyes. "It'll keep us busy forever." Wes sat back and looked at us expectantly.

"I like that story," said Mika. "Sort of."

"What's it mean?" asked Christian suspiciously.

Réal looked thoughtful, and Gabe punched his fist into the palm of his other hand. We were all quiet for a moment.

"Wishes," reminded Cydric, tapping his fingertips on the ground impatiently in front of him. "Back to the wishes."

"Let's wish for a million dollars," said Mika excitedly.

Wes made a strangled sound and we all looked at him. "Where would I get a million dollars?!" he exclaimed. After a second, he added, "If we all go down to the food court at the mall, maybe we could collect enough empties to go and buy a case. But we'll have to hurry – the LB closes by six on Saturdays."

"Today's Wednesday," said Gabe.

"No it's not," said Christian. "It's Sunday and the LB isn't open."

"I don't believe you," said Cydric. "You tried to pull that one before."

"Man, I'm getting hungry, and the bugs are bad. Can we move this along already?" Angel interrupted.

"Was that a wish?" asked Wes hopefully. I could tell he was still thinking about that case.

"Just wishful thinking," said Angel. "Not the same thing."

"Well if I had a wish, I'd wish not to be poor," said Cydric.

"But how do you know you're poor?" Réal piped up. I thought I heard Gabe groan. We'd heard this all before. "Is it just because we're supposed to be poor that we come to think of ourselves that way?" Réal prodded.

"I don't think of myself as poor," Mika piped in. Then I knew she was lying.

"Well even if you don't, everyone who sees you thinks of you as poor," said Réal.

"No they don't. They think she has bad breath and fleas." This helpful comment came from Angel.

"Hey!" Mika protested.

"Just jokes," Angel said lightly, which was her response to everything.

"I told you, it's because they expect you to be poor," Réal said, ignoring the tension between Mika and Angel. "So therefore you *are* poor. Get it?" Réal asked, raising his eyebrows. Then he added firmly, "But we don't have to accept it. I want you to know that."

"Réal, you should be a fucking professor," Cydric said with mock admiration. "Are you sure you're Métis? We're starting to think you're a white guy." We all laughed.

"Anybody got a smoke?" asked Wes, yawning. No one answered. "Some sacred tobacco?" he prompted again.

"You know I don't believe in that superstition," said Christian.

"What superstition *do* you believe in?" asked Wes, smiling.

"Tobacco is one of the four sacred plants to First Nations," said Angel knowledgeably.

"How would you know?" asked Mika. "You've only been an Indian for two weeks!"

"Good old Bill C-31," said Cydric. "Making Indians out of all of us."

"That's Eye-nac for you," said Angel.

"Eye-rack," quipped Gabe.

"Indian Nation Abolishment Commission – their job is to make policies to get rid of us." We all laughed.

"Isn't that what the Indian Act is for?" joked Wes.

"No, the Indian Act is in case we run out of toilet paper," laughed Angel.

"Seriously, what good is it?" asked Christian.

"Paternalistic," said Gabe.

"Sexist," said Réal.

"Outdated," said Christian.

"The Métis are lucky. We define ourselves," said Réal.

"*Otipemisiwak,*" said Gabe. "We're the people who own ourselves."

"Can we wish away the Indian Act?" asked Christian.

"What good would that do?"

"It might be bad, but at least it's something," said Réal.

"I'm afraid I can't get rid of the Indian Act anyway," said Wes, shaking his head. "It's too political. I try to stay out of the politics. I'm a lover, not a fighter." He winked at Mika and she blushed.

"I gotta take a leak," Réal said, getting up and heading for a dense stand of bushes closer to the water.

As soon as Réal was out of earshot, Angel whispered in a mock stage voice, "He's got cancer," she pointed to her throat. "Neck cancer. We should wish him better. Cured."

"Throat," Gabe interrupted.

"What?"

"Throat," he said, pointing. "It's cancer of the throat."

"Throat, neck, whatever. It's still cancer," Angel said, waving her hand in the air.

"That's an unusual place to get cancer," said Mika.

"Réal's not an ordinary guy," answered Angel simply.

"I predict his words will live one hundred years. Maybe more," said Gabe.

"He's a genius, a mastermind. We should save him if we can."

Réal returned and we fell silent.

And that's when a truly stupid thing happened.

"These mosquitoes are as big as helicopters this year," complained Mika, slapping the air. "I wish they would go away."

"Done!" Wesakechak shouted before we even realized what had happened. He jumped up and trotted to the water's edge.

"Idiot!" hissed Angel.

Stunned, we watched as Wes hauled a large stone to the centre of our circle and plopped it down.

Mika started to cry quietly.

"Well don't just sit there; could you give me a hand?" he asked us. He was sweating. We helped him bring the stones. No one spoke.

When we had created a small circle of stones, Wes had us collect twigs and dry grass. He dug into his backpack and brought out kindling, dry moss and a flint and steel. Réal looked dismayed. Mika cried silently. This was our wish, gone to shit. Still, we helped.

Wes showed Gabe how to work up a rhythm with the flint on the steel and all of us stood close together in a circle to block any stray breezes. Each time a flurry of sparks looked promising, we leaned in and blew gently on the tinder. Soon the sparks glowed themselves into a small flame under our breath and we murmured a collective sigh of satisfaction. Within a few minutes, the fire was going well, the smoke driving the mosquitoes away.

"One down," said Wes. He looked very satisfied.

Mika sniffed and wiped her eyes.

Angel was less bad tempered after we had successfully built the fire and she surprised us all when she reached over, patted Mika on the arm and said, "We still have two more. Could have happened to anyone. Just jokes, hey?"

Most of us laughed half-heartedly to show Mika we didn't have hard feelings, with the exception of Cydric. Angel was right. It could have been any of us.

"What's next?" asked Wes, looking around expectantly.

All eyes turned to Angel. We waited for her to ask for Réal to be cured. Instead, Cydric interjected in his abrasive tone.

"This changes everything. We only have two wishes left now. We need to rethink this."

"Rethink what?" asked Réal.

"Rethink our wishes. We need a strategy. I'm not sure I'm willing to waste my wishes on just one person – what if the rest of us have a problem that no one knows about? What if we're just not telling everyone our problems all the time so no one knows? What about Angel?" he asked, and all our eyes turned to Angel.

She scowled at Cydric, her eyes such small slits she might well have had them closed.

"She wants to have a baby but can't, did any of you know that?" Cydric paused for effect.

Angel looked like she might spring to her feet at any moment and kick the shit out of Cydric. But she remained still.

"Or Mika," Cydric said, and all our eyes swung to Mika's terrified face. "Mika, who can't stop having babies. Can't look after the ones she has." Cydric's tone was fierce. Mika looked as if she might burst into tears.

"What about Christian?" Cydric continued, and we all looked at Christian. "Sitting over there," Cydric said, pointing, "wanting you all to think he's perfect when he's done some of the worst things among us, has the most to be sorry for." Cydric paused to let this idea percolate. "It's usually the ones who turn to religion," he continued, talking about Christian as if he wasn't eight feet away. "He's repenting. At least that's what he thinks. Which of us really knows him? All of us have a past and most of us have things we're not proud of. Things we're ashamed of. Things that have driven us to religion, to seek salvation or to try and find forgiveness. Things we'd like to wish away if we could. Do any of you know what happened to Christian's family...?"

Christian jumped to his feet. "Shut up!" His face was red and his hands, balled into fists, trembled. "Shut up!" he cried, leaning forward and yelling. "Whatever you think you know about me, you know nothing. I want you to shut your dirty mouth. Just shut your dirty mouth." Christian's face was scarlet. His lips shook.

Cydric smiled at him, cool in the face of Christian's outburst. With that smile, Cydric appeared to be really enjoying himself. "Or what?" he finally asked.

Christian stood staring at Cydric, his mouth opening and closing, no words coming out.

In the impotent silence that fell over Christian, Cydric said quietly, "Tell us Christian, what are you repenting for? Is it the thought of your dead wife or your dead child that makes you most sorry?"

Christian found his voice and spoke slowly, through clenched teeth. To this day I believe Christian knew what he was doing – I believe he was answering Cydric's "or what" taunt. I imagine him thinking to himself, "This is what."

Out loud, Christian said what many of us might have thought at one time or another. Enunciating every word clearly, he said, "I wish you were dead."

Réal gave a sharp intake of breath.

Gabe groaned.

Wes hung his head. We all looked at him, waiting to see what would happen next.

Cydric shut up, for once. Then he said, "Take it back," in such a quiet voice I didn't know if he had really spoken.

Christian took a few steps from the circle and sat on the ground with his back to us. He put his head in his hands and rocked back and forth, moaning.

"I feel funny," Cydric said, patting his arms and legs. "Do I feel funny?"

Wes looked sadly at the ground, as if he was disappointed in us.

Réal told Cydric to lie down and to take deep breaths.

Gabe tried to quiet Christian and stop his rocking and moaning.

If anyone had cared to look, they would have seen Angel and Mika holding hands.

We were quiet as we waited to see what would happen next. Cydric closed his eyes. He appeared to be asleep. I wondered if it had happened, if he was dead. I didn't like Cydric, didn't like what he did to us or how his negative attitude infected our group, but I would have never wished that on him for real. And I couldn't believe Christian would either.

Gabe sat with his arm around Christian and spoke in a whisper. I couldn't hear what he said, but it sounded soothing. Christian had stopped rocking and making noise.

Wes sat very still and refused to make eye contact with us.

Réal was the first to speak. "We have no choice," he said, obviously talking about the third wish.

We knew. We all knew it.

After, when Cydric had been taken away in the ambulance, Wesakechak packed his things into his backpack and prepared to leave.

"Where will you go, big brother?" we asked, but he didn't answer.

I wanted to ask him to stay with us, but I knew it was no use.

Wesakechak shook our hands, kissed Angel on the cheek and Mika on the lips and left us, headed west, following the river.

"Do you see that?" asked Mika. We followed her eyes. With every step Wesakechak took, tiny purple flowers sprang up underfoot like spongy alfalfa. Where there were no flowers a second before, there was a thick bed of tiny flowers even before his foot had fully left the spot. The ground behind him was dotted with purple footprints. It was beautiful.

"We love you Wesakechak," we called after him. And we did. We truly did.

acknowledgements

I can't imagine where I would be without family (in all its forms), friends and community. Each has a vital role and influence in my life and has played a part in the making of this book. I want to acknowledge my family for their support and inspiration, especially Declan, my first reader, greatest encourager and most avid fan. I am also very grateful to my talented, ever-patient editor, Warren Cariou, for his shrewd editorial comments, constant enthusiasm and overall support for this book. Many people in the Saskatchewan writing community have mentored, supported, and taken interest in my work as a writer, especially my insightful Visible Ink compatriots and my good friend and first mentor, J. Jill Robinson. *Maarsii*, for believing in me and always being enthusiastic about the work. And my thanks, in general, to the many talented and amazing Aboriginal writers who set the example of how it's done. Finally, the Canada Council for the Arts provided me with a grant to work on these stories, a shot of encouragement for which I am grateful.

The following stories have been previously published or recognized:

"Ayekis" appeared in *Spring Magazine*, 2007, and in *New Breed Magazine*, Fall 2008.

"Billy Bird" appeared in *The Dalhousie Review*, Autumn 2008.

"Blood Memory" appeared in *Geist*, Spring 2010, and subsequently in *Best Canadian Essays 2011* (Tightrope Books, 2012). It was a finalist for a Western Magazine Award (2011) and nominated for the Journey Prize (2010).

"Just Pretending" appeared in *Prairie Fire*, Spring 2010.

"Mister X" received first place in the fiction category of the Short Manuscript Awards, Saskatchewan Writer's Guild, 2008.

"The Nirvana Principle" appeared in *Grain* Magazine, 2008, and was nominated for the Journey Prize (2009).

"Someone's Been Lying to You" appeared under the title "Cracker" in *Zaagidiwin is a Many Splendoured Thing* (Ningwakwe Learning Press, 2008).

about the author

Lisa Bird-Wilson is a Saskatchewan Métis writer whose stories have been nominated for the Journey Prize, among others. They have appeared in periodicals such as *Grain, Prairie Fire, Geist,* and in the anthology *Best Canadian Essays. Just Pretending* is her first book-length work of fiction.

Lisa is the author of one other book, *An Institute of Our Own: A History of the Gabriel Dumont Institute,* and has also written curriculum and other materials for the Ministries of Education and Advanced Education. Saskatchewan born and raised, she works as a director of the Gabriel Dumont Institute and lives in Saskatoon with her family.